y

MURDE
by Elsp

Also available in Perennial Library
by Elspeth Huxley

THE AFRICAN POISON MURDERS

MURDER ON SAFARI

ELSPETH HUXLEY

PERENNIAL LIBRARY
Harper & Row, Publishers
New York, Cambridge, Philadelphia, San Francisco
London, Mexico City, São Paulo, Sydney

A hardcover edition of this book was published by Harper and Brothers.

MURDER ON SAFARI. Copyright 1938 by Harper and Brothers. All rights reserved. Printed in the United States of America. No part of this book may be used or reproduced in any manner whatsoever without written permission except in the case of brief quotations embodied in critical articles and reviews. For information address Harper & Row, Publishers, Inc., 10 East 53rd Street, New York, N.Y. 10022.

First PERENNIAL LIBRARY edition published 1982.

ISBN: 0-06-080587-0

82 83 84 85 10 9 8 7 6 5 4 3 2 1

MURDER ON SAFARI

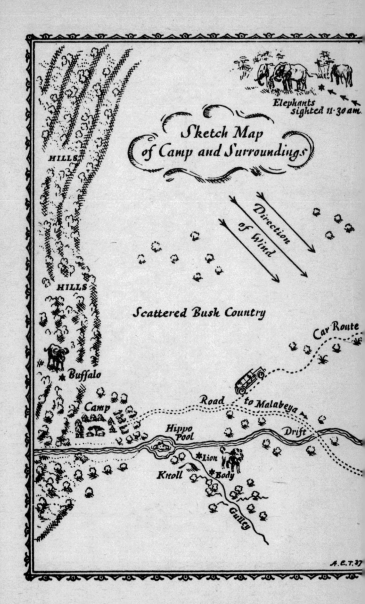

Elephants
sighted 11·30 am.

Sketch Map
of Camp and Surroundings

Direction
of Wind

HILLS

HILLS

Scattered Bush Country

Car Route

Buffalo

Camp

Road to Malabeya

Hippo
Pool

Drift

Lion

Knoll

Body

Gulley

A.E.T. 37

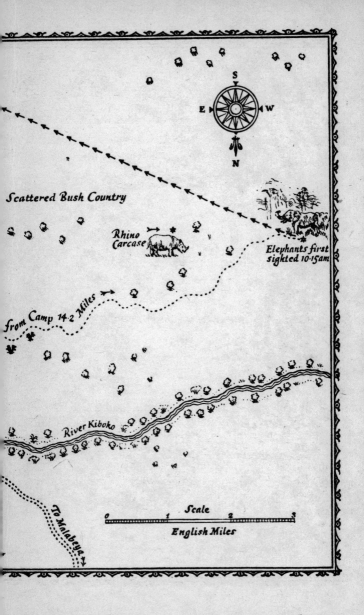

CHAPTER 1: Vachell looked across the desk at his visitor with a slight sensation of surprise. He'd never met a famous white hunter before, and he felt that a member of such a romantic profession ought to be big and husky and tanned, and to dress in shorts and a broad-brimmed hat. Danny de Mare was at the top of his profession but he didn't look husky at all. He was a rather small, slight man, with broad shoulders that dwarfed his height, and small hands and feet.

"Sit down, Mr. de Mare," Vachell said. "I read somewhere you'd gone up to the Western frontier on a job, but I guess I got the dates wrong."

Danny de Mare sat down in a high-backed chair and faced Vachell, Superintendent of the Chania C.I.D., over an untidy, littered desk. His face was lean and sallow and a long, beaky nose gave it a bird-like look. His expression was alert, like an animal ready to pounce if anything moved unexpectedly; he reminded Vachell of a small, compact hawk. His thick, dark hair, brushed until it shone, was grey at the temples. He wore a well-cut grey flannel suit with a white pin-stripe, a blue-and-white spotted tie, and carried a soft grey hat.

"You were right," he said. "I got down to Marula late last night, and I go back to the Western frontier district to-morrow. My safari's camped on the Kiboko river, safely at anchor, I hope. As a matter of fact, I came to see you."

Vachell slid a box of du Mauriers over the table and crossed his lanky legs. He was a tall, lean young Canadian, with sandy hair brushed back from a high-cheeked, bony face, and a large mouth which seemed ready to expand at any moment into a friendly grin.

"Anything serious?" he asked.

"There's been a burglary. Lady Baradale—she's rich as Rockefeller, and paying for the whole outfit—says she's lost a whole sackful of jewellery. I've got a description of it here. She puts the value at thirty thousand."

He took a sky-blue envelope out of his pocket-book and handed it over. A coronet was embossed on the flap and inside were two sheets of note-paper with "On Safari, Chania" in red letters at the top as an address. Vachell read through the list without speaking and rubbed the side of his nose with a nicotine-stained finger.

"She sure must like to put on the dog," he remarked. "What does she want with all this stuff on the Western frontier? There must be some native chief up there who's going to have a coronation. So some guy's swiped the lot, has he?"

"Or she," de Mare said. He spoke tersely, giving every word its full value, in a pleasant baritone voice. There was nothing aggressive about him, but his whole manner was quietly self-assured. "I'd better tell the story properly. Lady Baradale sent for me the day before yesterday, about eight p.m. She said she'd just opened the portable safe she keeps in her tent to get out some jewels to wear at dinner, and she found that practically everything had gone.

"She was in a frantic state, of course. I wanted to hold an

inquiry there and then, but she turned that down flat; said, I suppose with truth, that the thief had probably had all day to hide the stuff and all East Africa to do it in, and that it was better policy to say nothing and keep him guessing until the police arrived. So I agreed to drive down to Marula next day. I got in after midnight, and came here first thing in the morning."

The Superintendent lit a cigarette and stared thoughtfully out of the open window. Sunlight flooded the small square of lawn that lay between his window and the row of eucalyptus trees that sheltered the road. Africans strolled without haste and apparently without objective along the highway. The bark of a sergeant's voice came to his ears from the parade ground behind the headquarters of the Chania Police.

"What's your opinion?" he asked his visitor.

"She's not the sort of woman to mislay thirty thousand quid's worth of jewels through carelessness. Enormously rich American—her money comes from things like caffeine-less coffee and tanninless tea, I believe—but she's like God and the sparrows: knows every dollar by name. She always locks her jewels into this travelling safe, and keeps the key herself. She told me that even her maid isn't trusted with the key. But some one must have pinched it, because the safe wasn't forced. There's only the one key, apparently, and you can't cut duplicates on safari."

"Who's on the roll-call in this safari outfit?"

De Mare smiled. He had very white teeth, and the smile made his face come alive. Vachell noticed his eyes for the first time: light brown and large, with long, curved lashes. He looked much more human when he smiled.

"Uncle Tom Cobley and all," he said. "Lady Baradale first; she pays. I've told you about her. Then Lord Baradale; he takes pictures, and plays about with camera gadgets, and thinks out Heath Robinson inventions. His daughter by a previous marriage, Cara Baradale. One of these hard-boiled, prickly girls; I don't know what she does. Her fiancé, Sir Gordon Catchpole—he decorates London interiors, I believe. Then there's Lady Baradale's maid, Paula, and Rutley, the chauffeur-mechanic. He's as pleased with himself as a peacock—he once had a small part in Hollywood, I believe, in fact Lady Baradale picked him up there—and he's got a filthy temper, but I must say he's a good mechanic. That's all the Europeans. Then there's a whole tribe of native retainers—gun-bearers, trackers, cooks, personal boys, drivers, skinners, and just plain porters. No expense spared."

"Do you look after all those babies single-handed?" Vachell asked.

"There's a second hunter, of course—a young fellow called Luke Englebrecht, a Dutchman. A new-comer to our racket, but he knows his stuff; he was born in Chania and brought up rough, and it's as natural to him to shoot as to breathe; his only trouble is, he's a bit of a butcher. And then there's me. Oh, and Chris Davis—you've heard of her, I expect. She brought her plane along to join the three-ring circus."

"The dame who spots big game from a plane and then comes back to tell on them?" De Mare nodded. "That's always seemed kind of mean, to me. Well, that's nine Europeans—four to hunt and five to smooth their path through the bush. How about the African staff?"

"I don't think any of the gun-bearers or trackers are likely to have turned into jewel thieves. It isn't as though the safe was forced; whoever did the job borrowed the key. I suppose it's possible that one or two of the personal boys might be mixed up in it. Lord Baradale's pet valet, a Somali called Geydi, for instance. I don't trust him a yard. When it comes to conceit he makes Rutley look like a small child, and he's ultra-sophisticated; he's even been to England. But it's no good my sitting here and trying to give you potted biographies of all these people. You'd better come up to the camp and see them for yourself."

Vachell smoked for a few moments in silence, his eyes on two natives squatting on their hams under a gum tree across the lawn and tossing coins. The chance of an assignment in the Western frontier district, away beyond the civilized parts of the colony, seemed too good to be missed. He was new to his job, to the colony, even to Africa. It would break new ground.

"I might get up there," he agreed, "so long as it isn't a wild-goose chase."

"There's one thing in the police's favour," de Mare said. "The stuff must still be up there, hidden somewhere in or near the camp. No one has left in the last week, so there's been no chance to get it away."

"What about mail?"

"We send a lorry into Malabeya at intervals for supplies, but we haven't done so since the theft. It's the nearest

Government post, about a hundred miles away—too far to
walk to post a letter. Lady Baradale's got a suggestion
about police investigation. She thinks you'd find out more
if you came under false pretences—if no one knew you
were a detective. Then people wouldn't be so much on
their guard."

"What do I pretend to be?" Vachell asked. "A man
come to read the gas meter, or a college boy trying to sell
Lady Baradale a subscription to the *Saturday Evening Post*
to help earn my way through school?"

De Mare looked grave and shook his head. "Nothing
so respectable. She wants to get rid of Englebrecht. She's
got nothing against him as a hunter; it's a personal matter.
She wants him to fade out and you're to take his place, disguised as a white hunter. I could manage for a week without assistance, I think. I expect you're a good shot, and if
it came to a pinch you could deputize. How does the idea
appeal?"

"It appeals like a swim in a pool full of starving crocodiles," Vachell answered. "What do I do when I meet a
herd of elephants head-on? Make a noise like Sabu the
elephant boy, or show an honorary membership ticket in
the White Hunters' Association? I'm here to chase crimi-
nals, not to be chased by wild animals."

"We wouldn't send you out after anything savage," de
Mare said reassuringly. "A kongoni or two at the worst.
A second hunter's job is mostly checking over Fortnum and
Mason chop-boxes and writing requisition forms for new
supplies of shoe-polish, these days. You might pick up
some sort of a lead, if you come as a hunter. If you come

as yourself no one will want to gossip to you. I propose to leave Marula at four a.m. to-morrow. I'd be delighted to take you if you decide to come."

De Mare stood up, adjusting his tie. Again Vachell felt irrationally surprised that he should be so small, slender and spruce.

"You'll want rifles and some camp kit," the hunter added. "I'll help you choose them this-afternoon, if you like."

"I'll have to think it over," Vachell said.

De Mare nodded, and made towards the door. "Lady Baradale will pay the extras, of course," he said. "I'll be in the lobby of Dane's at two-thirty, if you want to do any shopping."

His step, as he walked out, was light and springy. The word jaunty came into Vachell's mind. Its slightly Edwardian flavour seemed to fit the hunter well.

Vachell had heard of him often, but had never run across him before. There were only three white hunters in East Africa, it was said, worth a salary of £200 a month, and de Mare was one. He was middle-aged now—round about the fifty mark—but they said he was as skilful a hunter and as infallible a shot as ever. He knew the game districts inside out, from the Sudan to Rhodesia.

He had other assets, too, just as important on modern safaris—social assets such as ease of manner, ability as a raconteur, and attraction for women. He wasn't good-looking, Vachell reflected, but from all accounts women fell for him like ripe coconuts. He had been married once, but there had been a divorce.

He had a reputation for reckless courage and for a sort

of bravado which belonged to a past age and generation. He had speared a lioness from a pony's back, and once the Masai had permitted him to join a warrior's lion hunt, armed with a long shield of buffalo hide and a native spear. The hunted beast had charged the line between de Mare and his Masai neighbour and had fallen a yard from either with two spears, the white man's and the warrior's, quivering in its body. He had hunted elephant in Abyssinia in the Emperor Menelik's days, and once, according to legend, entertained an Ethiopian chieftain, who had been sent from Addis Ababa to arrest him for poaching ivory, to a sumptuous feast of raw meat in his tent, while the tusks for which the potentate had unsuccessfully searched all day were buried underneath the table at which the banquet had been held.

There were stories, too, of his extravagance. Sometimes, after a safari, he would spend a month's salary on a couple of wild parties in Marula, and he was said to be always in debt. He once got out of the country wearing a red beard and a turban, having disguised himself as a Sikh merchant and joined a party of his own creditors travelling down to the coast to intercept his flight. He left in an Arab dhow and came back in a private aeroplane chartered by one of the Vanderbilts, so no one liked to intervene.

An interesting guy, Vachell reflected. In the meantime, there were Lady Baradale's stolen jewels. Some one, clearly, had to investigate. He picked up the telephone receiver off its cradle and asked for the Commissioner of Police.

CHAPTER 2: THAT AFTERNOON DE MARE took Vachell on a rifle-buying expedition. The Superintendent had learned to shoot in the Royal Canadian Mounted Police; sporting guns, however, were new to him. He had wandered over North America from the Arctic Circle to the Gulf of Mexico, working on all sorts of jobs, but hunting big game had never been among them.

"You'll want two rifles," de Mare told him. "One heavy and one light. Every one has their own ideas, of course. I'd recommend a double-barrelled .450 or .470, in case you do meet anything large. I don't believe in medium bores for big game myself; bullet weight's more important than velocity when you're trying to stop a rhino at fifteen yards. But with any luck you won't need to use it. There are half a dozen high velocity medium-bore rifles for smaller game to choose from, all good. Come along and try them out."

They spent the next hour in a cellar underneath a gunsmith's shop, talking about muzzle velocity and bullet weight and foot-seconds with a Mr. Capstick, and testing rifles on a miniature range. Vachell settled on a double-barrelled .470 Rigby for the heavy rifle and a .275 Magnum Holland and Holland for the light.

They looked beautiful, he thought, as Capstick wiped them over and laid them gently in their felt-lined cases—blue-black and shining, with dark, smooth stocks, models of precision and efficiency. Capstick charged them to Lady Baradale without demur, and added ammunition, cleaning materials, sight-protectors, and slings.

"How about a cartridge-belt?" he went on. "With one of these, there's no risk of getting your ammunition mixed and trying to load your .470 with your .275 ammunition when an elephant's coming for you bald-headed at twenty yards. You ought to have one of these, Mr. de Mare."

"More frills," de Mare said. "I'm not going to go about looking like a Texas Ranger or something out of the films. I use a clip to reload my magazine and keep my heavy ammunition in a separate pocket. It's quicker, simpler, and just as effective."

Capstick looked a little dashed and laid a wide leather cartridge-belt on the counter. On each side of the buckle was a row of slots to hold the cartridges.

"Takes two sides, large and small bore, you see," he went on. "Solids one side and soft-nosed on the other, so that you can't get them mixed."

Vachell, growing reckless, decided that Lady Baradale would have one.

"Guess I'd better look the part, even if I don't know how to act it," he remarked. "When do I use soft-nosed bullets, and when the solids?"

"Solids for elephant, rhino, and buffalo," de Mare said. "Soft-nosed for lion and everything else—anything thin-skinned, in fact. You must have a solid to penetrate the hide of an elephant or rhino."

"Where do you stand on the buffalo issue, Mr. de Mare?" Capstick asked earnestly, wiping his glasses.

"Solids," de Mare answered decisively. "If you shoot straight you can find a vital organ, and if you don't an expanding bullet won't bring him down anyway—only annoy him. And if he comes, he needs a solid as much as a rhino does."

"Ah, well, so long as you can take the neck or brain, that's all right," Capstick said. "If you're taking the heart there's an advantage in a good mushroom. A bit in front and you splinter the shoulder, a bit behind and he won't go far. Gives you more margin."

"This is an old controversy," de Mare explained to Vachell. "Buffalo are midway between thick-skinned and thin-skinned classes of game. So the hunters' world is split into two camps as regards the right type of ammunition to use. If you take my advice you'll use solids, but even more will you avoid buffalo. They're tricky beasts to hunt."

On the counter was a small pudding-basin full of irregular-shaped scraps of twisted metal. Capstick took out a handful and spread them on his palm.

"You know how bullets look when they've done their job," he said. "These have all been recovered from dead animals. Here's a solid; you see, it's kept its shape almost intact. Solids will go through a bone without splintering it, and sometimes you can hardly see the hole where they pierced the skin. Now, here's a soft-nosed bullet. See how the lead has splayed out into the shape of a mushroom, and split the cupro-nickel coating into phalanges? This will tear a great hole in the soft tissues and splinter a bone to bits."

"It's the shock that kills more than the injury," de Mare

put in, "unless, of course, you get him straight off, plumb in a vital spot. After the first hit an animal's power to experience shock is diminished. Remember that if you ever get into a tight corner—it's the first shot that counts. Take your time, and don't rush it. That's one reason why a heavy rifle kills more surely than a light one. The bigger the charge in the cartridge, the higher the striking energy of the bullet in foot-pounds, and the greater the shock. These small bores have all the velocity you can want and a trajectory so flat they'll only drop about seven inches in three hundred yards, but they haven't the same powers of shock. They break up too quickly after impact, too. Give me bullet weight—and remember, it's the first shot that counts."

They said good-bye to Capstick and walked through the crowded streets, lined with two rows of angle-parked cars, towards the offices of Simba Ltd., the leading safari outfitters of Chania. The firm had equipped the Baradale safari, and de Mare was one of their hunters.

"I guess there's a lot of angles to this hunting racket the ordinary guy doesn't know about," Vachell said. "I shall feel as dumb as hell when I get up there, not knowing the ABC of the game. I'd be grateful if you'd give me a few wrinkles."

"It's just common sense," de Mare said. "You can't lay down a lot of rules, because each case is different. It's all experience. You develop a sort of instinct about how animals are going to behave. Watch the wind: that's the first rule, of course. It sounds simple, but it isn't—like keeping your head down in golf."

"And just about as vital, I guess, in this game."

"Exactly. Winds have a way of getting puffy and temperamental after about eleven o'clock. That's why most successful hunting is done in the early mornings. I always carry a little sack of wood ash myself, and test the wind every few minutes, especially if I'm after elephant. They can get your wind up to about eight hundred yards, though they can't see more than about thirty. And always get as close as you can—never take a shot you aren't certain of. All the work is done before you press the trigger."

"I shall stick to jewel hunting, if I can."

"Yes. I don't suppose you'll need to worry much about game, unless you want to go after some of the smaller stuff. You can never be certain, though. Never forget to watch the wind, and try to pass down-wind of any patch of bush that looks as though it might conceal a rhino. If you ever have to use the heavy rifle, keep your left barrel in reserve as long as you can, reloading the right after the shot. And another thing—look out for the man behind you. These inexperienced safari people are often more dangerous than a wounded buffalo. There are some wild shots in this party. Old Baradale's all right—a first-class shot, as a matter of fact—but young Catchpole and the girl are awful."

The name of Simba Ltd. was well known in London and New York as well as in East Africa, but its offices were unpretentious. They consisted mainly of a large warehouse with a corrugated iron roof, crammed with the relics of every kind of animal. Long shelves round the wall were piled high with a twisted mass of horns. Stiff, untanned lion and leopard skins lay in rolls on the bare board floor, and dried rhino and elephant feet littered every odd corner. The peculiar musty smell of semi-treated animal trophies permeated everything.

Vachell shook hands with a preoccupied-looking man in a dust-coat who was supervising the packing of some greater kudu horns destined for Czechoslovakia. He thought with horror of the many blameless walls that had been made hideous with the severed heads of dead animals dispatched to Europe and America from this warehouse in Marula.

"The boss said something about you this morning," the man said. "My name's Brett. You're new to Chania, aren't you? Done a lot of hunting in Tanganyika and Rhodesia, I understand?"

"Well, a bit," Vachell said modestly.

"Knowing the country is nine-tenths of the game, I always say. However, you've got a boss who knows what's what in Mr. de Mare." Brett led the way to an office which had been made by partitioning off a corner of the warehouse, pushed a roll of leopard skins off a desk, and pulled down a fat ledger.

"Here's the Baradale safari," he went on. "It's slap-up, believe me. Fourteen Chev lorries, all light buff with a red stripe and the Baradale crest on the side. Two Ford V 8 saloons and two Plymouth box-bodies, for running about. And all the doings—a big electric frig, light off the car batteries, pull-and-let-goes, an outfit for the mechanic fellow that's like a young machine shop, and a twelve-valve radio. You won't exactly be roughing it up there."

Vachell looked over Brett's shoulder at a long list of

provisions and equipment ranging from sugar castors and fruit-juice extractors, through grocery delicacies such as Comice pears preserved in *crème de menthe* and chicken breasts in aspic, to a screen for projecting movies and a taxidermist's outfit.

"Yes, it looks like we shall make out somehow," he said. "I don't have to order the meals, do I?"

"Not if Juma knows it," Brett replied. "He's the best safari cook we've got. He's been out with the Duke of Windsor, one ordinary duke, three earls, four maharajahs, and six American millionaires. The maharajahs were the worst—all those curries. We had a lot of hot-stuffs flown out special from Karachi that time. But Juma took it all in his stride. He'll do the meals, but you have to go through the stores with him every other day to see everything's okay, and send in a weekly return to us."

"And the liquor?"

"You're in charge of that too. It's kept locked up, and you issue it every evening. That's one thing you must look out for—never let the drink run low. Nothing gives safari people chilblains on the temper so much as running out of their favourite liquor. They all have their fancies, you know. Take this chap Catchpole; we've had a lot of trouble getting hold of some French drink he set his mind on, Amer Picon, it's called. And we've got a special order to send fresh mint packed in ice every time a lorry goes up to Malabeya, to make mint juleps, I understand."

"There shouldn't be any risk of a liquor shortage on this safari," Vachell remarked. He noticed an indent on the books for two cases of claret, two of Pouilly, four of gin, four of whisky, six of champagne, and assorted bottles of curaçao, liqueur brandy, Cointreau, and van der Hum.

Brett closed the ledger with a snap. "It's my job to see there isn't," he said. "People laugh at these modern slap-up safaris, but you and I get our living out of them. These rich blokes want their luxuries, and they're ready to pay handsome for them. Well, so long as their money's good, let 'em. That's what I say."

"Sure," Vachell said.

"Don't you go running away with the idea that hunting's the important part of these safaris," Brett went on. He was scribbling something on a pad. "It isn't. The commissariat is the part that counts. Give your clients a full belly and they won't mind how many lions they miss, but let the cook run out of tea or butter and if they get an eleven-foot black-maned beauty they'll grouse like the devil because it isn't a world's record. I know."

He tore a piece of paper off the pad and handed it to Vachell. "You can take over Englebrecht's tent and camp-bed; they belong to us. And you can keep his gun-bearer, too, but you'll need to take your own personal boy. If you give this chit to one of the clerks at the store he'll fix you up with bedding. You'll excuse me if I rush. I've got a safari due in a few minutes with a live elephant calf and two lion cubs that I've got to ship to Honolulu."

Brett zigzagged away through packing-cases and discarded horns towards a yard where native carpenters were busy making crates. Vachell wiped his forehead and remarked:

"Gee, these boys know how to hustle. Am I a hunter

now, or do I have to take a course in making *crêpes suzettes* and mixing cocktails?"

De Mare smiled, and led the way out into the street. "That's all for the present, I think. Simba Ltd. has changed a lot since I first knew it. They started life by taking foot safaris from the coast to the Great Lakes before the days of railways. It took six months for the round trip. There were three or four hundred porters, sometimes, each one with his sixty-pound load and a pair of boots slung round his neck. They had to carry beads and cloth to trade for food with the up-country natives. Now, of course, everything's done in lorries, even planes sometimes, with all home comforts laid on. Simba Ltd. do everything, from the moment you get to Chania with your cheque-book to the moment you leave with your trophies. That's the demand, and they meet it."

"With so much efficiency," Vachell said, "they should make nothing of finding Lady Baradale's jewels."

"She was a fool to take them on safari," de Mare answered. "She'll live to regret it, I think."

Neither of them knew, of course, that de Mare was wrong.

CHAPTER 3: THE LAST GLOW OF THE SUNSET
was fading out of the sky above a grey and darkening plain
when de Mare and Vachell reached the Baradale camp at
six-thirty the next evening.

The camp was pitched on a flat and grassy piece of land
on the left bank of the Kiboko river, facing north. A cluster
of large tents was centred round a magnificent flat-topped
acacia tree which stood on the edge of the bank. Ten feet
below it lay a broad white ribbon of sand, so white and
gleaming that it hurt the eyes when the sun beat down at
noon. The Kiboko river, a shallow stream nowhere more
than twenty yards wide, had cut a channel down the middle and flowed smoothly over rocks, eddying in and out
of little pools. At the far side the bank rose gently out of
the sand and merged into a wide bush-speckled plain
which rolled away to a far flat horizon.

To the east, a range of hills towered above the camp.
Thick bush grew up the sides, and the summit was
crowned with forest. Many watercourses straggled down
the hill-side, cutting the slope into smoothly rounded shoulders, and gentle foothills ran almost to the edge of the
camp. Behind, to the south, lay a stretch of broken bush-
clothed veldt, rising in the distance to form a long, low
range of hills. The Kiboko river flowed past the tents from
east to west.

The camp was symmetrically arranged, and kept tidy

18

as a London square. A big mess-tent near the acacia was
partially surrounded on the landward side by a group of
four more tents which housed the four principals of the
party. To the east, the far side of the acacia, was a cluster
of three more tents occupied by the two hunters and the
European chauffeur. The maid and Chris Davis, the game-
spotting pilot, comprised a third group on the other side
of the Baradale party. All these tents faced the river. Behind them lay an open grassy space, and beyond that,
partially concealed by some scattered bush, was a group
of a dozen smaller tents where the natives slept and where
the cooking was performed.

The car park was perhaps the most impressive sight. A
long line of shining trucks and cars was drawn up along
the western boundary of the camp, at right angles to the
river, their ranks as straight as a row of French poplars.
Two trucks stood apart, drawn up close to the tents. They
were the power-houses. One operated the refrigerator, and
the other was joined to the tents by long flexes carrying
electric current.

"I guess the tents of Israel had nothing on this outfit,"
Vachell said.

De Mare drove the car, one of the Baradale Fords, into
its place in the line, and switched off the engine.

"When you've got half East Africa to spread over,
there's no point in being too matey," he said. "We've arrived at the right time. The sun's gone down, and it's time
for the shy, retiring whisky bottle to emerge."

Several natives materialized round the car and a brisk,

clean-shaven young European in shorts and a dark red sports shirt came up, swinging a stick in his hand.

"Evening, Mr. de Mare," he said. "Have a good trip? Car all right, I hope? I'll give you a hand with the kit." He took a suitcase out of the back and handed it to an African. He was dark-skinned and good-looking, with healthy ruddy cheeks and thick black wavy hair that refused to lie down properly.

De Mare looked at him in surprise. "Kind of you, I'm sure, Rutley," he said. "This is Mr. Vachell. He's taking Mr. Englebrecht's place."

"Evening," he said. "Yes, I know. Englebrecht's leaving first thing to-morrow. You had a puncture, I see. Have any trouble with it?"

"I managed to change the wheel, thanks," de Mare said dryly. Rutley opened the tool-box on the running-board and rummaged about it. Then he straightened up, looking sullen.

"There's a spanner missing out of here," he said. "And you've brought back a different foot-pump. This one isn't ours."

De Mare looked up from extracting baggage out of the back of the car. "The foot-pump was missing out of the Ford when I started," he said, "so I borrowed a pump out of one of the trucks. I left the car at the garage in Marula to be greased and oiled. I expect they put back the wrong pump after they'd mended the puncture, and pinched a spanner."

"That pump belongs to one of the trucks," Rutley said. "You've no right to go changing the tools without telling me. I get the blame if anything's missing. This pump isn't half as good as the one you took down. And what became of that spanner?"

De Mare took his pipe out of his mouth and spoke sharply. "These cars belong to Simba Ltd.," he said, "not to you. This camp is lousy with pumps and spanners. What the hell's the matter with you?"

"Nothing's the matter with me," Rutley answered aggressively. "I'm responsible for these tools, that's all. I ought to be told when things are shifted about and lost through other people being careless. What's happened to that foot-pump and that new spanner?"

"I dug a hole ten feet deep on the top of Mount Kilimanjaro and buried them in a Union Jack," de Mare said. His voice was curt and strained. "You can dig them up if you like." He turned on his heel and stalked angrily away towards the tents.

"I shall lose my temper with that bastard," he remarked, "one of these days. He's getting more and more intolerable. I suppose one can't expect anything else, in the circumstances. But it's getting very hard to bear."

"What do you mean, in the circumstances?" Vachell asked.

"You'll soon see," de Mare said.

They found the party sitting round a table outside the mess-tent, looking over the river towards the shadowy veldt beyond. The water below them glowed softly, reflecting the last pink from the western sky. A newly lit camp-fire was beginning to crackle nearby, and a blue spiral of smoke rose through the still evening air.

Vachell got the impression that restraint and a little awkwardness were in the air as he shook hands all around. It didn't surprise him. Although no one but Lady Baradale knew he was a detective, every one knew that he'd come to replace Englebrecht. And Englebrecht was still there—a hefty, flaxen-headed, coarse-boned lad, with a trace of Dutch accent, good-looking in a commonplace sort of way. He had a clear, healthy complexion, and his bare brown arms and legs looked as hard as marble. After he greeted the two new arrivals he hardly spoke half a dozen words all the evening, except when he asked Vachell what sort of rifles he had brought; and he got up and left the group shortly after de Mare joined it. Vachell couldn't tell whether he was sulky or just shy.

But he could tell who was boss around the camp before he'd been there ten minutes. Lady Baradale let there be no mistake about that. She had a face like a mask, and rarely smiled; when she did, it looked more like a deliberate facial contortion than an expression of amusement. She had regular, even features, high cheek-bones, and deep-set eyes. She was lavish with make-up and her perfectly waved silver hair was set in a wide sweep off the forehead. It was a humourless, calculating face, with a mouth like the slit between the shells of an oyster. She was thin, and held herself very upright. She looked well in khaki slacks and a drill shirt, the uniform of safari.

"Very glad to know you," she said to Vachell. She had a metallic voice, and spoke slowly. "It's too bad Mr. Englebrecht can't stay on with us, but we're all delighted to have you take his place. I want you to meet my step-daughter, Cara Baradale."

Vachell glanced at Englebrecht. The young hunter stirred slightly in his canvas chair, and reached for his glass. The table was covered with bottles. That was a dirty crack, Vachell thought.

Cara Baradale nodded to him across the table and said, "How d'you do," curtly. She was lying back in a camp-chair with a tall glass clasped in both hands, and a pair of perfectly shaped legs, smooth and white below navy-blue shorts, stretched out in front. She looked up at him for an instant and returned to a concentrated study of the contents of her glass. She's a good-looker, Vachell thought, but sulky as a thunderstorm that won't burst. The light was fading quickly and he couldn't see her face distinctly, but he could tell that she was pale and clear-skinned, and that her eyes were large and dark. One lock of dark hair had fallen over her forehead, but she did not trouble to push it out of the way.

"Cara is engaged to be married to Sir Gordon Catchpole." Lady Baradale gave the impression of dropping the words, one by one, into the silence, like stones dropped into a pond to create a ripple. A young man seated in a chair next to Cara Baradale nodded his head and said: "Pleased to meet you, Mr. Vachell." He sounded affable, but his voice suggested affectation. He was fair and slender and looked delicate. He hadn't been hunting that day, evidently, Vachell thought; he wore rust-red corduroy trousers, a chocolate-brown linen sports shirt, and a red-and-yellow silk scarf knotted round the neck.

Lord Baradale was left to the last. Not that he seemed to notice; he was too absorbed in the dissection of a small camera to be conscious of his surroundings. It lay in bits all over the table. His wife had to repeat his name twice before he came to.

"Good evening, good evening, delighted you were able to come." He shook hands warmly and pulled up a chair. He was a short man, not more than five foot six or seven, and rather stout. He was clean-shaven and nearly bald, and the dome of his head shone like a billiard ball. His face was fleshy, his nose long and slightly hooked, his eyes small and pale. She didn't marry him for his looks, Vachell thought. His title, probably. He poured out two highballs for the new-comers with hands that were deft, restless, and neat.

Conversation was not, at first, very lively. Catchpole asked for news of Marula. De Mare, in no doubt as to the type of news required, responded with a summary of such gossip about visitors and local celebrities as he had managed to collect in the capital.

"Marula's crop of ripe, rich scandal never fails," Catchpole said. "It's my favourite city. It's so *baroque*. A good, mid-west, Main Street town with delusions of Mayfair grandeur—the sort of place where the bartender of Dane's claims to have been the head waiter at the Café de Paris. Don't you think, Mr. Vachell, it has a sort of jejune *charm*?"

"I never got just that slant on it before," Vachell said cautiously.

Lady Baradale came to his rescue. "I hope you will

enjoy being with us, Mr. Vachell," she said. "Cara will monopolize most of your time, I expect. She likes to start at dawn and be out all day." There was a dash of malice in her tone, like the flavour of bitters in a cocktail.

Cara Baradale slumped down a little farther in her chair. "It's a nice change from being out all night," she said. "Anyway, I shan't monopolize Mr. Vachell to-morrow. I'll leave a clear field for you, Lucy. I'm going into Malabeya with Luke to drive the car back."

"You are not!" The command came from Lord Baradale like a small explosion. He lifted himself half out of his chair. "You'll do nothing of the sort, Cara. I've never heard such damned nonsense in my life. Do you think I'm going to let you go driving cars all over Africa by yourself?"

"Cara would be perfectly safe for the part of the trip she made by herself." Lady Baradale's tone was quite expressionless. "I will talk with Cara."

"You can talk yourself sick," the girl said. She tossed the straying lock of hair out of her eyes with a jerk of the head, and drained her glass. "You make me tired. I can't prevent you giving Luke the sack, but if you think you can stop me seeing him when I want to, you're crazy. I know perfectly well what's going on here. You're such a lot of damned snobs you want to get Luke out of the way. Well, you're wasting your time, and you'll soon know it." She jumped to her feet and walked, quickly but unsteadily, towards her tent.

"Good Lord," Catchpole remarked. "Cara gets more and more like Katharine Hepburn every day. Some one ought to warn her, or she'll wake up and find she's been turned into a lonely little *gamin*." He got up and helped himself to another gin-and-French.

"Some one!" snorted Lord Baradale. "Some one be damned! If you had the guts of a ferret, Gordon, you wouldn't stand back and let this sort of thing go on in front of your nose. Why don't you ——"

"Thomas! Remember where you are!" Lady Baradale's voice was sharp and peremptory. Her husband checked himself and subsided into his chair. His face looked flushed and angry and, somehow, frustrated.

"Whose fault is it?" he asked. He was still breathing heavily. "This trip was your idea. You've driven her into it. It was you who ——"

"Be quiet, Thomas!" The drawl in Lady Baradale's voice had given way to the snap of command. "You can't blame it on me if your daughter prefers to go around with an illiterate Boer instead of with a boy from her own class. Mr. Vachell, we dine at eight-thirty. Thomas, please light me to my tent."

Lord Baradale picked up a safari lamp from a row on the ground and escorted his wife to her tent. De Mare, remarking that he needed a bath, took another lamp and disappeared into the darkness, leaving Vachell and Catchpole alone.

"I'm so glad you've come," the young baronet remarked. He smiled a little wistfully, and poured out another gin-and-French. His face was finely moulded and effeminate, his body slim and willowy. He had soft blond hair with a slight wave. "You look so *sensible*. To tell the truth, this safari has begun to get on my nerves. I'm sure Luke Engle-brecht is highly satisfactory as a lover, though he doesn't seem to me to have a *spark* of imagination, but I must admit that *I* find him boring. Of course, I should be the last person in the world to try to prevent Cara, poor sweet, from having a bit of fun, but I can't pretend the situation's easy."

"I should say not," Vachell agreed. Catchpole's voice was growing a little squeaky, and there was no doubt that the numerous gin-and-Frenches he had put away were having their effect.

"You know, I like you," he went on expansively. "I know *instinctively* when I meet some one I can trust. It's all very awkward, as I was saying. Lucy's a dear, but she hasn't an *atom* of tact. I really can't blame Cara for re-senting the whole thing. After all, she never pretended to be in the *least* in love with me. But she hasn't a *bean* of her own, poor sweet. I'd drop this marriage idea to-morrow, but Lucy's so *dominating*. And then, of course, I've got a very expensive interior decorating business to keep up. I must say, Lucy's been an *angel* over that."

Vachell was uncertain of the correct response. He drained his highball and ventured: "I guess you can't let Lady Baradale down."

Catchpole nodded his head emphatically and groped for his glass. He was having difficulty in focusing his eyes. "That's just *it*," he said. "I knew you'd understand. It would break Lucy's heart if I left Cara to that *handsome* clod. Poor dear Lucy *such* a snob. I can't desert the sinking ship, can I? That's what Lucy is, stinking—sinking, I mean."

"How do you mean, sinking?"

Catchpole looked melancholy, and wagged his head. "Age has withered her, and custom staled her infantile— infinite variety. After all, even with all that money, you can't expect these things to last for ever, can you? *I* think she's being very unreasonable. He's awfully attractive, and after all he's twenty years younger, and you can't expect him to stick to one job for the rest of his life, however well he does out of it."

"Who are you talking about?"

"Don't you know?" Catchpole looked surprised. "Rutley, of course. He's Lucy's boy-friend. She picked him up on the lot and made him into a day-time chauffeur."

"I see," Vachell said slowly. "And now he's beginning to tire of the night-time part of the job?"

Catchpole nodded. "Poor dear Lucy made an awfully stupid mistake. She *had* to bring a maid, of course, but instead of a *hideous* old hag she brought an attractive young *thing*. And now, of course, her precious Rutley has gone and fallen for the lovely Paula."

CHAPTER 4: IT WAS NINE O'CLOCK BEFORE
dinner began. The meal was not so difficult as Vachell had
expected. Hot baths seemed to have restored everyone to
a more mellow frame of mind. They appeared in heavy
silk dressing-gowns over pyjamas and mosquito boots, and
ate in the open under the big acacia tree. The night was
balmy without being too hot, and a myriad of stars glit-
tered in a cloudless sky.

The meal was rich and excellent and the champagne
superb. Glasses were kept constantly replenished by a tall,
slim young Somali with a beautiful, disdainful face and a
proud bearing whom Vachell identified as Geydi, Lord
Baradale's personal boy. He wore a white silk robe with a
red sash and a coloured turban. Other native servants,
deft and silent, came and went with plates and dishes, and
miraculously managed to serve the meal hot and steaming
from a kitchen fifty yards away.

Vachell said little, and admired the skill with which de
Mare kept the conversation under full sail but steered it,
on occasion, away from the rocks of controversy. A dis-
cussion on the coloration of game animals occupied most of
the meal. Lord Baradale defended the protective theory
of coloration vigorously, while de Mare quoted Stigand
and Selous in support of his contention that the theory, as
applied to game in Africa, was in the main a fallacy. All
beasts of prey, he pointed out, hunted by smell and not by

sight, and in any case at night; and an elaborate system of coloration to avoid natural enemies by daylight was therefore unnecessary. As for man, it was probable that primitive people were to a large extent colour-blind and in many case insensitive to tones and shades, so that subtleties of marking were equally wasted on them.

Catchpole joined in with some remarks on the contribution of African game to the art of interior decoration. He was designing, he said, a material for curtains based on the colour scheme of Grant's gazelle, and was planning to launch two new shades for sitting-room interiors; one, "Cobus grey," copied from the coat of the waterbuck, and the other, *Pachyderm* pink, from the inside of the hippopotamus's nostrils. He was very excited over his discoveries.

"Africa is so magnificently *modern!*" he exclaimed. "We've neglected it for far too long. Now, at last, it will come into its *own* as a wonderful source of original design in decoration."

"I saw the Game Warden in Marula," de Mare intervented hastily. "He says we're to keep a sharp look-out for a gang of Timburu rhino poachers in these parts. They've just killed a game scout who was trying to round them up. They're ugly customers, it seems."

"But how thrilling!" Catchpole said. "Fancy poaching rhinos! So much more *unwieldy* than pheasants or rabbits. Why do they poach the poor dears?"

"For aphrodisiacs," de Mare replied.

"Good heavens!" Catchpole exclaimed. "I should never have thought that a rhino would have *that* effect. Of course, they are *primitive* looking things."

"You don't look at them," de Mare explained. "The Timburu sell the horns to Somali traders, who smuggle them down to the coast, and they—the horns, I mean—finally get shipped to China and made into a powder."

"What a *shame*!" Catchpole said. "To think of those poor prehistoric dears laying down their lives to stimulate the jaded appetites of the teeming millions of China! Could they know that they were being sacrificed on the altar of Venus, would they die more gladly, I wonder?"

"I doubt it," de Mare replied.

"You ought to try it, some time," Cara Baradale said. Her voice was low and husky, with an undertone of exasperation. "In small doses, not too strong."

"There's nothing I should love more. But I think you would be better without it, don't you, my sweet?"

Cara didn't answer, and Lord Baradale quickly switched the conversation back to the Timburu. He asked de Mare a string of questions about their methods of hunting. They used poisoned spears, mostly, de Mare explained; rhino's hide was generally too thick for arrows. They were young warriors, as a rule, newly circumcised and anxious to obtain trophies of their own prowess, and money to exchange for camels and cattle with which to buy wives. Three or four would stalk the rhino to within fifteen or twenty yards and then hurl their spears simultaneously into its side. It was really murder, de Mare said; rhinos were easy game, and sometimes the poachers would get six or seven in a week.

Liqueurs were served with coffee, and afterwards the party sat out under the tree and watched the starlight on the river and the mysterious misty veldt beyond, where

a thousand invisible forms crept and stalked, fed and
mated, listened and sniffed for smells, in the busy darkness.
A slight breeze stirred the acacia branches and cooled the
faces of those who sat, replete and rather sleepy, beneath it.

Lady Baradale was the first to say good-night. When
she had gone, de Mare leant over the back of Vachell's
chair and said, in a low voice: "She wants to see you in her
tent." A little later Vachell pleaded fatigue and walked off
with his lamp to his tent. He left the lamp inside and
made his way cautiously across the grass to obey the
summons.

Lady Baradale was waiting for him, seated at her dressing-table. She wore deep green velvet dinner pyjamas that
glowed like *crème de menthe* in candlelight. The scent
of perfume mingled with the smell of sun-bleached canvas.
Vachell sniffed with interest, and diagnosed Chanel No. 5.
The tent was a large one, with a veranda at one end and a
bathroom partitioned off by a canvas flap at the other. To
the right was a camp-bed with mosquito-net, to the left a
green-and-white striped curtain that concealed a row of
hanging skirts and dresses. The dressing-table, with a three-
piece jointed mirror, was between the entrance and the
bed. An electric bulb dangled from the ridge-pole above it,
and a reading-lamp stood beside the bed. A small leather
travelling-clock on the dressing-table told him that it was
a few minutes past eleven.

"Please sit down," she said. He pulled up a camp-chair
and obeyed. She kept her profile towards him and smoothed
her silvery waves with a skinny hand. "I guess Danny de
Mare has talked with you about the burglary. There's one

hundred and fifty thousand dollars' worth of jewels missing, Mr. Vachell, and I want to get them back."

"Where were the jewels kept?" Vachell asked.

She pointed to a small square safe standing on the ground beneath the table at which she sat.

"In there. It weighs heavier than it looks, and it has a burglar-proof lock. The safe wasn't busted open, though; some one used the key."

"Where did you keep the key?"

"In my pocket-book. It stays there all of the time. I keep the pocket-book in the pocket of my slacks all day, and at night I sleep with it under my pillow."

"And you've never loaned the key to any one?"

"Never. These jewels are genuine, Mr. Vachell, not copies, and they're worth too much money to trust any one with the key. Even my maid isn't allowed to open that safe. I'm certain I haven't had my pocket picked, and I can't figure out how any one can have taken the pocket-book from under my pillow without waking me. I wonder if the thief could have drugged my after-dinner coffee, or something? I'm counting on you to find out."

"I'll do my best," Vachell said. "Have you had a thorough search made in the native quarters?"

Lady Baradale shook her head.

"Why not?"

"Because I don't believe a native stole my jewels. Look, I'll show you." She knelt down by the table, twiddled the key, and flung open the doors of the safe. Inside were two compartments. The top one was occupied by a red leather jewel case. The lower section was filled with papers done up in bundles in elastic bands, some of them obviously personal letters.

Lady Baradale pulled out the jewel case and opened it, and Vachell looked over her shoulder. He saw that none of the drawers in the case was empty. Diamonds, sapphires, topaz and zircons gleamed at him invitingly from the shadows. There were no emeralds, rubies, or pearls.

"I get it," he said. "This was a selective burglary. He knew enough to pick out the plums and leave the small-time stuff. A native would have cleaned out the lot—anything that sparkled."

Lady Baradale locked the safe again and stood up. "That's how it looks to me," she said. "I hate to have to admit it, but I'm afraid you won't have to look farther than the white section of the camp for the thief."

"How about this maid?" Vachell asked. "How long has she been with you?"

"Two years. I like her, but I guess I don't know a great deal about her history. She claims to be a Russian of good family. Her father was killed in the revolution and her mother brought her over to the United States when she was a baby. She was raised in Los Angeles. My daughter, whose home is in Hollywood, found her for me. She's had opportunities to steal from me before, but she hasn't used them."

"And the chauffeur, Rutley?"

Vachell watched her face carefully as he spoke. The mask remained expressionless, under perfect control.

"He came to me with excellent references, and I have

no cause to doubt his honesty. He has no need to steal. I see no reason to suspect him of this."

"What are his relations with the maid?" Vachell leant forward in his chair and kept his eyes fixed on Lady Baradale's face.

"He has nothing to do with Paula." A new and harder note had stiffened her voice. She took up an orange-stick from the table and started to treat her nails. Her lips were pressed together in a hard line.

"Looks like most any one could have sneaked in here and extracted the key while you slept," Vachell commented. "Is there any lead on that dope angle? Do you remember any occasion on the night before the theft when a member of the party might have had a chance to monkey with your coffee?"

"I've thought of that," she answered. "I can't call anything to mind."

"Why did you fire Englebrecht?"

"I should have thought that was obvious, Mr. Vachell. My stepdaughter has gotten herself into a very foolish state of mind about that young man. It's nothing serious, of course, but both Lord Baradale and I feel that in Cara's own interests it would be best to dispense with his services. Although he has not behaved honourably, I have no reason to suspect him of theft."

"I shall search his baggage before he leaves, of course," Vachell said, "but if I use a microscope on everybody's kit it isn't likely to do any good. If the thief has any sense he buried the stuff a foot deep in the bush an hour after he took it. If he left any prints on the safe, which isn't likely, they're all mussed up by now. Will you help me out, Lady Baradale? Do you have any suspicions?"

Lady Baradale kept her attention fixed on her nails. The mask was still without expression, but her nostrils and the muscles of her mouth contracted slightly.

"None that I can substantiate—yet," she said. "I'd prefer that you use your own judgment. I'd like to make one thing quite clear. I want my jewels back, whoever took them. If your enquiries lead you to some—well, distasteful results, go right ahead and don't spare any feelings."

"The police aren't very squeamish over feelings," Vachell said.

He said good-night and walked thoughtfully back across the grass, the clinging scent of Chanel No. 5 still in his nostrils. One thing, at any rate, he thought, was clear. Lady Baradale had made her own guess as to who had stolen her jewels; and she was reluctant to admit the truth of her suspicions.

CHAPTER 5: KIMOTHO, A SMILING, STURDILY built native with the usual close-cropped woolly head, flat nose, and prognathous lips of his kind, brought his master's tea at five o'clock next morning. Through the triangle formed by the end of his tent Vachell could see night and stars and a faint thinning of the blackness that meant that dawn was spreading behind the hills.

"It is very early," Kimotho remarked in Kiswahili. He spoke with feeling. "But you told me to wake you when the other bwana was called. He has had his tea, and now his boy is packing his bed. Why does he want to leave before the lions go to sleep?"

Vachell extricated himself from his mosquito-net and gulped his steaming tea. He slipped into a shirt and shorts, pulled on a couple of woolly sweaters, and stepped out of the tent. The sky was oyster-grey behind the towering hills to the right. Shapes of trees began to loom mysteriously in the half-light. There was a heavy dew and the grass felt chilly through the soles of his shoes. The air was sharp and cold in his lungs.

He found Englebrecht loading the last of his possessions into one of the Plymouths by the light of a safari lamp. Vachell explained the situation briefly. The hunter's face was invisible in the darkness, but his surprise at the news of the jewel theft seemed to be genuine. He raised objections, however, when he heard that his luggage, his person, and the car would have to be searched.

"It will take too long," he protested. "I am no thief."

"What's the hurry? You haven't a train to catch," Vachell observed.

Englebrecht shrugged his shoulders. "Oh, well, all right," he said. "You'd better be satisfied."

He stood by, scowling, while Kimotho held up a lamp and Vachell opened bags, gun-cases, bedding, and boxes and spread every item on the ground. The hunter's armoury consisted of a Westley-Richards .318, a 9.3 m.m. Mannlicher-Schonnauer, and a shot-gun. Vachell asked him, casually, why he hadn't a heavy rifle.

"I've got a .470 like yours," Englebrecht answered. "I've lent it to Rutley, though. The clients on this safari are so mean they never let him do any shooting, and he hasn't got a rifle of his own, so he borrowed mine. I'm not sorry to be leaving."

The bright stars faded and the dark night paled to a rich blue as the hunt proceeded. Vachell took his time, searched carefully, and found nothing. Inspection of the car and of the hunter's clothes yielded no more. Englebrecht grew more and more impatient.

"Okay," Vachell said at last. "You've nothing to declare. Hope I haven't made you late for an appointment."

Englebrecht only grunted in reply. He and the driver, who was going to Malabeya to return the Baradale's Plymouth, threw the luggage into the back and jumped into the front seat. (The hunter had left his own car in

Malabeya.) Englebrecht let in the clutch with a bang and the car shot at high speed into the bush.

"Luke seems in a hurry to leave us," a woman's voice said. "Are you ready to go?"

Vachell turned to greet Chris Davis, the game-spotting pilot. She had been instructed by de Mare to take the new-comer out to look for elephant before breakfast. This was part of the second hunter's job, and it had been agreed that Vachell had better act the part as realistically as he could.

He had hardly had a chance to speak to Chris Davis at dinner the night before. Like de Mare, she was quite different from the picture that he had unconsciously built up in his mind. He had heard, vaguely, of her history, and knew that it was not a happy one. She had been mar-ried very young and her husband, a local farmer, had been killed in a motor smash on their honeymoon. She had struggled, single-handed, to carry on his farm, but bad luck and bad seasons had forced her out, and for a time she had made a living by capturing wild animals for Ameri-can zoos. She had learnt to fly, and become obsessed with aviation; and now she supported herself precariously by taking any flying job she could get. She had operated her second-hand Miles Hawk for a while as an air taxi, and had once held a job as a parachutist in an air circus in Eng-land. Vachell had expected some one masculine and hard-boiled and weather-beaten; but there was nothing tough about her outward appearance. She was slight, slender and fair, with thick corn-coloured hair and a pale clear com-plexion. Her thin, rather delicate-looking face wore a grave expression, but there were little puckers at the corners of her mouth and eyes which suggested indulgence in a private amusement at the world.

The ball of the sun was rising over the hilltops as the Baradale Plymouth rattled along a rough track that de Mare had cut through the bush to connect the camp with the main road. The car twisted and turned among stunted thorn trees and lurched up and down rocky gulleys apparently at random, but Chris, who was driving, seemed to know exactly where to take it.

A five-mile shadow lay across the bush-covered flats like an immense dark stain, and beyond it the open plains were flooded with sunshine. Below them Vachell could see the shadow rolling up like a carpet and the sunlight racing after it up the slope. A few minutes later the sun burst over the summit, and suddenly he felt warmth on his bare arm and saw the car's shadow in front. Birds twittered excitedly in the green acacias, and steam started to rise out of the bush as the dew evaporated.

They crossed the drift, abandoned the car, and plunged on foot in the long grass on the right-hand side of the river. Vachell stripped some grass seeds and florets off a handful of stems and threw them into the air to test the wind. They floated gently down to his right.

Their intention was to search for spoor around the drinking pools along the river. Vachell led the way, gripping his new .470 in one hand. The grass reached nearly to his waist and he was soaked to the skin in the first few minutes. He followed the swing of the river, moving with caution and straining his eyes to see around each clump of bush. The grass swished against his knees as he walked.

After ten minutes he caught sight of something grey moving behind a bush to his left. He stopped dead in his tracks and watched an animal about the size of a donkey stalking majestically across his field of vision. It must be a waterbuck, he decided. It was a fine male, holding its forward-curved horns high and sniffing the air with soft black nostrils.

A little farther on his eye caught a movement to the right and he stopped again, this time with more abruptness. Thirty yards away, through the long grass, he saw a face: the tips of two tawny ears, a black nose. The rifle went up to his shoulder in a flash. A lioness! She had seen them, and was staring fixedly in their direction. He felt his heart pounding quickly, and pressed the stock into his shoulder. It looked as though she might be crouching for a charge. His finger tightened on the trigger. Then the face moved: disappeared. It bobbed up again through the grass to the right and he swung the rifle round and sighted again. No, it was all right: she wasn't coming. He lowered the rifle in relief and watched the grass wave as she lolloped away.

"I'm glad you didn't shoot the poor little waterbuck calf," a low voice behind him said.

Vachell experienced a sinking feeling in the pit of his stomach. For crying out loud, he thought, a waterbuck calf!

"Just trying out the sights of a new rifle," he mumbled. They moved forward again, slowly.

A few hundred yards farther on they came to a pool in the river with a game path leading down to it. The wet

sand around the edge was pitted with spoor. They examined
it silently, bending over the criss-crossed tracks. Vachell
felt a fresh wave of misgiving. They all looked the same
to him. How was he to know an impala from an orbi?
There was the mark of a pad with five toes. Was it a lion
or only a hyena?

A low whistle came from his companion. She was bending over a large, clear impression in the sand, about
twenty inches across, with a slightly corrugated surface.
Well, he could recognize that. There wasn't anything else
that *could* look like an elephant.

He bent over it, nodded, and tried to look knowing. De
Mare, he reflected with envy, could probably tell the animal's age, sex, and the size of its tusks from that spoor.
The hunter had explained a bit about tracking on the way
up. You could tell sex from the size and age from the
imprint, he had said—the corrugations on the sole of the
foot were sharper and deeper in the case of a young animal
than with an old one. And sometimes a heavy tusker could
be distinguished by the deeper imprint of his toes. Hell,
Vachell thought, that guy could probably tell the colour
of its eyes and its views on the Chinese war and whether
it goes for blondes or brunettes by looking at its footprints.

"Two big bulls," Chris said in a low voice. "We'd better
see which direction they've taken."

There was a steep sandy bank above the right-hand
margin of the pool, and Vachell had no difficulty in picking out the marks the elephants had made in scrambling
up it. On top of the bank a game track led back into the
bush. He could make out the great round impressions

distinctly in the dust. A little way along he came to a pile of droppings, still slightly warm. He wondered how long droppings kept their heat, and how you told their age. Chris, behind him, turned over part of them with a stick and he observed a number of large beetles rolling the dung inside into neat balls. "About two hours old," she whispered.

He led on, wondering whether the bulls were feeding just ahead. If only they'd keep to the sand it would be all right. But of course they didn't. Soon after they passed the droppings he lost the spoor. He cast about in the bush ahead and found a faint trail which led over a patch of dry grass and then petered out in a rocky gulley. Although he searched for ten minutes he couldn't pick it up again. The stony ground seemed to stare back at him blankly, utterly uninformative.

How could any one, he asked himself, spoor an animal over a lot of rocks and stones? There just weren't any traces. In the back of his mind he knew that a native tracker could follow those bulls as easily as a passenger changing stations on the London Underground could follow the red light for Piccadilly. Where animals had walked, there must be traces—crushed grass stalks, torn-off leaves, little stirrings in the dust; invisible to the unskilled eye, but crying aloud to the initiated. That was the way a detective went to work. Where a man had committed a crime, there must be traces—imperceptible, probably, to any eye but the trained one. This jewel theft, now . . .

He jerked his mind back to the elephants. That damned woman was watching him. She seemed pleasant enough,

quiet, didn't say much, but she was just a shade too observant.

"They've gone up the gulley and down towards the
plains, I guess," he said. He tried to make his voice sound
confident.

She looked at him in a peculiar way, half puzzled, and
he thought he saw her mouth twitch a little.

"I expect they have," she said.

For some reason her tone annoyed him. To hell with
the elephants, he thought. He decided to climb to a rocky
knoll on top of one of the gulley's shoulders. There was
just a chance that they might be visible from there, if they
had halted nearby. There was a red ant-hill near the
crest that might serve as a lookout post. He clambered up
a bank covered with thick bush, cursing all elephants as he
went, and steering for the ant-hill.

He emerged into an open grassy space on the edge of
the knoll and saw the ant-hill a little way ahead. Then,
suddenly, a violent crash made him jump convulsively and
jerk the rifle up to the ready. Simultaneously it occurred
to him that he must have gone crazy. The ant-hill had
apparently detached itself from the knoll and was crashing towards him with the noise of a thunderbolt and the
velocity of a shell. He flung himself sideways into a bush
and the object hurtled on into the gulley like a big tank run
amok.

He disentangled himself slowly from his thorny refuge
and emerged cursing, pulling thorns out of his bleeding
legs. He realized with devastating clearness that he had
been walking down-wind in thick bush with his rifle slung

on his shoulder, making straight for a rhino that had just completed a mud-bath in the river and was standing in the open, in full view. He had mistaken the rhino for an ant-hill.

Chris Davis was waiting at the bottom of the gulley. He walked towards her slowly and reluctantly, his bare arms and legs criss-crossed with scratches. No doubt about it, she had caught him with his pants down this time.

"Next thing you know we'll be running into Mrs. Roosevelt," he said heartily. "Plenty of activity around here. How about getting back for some breakfast? The elephants will keep."

"We certainly didn't disturb them," his companion said. It was clear that she thought him either a fraud or a flop; and Vachell was afraid he knew which.

Breakfast was set in the shade of the giant acacia. The tree was in flower, and the scent of its pale lemon-yellow blossoms was sweet and fresh. Vachell decided that charging rhinos made you hungry. He ate a mango, a slice of pawpaw, scrambled eggs and sausage, and a great deal of toast. De Mare and Chris were his only companions. The Baradales, and sometimes Catchpole, it seemed, had breakfast in bed, and Lady Baradale never appeared before ten or eleven. Her husband sometimes got up in time to photograph the dawn, and sometimes fooled around in pyjamas with his films till noon.

"I'm going to take Catchpole out after lion this morning," de Mare said. "There were two hunting down the river last night. I sent the trackers out first thing and they found a fresh kill about a couple of miles away.

Catchpole is just too *thrilled*, my dear. He must have a
beautiful lion with a proud, flowing mane. Uh."

"There's no justice," Chris remarked. "Why should a
man like that be allowed to kill a good, honest lion?
Or, rather, employ you to kill it for him, Danny. It
ought to be the other way round."

De Mare grunted and filled his pipe. He looked as
spruce in a pair of khaki shorts and a bush shirt as he
had in a suit in Marula. His shiny hair was brushed
neatly off his forehead, and his clothes were carefully
ironed.

"How many baronets would you give a lion on its
license?" he mused. "Some people could be classed as
vermin. . . . There'll be a murder in this camp one of
these days. Half the people are at each other's throats,
and the other half in each other's beds. What with Cara
Baradale and young Englebrecht disappearing into the
long grass together all day, and our respected employer
dallying with her sulky boy-friend, the camp's practically
a damned brothel." He lit his pipe, picked up his felt hat,
and rose to go.

"A couple of elephant watered below the drift this
morning," Chris said. "I thought I'd take the bus out
later on and look for them."

"Good idea," de Mare agreed. "Take Vachell along
too. Give him an idea of the lie of the land. I must go
and butcher this wretched lion to make Catchpole's holi-
day, I suppose. It'll probably give him some new ideas
for mural design in cocktail bars."

"Good luck," Chris said. She smiled at him, and Vachell

noticed that it made her face look young and vivacious, and that her teeth were white and even.

"Thanks," de Mare said. "Oh, and by the way—watch your step if you see Lord Baradale this morning. He's in a tearing rage. Cara kept her word, and went off to Malabeya with Englebrecht before dawn in one of the Plymouths."

Vachell sat up abruptly in his chair. "She did?" he asked incredulously. "She didn't leave here with him in the car."

"No; she used low cunning. She was waiting for him about a mile down the road, according to the driver, who was turned out and came back on foot. Lord Baradale is not amused."

Vachell leant back and lit a cigarette, his eyes on the morning sunlight sparkling on the river. He'd got away to a bad start, he reflected. Cara had outsmarted him already. She'd got away from the camp without being searched.

As he lay there, his muscles relaxed, it seemed to him that a cloud passed swiftly over the sun. He shivered, and goose-flesh rose on his arms. "A goose walking over my grave," he said to himself, and smiled at the superstition.

Afterwards he wondered if he had, for the first time in his life, experienced a premonition—a warning that before the sun had reached its zenith, death's cold shadow would have fallen across these bright surroundings.

CHAPTER 6: A LITTLE BEFORE TEN O'CLOCK
Chris and Vachell drove in the remaining Plymouth to
the roughly cleared air-field just outside the camp. The
blue two-seater Miles Hawk looked a flimsy little object
for such tough conditions—more like an outsize locust,
Vachell thought, than anything else. He climbed up on
to the wing, pulled a flying-helmet over his head, and
settled into the front seat. Chris swung the propeller and
clambered into the pilot's seat behind. There were two
rifles, a heavy one and a light, by her side—a wise pre-
caution, he imagined, in case of a forced landing. A native
guard kicked the blocks away from under the wheels, the
engine roared, and they bumped forward over the veldt
and into the wind.

They flew first down the river bed, a dark green ribbon
on a speckled light green field, at about five hundred feet.
When they came to the drift the plane banked and started
to climb to the left. That was funny, Vachell thought;
the elephants were on the right bank of the stream.
A herd of antelope in the thin bush just below looked
like a swarm of red ants. He wished that he knew what
they were. The plane rose higher and Chris took up a
pair of field glasses and peered down at them through
the open window.

They swung away from the river in a wide sweep
to the south. The country below was rolling, fairly open

bush. Chris kept on banking the Hawk slightly to the
left so that she could examine the ground beneath.
They came to dark patch of trees and she circled over
it, using the glasses. Then she switched off the engine
and then drifted silently down towards the splodge of
vegetation.

"There they are," she said.

Vachell leant out as far as he could and saw what
looked like a collection of grey boulders scattered about
in some thick bush. Each boulder had two white knobs
at one end. As the plane swooped lower the lines of the
spinal cords and the huge flapping ears became visible.
The Hawk's shadow glided silently over the backs of
the herd, but they noticed nothing. The plane went on
past them, losing height, until it was skimming over the
tops of twisted acacias and the dark fleshy arms of
euphorbias. One wing-tip missed a tall ant-heap by inches,
and then the engine roared. The plane gave a jump like
a startled horse and leapt forward, climbing sharply.

"I didn't want to scare them," the pilot explained into
the speaking-tube attached to Vachell's helmet. "They
were feeding. They'll stay where they are now all day,
unless anything disturbs them."

"That's swell," Vachell said with feeling. "We don't
want to risk disturbing them again."

The country looked like a grey-green rug thickly
dotted with dark knots. They flew on at about two
thousand feet, swooping down at intervals to inspect a
family party of giraffe and two rhino; herds of Grevy's

zebra, kongoni, and Grant's gazelle; a group of animals resting in the shade that Chris identified as oryx beisa and eland; and some black objects in a ravine which caused her to exclaim: "Look, buff." There seemed to be no end of it, Vachell thought; it was like a lesson in zoology.

Half an hour later Chris turned and headed for home, setting a course to pass over the elephants. She located the right patch of bush and flew low, but the herd was no longer there. She circled widely, using the glasses, but they were nowhere in sight.

"Something must have alarmed them," she said into the tube. "They looked settled in for the day. I'm going to have a look."

The Hawk turned eastwards, towards the hills, and flew low in big circles. Five minutes later Chris spotted something, pulled back the throttle, and swooped down to have a look.

"There they go," she said. "They're moving in towards the hills. Something must have scared them all right."

This time they looked like grey lice crawling over a flat surface. An aerial view, Vachell thought, robbed elephants of all their majesty. They looked undignified and insignificant.

"They're doing eight or nine miles an hour, I should think," Chris added. "They've travelled five or six miles and it's now nearly half-past eleven. That means they must have started moving about a quarter to. So it wasn't us that disturbed them, thank goodness. We flew over them about half an hour before that."

Chris swung the plane back on to a northern course and in a short time the dark bank that marked the Kiboko river came into sight. The heat-haze below gave it the illusion of wriggling slightly, like a snake. Each of the countless specks of bush seemed to waver like black stars in an inverted dust-white sky.

They crossed the river and turned, and Chris switched off the engine. They floated down towards the camp, crossing the river again above a pool that lay about a mile downstream and shone beneath them in the sunlight like a new coin. It was said to be the haunt of hippos. Vachell leant out as far as he could and gazed down at the fat, sleek back of one of the huge beasts standing, oblivious of inspection, by the pool's edge. It raised its head and gave him a clear view of its round pink nostrils. They reminded him of photographs of craters on the moon. As the plane flew over the water the engine started up again with a roar, spat two backfires in rapid succession that smacked against the air like rifle reports, and settled into its steady drone. The hippo plunged wildly into the water with a splash and a snort and disappeared completely from sight. The Hawk rose to clear the trees around the camp, skimmed over the neat symmetrical rows of tents, and drifted gently to earth on the bumpy air-field beyond.

It was noon when they landed, but they did not reach camp until half an hour later, for Chris announced that she had to clean out the jets. She crouched on a wing and went to work on the engine, the hot midday sun beating down on her bare head and causing her thick, windblown hair to gleam like honey. Vachell waited for her, strolling around in the biting heat, his thoughts veering between elephants, jewel thefts, and the involved personal relationships between the principals of the safari. Being a white hunter, he decided, wasn't all gravy from any point of view.

Chris finished her job on the plane and stood for a moment wiping her hands on a wad of cotton waste and looking down at him, curiously.

"Have you done a lot of hunting?" she asked.

Vachell's heart sank. Now it's coming, he thought. He tried to sound off-hand.

"Fair amount," he said.

"Had much to do with elephants?"

"Sure. I did some elephant control for the Tanganyika Government."

Chris threw the cotton waste into the Hawk's cockpit, jumped lightly off the wing, and walked over to the car. Vachell followed, carrying the two rifles.

"The Tanganyika elephants," she remarked, "must be very queer in their habits."

"What do you mean, queer? I once saw a bull that had red lacquered toenails, but that was in Billy Rose's circus in New York. These were standard models."

"I thought perhaps they all walked backwards," Chris said.

Vachell gulped, and it seemed as though the earth had quaked beneath him. He stood still, engulfed in a wave of dismay. He felt as small as a lost field-mouse in a desert.

Chris threw back her head and laughed uproariously.

Vachell's usually impassive face turned pink. He could think of no retort. He felt his mouth go dry and his palms moist with an unexpected wave of anger, and at the same time he noticed that when Chris laughed her rather solemn face looked as young and carefree as a seventeen-year-old's.

"I'm sorry," she gasped, "but it *was* funny. You mistook a waterbuck calf for a lioness, you walked downwind into a rhino and that you thought was an ant-hill, and you spoored those elephants backwards. It's a bit unconventional for a white hunter, you must admit."

"I admit everything," Vachell said, climbing into the car. "I was a dope, I guess, to think I'd ever get by. I'm a policeman."

"In disguise," Chris said, letting in the clutch, "but without false whiskers. Another illusion gone. Now I'll test my detective skill. You're here to investigate the theft of Lady Baradale's jewels."

Vachell felt a slight shock of surprise. "How did you know?" he asked.

Chris laughed again. "For three weeks Lady Baradale appears at dinner every night glittering like a Christmas tree with priceless gems—lovely ones, some of them, I must say, even if they did look ridiculous on safari. One night she appears without them. The following morning Danny rushes off mysteriously to Marula, and turns up again on the next day but one with a new white hunter that I've never even heard of, who has the original habit of tracking elephants backwards. It isn't very difficult."

"You're a smart girl," Vachell said, "and very observant."

They parked the car and found de Mare and Catchpole in the mess-tent, drinking gimlets. The lion hunt was just over and Catchpole was celebrating a new triumph.

"Come and drink with me to the great Danny!" he invited, waving a gin bottle in the air. "I asked him for a beautiful lion with a proud, flowing mane and he found me one—but a *beautiful* beast, with the flowingest mane you ever saw. And now his pride and beauty are no more. Let us drink to the destructive element in man!"

Vachell and Chris congratulated him suitably and toasted his success.

"We were lucky," de Mare said. "We found last night's kill and beat two or three gulleys down the river. My gun-bearer spotted the lion slinking out of the bottom of one of them. We marked him into a patch of bush, and the bearers beat up the gulley until he came out, and then Gordon got him with a peach of a shot. He dropped like a stone and never moved."

The noise of the celebration attracted Lord Baradale, who emerged from his tent looking hot and red-faced, with developer stains on his fingers. They all had another round of gimlets and heard the story over again, in more detail and with dramatic embellishments, from Catchpole. Lord Baradale only grunted and muttered something under his breath. It was clear that his temper was on edge. He even spoke sharply to Geydi when the young Somali, moving as though the very earth he trod on was beneath contempt, rattled the trays of the refrigerator when extracting ice cubes in readiness for the white wine at luncheon.

"It's past one," he said peevishly, after a third round of

gimlets had been consumed. "Time for lunch. Where's Lucy?"

"I haven't seen her since our triumphant return," Catchpole said. "She must be brooding enviously in her tent." Lord Baradale heaved himself out of his chair and went off to fetch her. He strutted along on his short legs like a bantam in a hurry, too rotund to look impressive.

A few minutes later he returned to the table by himself. "She must have gone off somewhere," he said. "I've been in my tent all the morning developing, and I haven't seen her. It's damned inconsiderate. She knows I don't like a late lunch. Well, we won't wait."

It was not until they had finished the cold guinea-fowl and canned Bradenham ham at two o'clock that any one started to worry. Then de Mare slipped away from his seat and disappeared behind the tents. He came back looking perturbed and anxious. Chris Davis jumped to her feet the moment she saw his face.

"Rutley says he took her out in the car this morning and dropped her at the drift about eleven," he announced. "She told him that she wanted to walk home along the river, and no one seems to have seen her since."

"By herself?" Lord Baradale asked sharply.

"I was out with Gordon, and Vachell had gone off in the plane with Chris. She shouldn't have done it. She knows that no one's allowed out of camp without one of the hunters."

"Rutley had no business to let her go off alone!" Chris exclaimed.

"No. He's behaved like a fool. Vachell, take a car and

a gun-bearer, go down to the drift and work back along the river. I'll start from this end. You'd better go with him, Chris."

"I'm coming with you, de Mare," Lord Baradale said. "This isn't your fault. At last I'll be able to get that bloody chauffeur sacked!"

At half-past two de Mare, Lord Baradale, and three natives, moving in open formation down the river, were halted by a shout from the hunter's gun-bearer, a sturdy native by the name of Japhet.

"Look at the birds, bwana," he said.

A cloud of vultures was hovering and wheeling in the sky, black against a brilliant blue. De Mare squinted up at them in the strong light.

"Yes," he said impatiently. "They are eating the lion which bwana Catchpole shot this morning."

"There is another kill beyond," Japhet said.

De Mare pulled out his glasses and focused on the hovering birds. He could see then that there were two separate points of attraction in the bush beneath. Sometimes the vultures settled in one spot, sometimes in another. He sprinted towards them up the gulley, dodging like a duiker through the bush.

A few minutes later he found all that remained of Lucy, Lady Baradale—a skeleton half covered with shreds of torn flesh and tattered strips of clothing, lying in a bloody trampled circle in the bush. Vultures wheeled overhead, angry at the sudden interruption. Lord Baradale panted up, and checked his impetus abruptly. He stared down at the gruesome remnants, his chest heaving, the sun shining hotly on to his bare and polished head. Then he lifted his rifle and emptied the magazine into a cluster of vultures perched like obscene black fruit in the branches of a nearby tree. Three birds thudded heavily to the ground, and lay still.

CHAPTER 7: HALF AN HOUR AFTER DE
Mare's gun-bearer reached them, panting, with the news,
Vachell and Chris Davis were back in camp. There was a
tense air of expectation everywhere. Crowds of natives
seemed to have sprung out of the ground. They stood
about in little clusters, chattering excitedly, and turning
their heads at intervals to gaze towards the mess-tent where
the Europeans had assembled.

They were all there except Lord Baradale. He had retreated into his tent, and no one liked to disturb him. De
Mare was pacing up and down with nervous, jerky strides,
looking white and unhappy. He was responsible for the
safety of the party; the death of one of them might mean
the end of his career. Gordon Catchpole sat limply in a
chair, drinking gin straight. Rutley lounged by the opening, impassively smoking cigarettes. His ruddy-cheeked,
handsome face betrayed no expression. Occasionally he
raised his eyes and glanced at Paula, who sat rigidly with
her hands clasped on her crossed knees, pale and nervous.

Vachell looked at her quickly as he stooped to enter
through the open flap. Her face was heart-shaped; high,
wide cheekbones, a pointed chin, and dark wavy hair with
a widow's peak. Her skin was chalk-white and she had
long eyes with heavily mascaraed lashes. She was small-
boned, and wore a tight cream-coloured linen skirt, a navy
open-necked linen shirt, and sandals.

De Mare halted abruptly in his stride as Chris and Vachell entered. He nodded towards the table and chairs in the centre of the tent.

"Sit down," he said. His voice was low and incisive. "We've got to get to the bottom of this. It won't be pleasant, but we've got to face it. We've got to find out how Lady Baradale died."

"Can't we send to Malabeya for the D.C.?" Catchpole asked. His voice was edgy and plaintive. "Surely it's his job to deal with *legal* things like this."

De Mare turned and stared down at him. "Yes, it is. But the D.C. isn't at Malabeya. Vachell and I called at his office yesterday and he's gone out on a camel safari. No one knows when he'll be back."

"What a god-forsaken country," Catchpole said. He reached for the gin bottle and poured another drink.

"Lady Baradale must have been dead for at least two hours when we found the—her," de Mare went on. "Probably more. That would mean she died sometime between eleven and twelve-thirty this morning. I don't think we can put it closer than that."

"How about the vulture?" Vachell asked. "Couldn't we fix the time of the . . . accident, if any of the boys noticed when they started to, well, come around?"

"We could have," de Mare answered, "if it hadn't been for Gordon's lion. Lady Baradale's remains were found about a hundred yards from where we killed the lion this morning. The vultures started to gather at once, of course, and they were all round the place while the boys were skinning it. From a distance you wouldn't be able to tell that they'd found a second kill!"

Paula gave a convulsive shudder and buried her face in her hands.

"My God, it's awful," Gordon moaned. "I can see it all now! Poor dear Lucy came walking along after we'd shot the lion, not a thought of danger in her head, and met his infuriated mate! The lioness charged, intent on vengeance; she sprang on poor unsuspecting Lucy; she buried her claws in . . . oh, I can't bear it!" He rocked to and fro in his chair.

De Mare stared at him grimly, and with some disgust. "That theory had already occurred to me," he said, "in a rather less dramatic form. Unfortunately the vultures got too long a start. I couldn't see any traces of lion-mauling, but there's very little left to show traces of anything."

Paula shivered and cried out: "Oh, this is horrible!" Chris Davis patted her on the shoulder and said: "Spare us the details, Danny."

"I propose that Vachell and I should examine the remains shortly," de Mare went on. "In the meantime, we must trace her movements as well as we can. Rutley, it looks as though you were the last to see her alive. What time did you drop her at the drift?"

"We left here just after ten," Rutley answered. His voice was sulky and he spoke with an air of defiance. "She said she wanted to go for a ride. We went along the Malabeya track for six or seven miles until we came to a herd of giraffe. We watched them for a bit, and then we turned back. When we got to the drift she said she wanted to walk back to camp from there for the exercise. I suppose that was about a quarter to eleven. I didn't look at the time."

"Did Lady Baradale often walk home when she went out for a drive with you?" de Mare asked. His voice was as even and precise as ever.

Rutley shifted on his feet and flushed slightly. "Sometimes," he said. "She said she wanted the exercise."

Vachell, his eyes fixed on the chauffeur's face, asked: "Did she intend to take that walk when you started out?"

Rutley turned on him with something like a snarl. "How the hell do I know what she meant to do?" he snapped. "She didn't tell me her intentions, did she? All she said was she wanted a drive. What's it got to do with you, anyway? You keep——"

"Shut up, Rutley," de Mare said. "You know perfectly well you had no right to let Lady Baradale walk back alone. It was criminal carelessness, if not worse. It's you who are responsible——" He checked himself in mid-sentence and went on with his striding to and fro. "What did you do after Lady Baradale got out of the car?"

"I drove back to camp."

"What time did you get in?"

"Just after eleven."

De Mare jerked his head up sharply and looked at the chauffeur.

"It's about three miles to the drift," he said. "How could it take you twenty minutes or more to drive three miles?"

Rutley glared at him and fingered the wide brim of his double-felt hat in his hands.

"I keep telling you, I didn't watch the time, particular," he said. "I wasn't hurrying. I stopped a few minutes for a smoke when I left her at the drift."

De Mare stared at him for a few moments without speaking, and then resumed his pacing. The chauffeur looked as though he was going to take a swing at his questioner at any moment.

"After you got back to camp," de Mare went on, "what did you do?"

"Adjusted the timing on one of the trucks."

"Were you in camp all the rest of the morning?"

Rutley's eyes flickered quickly in Paula's direction, and again back to de Mare.

"Yes," he said.

Vachell was watching Paula. He saw her raise her head sharply to glance at the chauffeur, and then lower it again to stare at her clasped fingers.

"Then Lady Baradale left the drift at about a quarter to eleven," de Mare continued, talking aloud. "The spot where we found her body is about two miles from the drift. If nothing occurred to delay her, she'd have reached it between 11.15 and 11.30—say 11.30. Paula, did Lady Baradale say anything about going for a walk when she left camp in the morning?"

Paula looked up with an anxious face. "I don't believe so," she said. Her voice was rather shaky. "She said she was going to take a ride with George—with Mr. Rutley."

"What time did she leave?"

"Right after ten, like George says."

"Did you see Rutley when he came back?"

"Sure. I saw him fixing the motor on the truck."

"And after that?"

The girl hesitated and passed her tongue over her brilliant carmine lips. "I guess he was around," she said. "Yes, I remember now. I saw him over at his workshop. I was in my tent all morning."

"Where was Lord Baradale? Did you see him?"

Paula seemed relieved when the questioning took another turn. "He was right here in camp, I guess. Why don't you ask him where he was?"

De Mare, still pacing up and down, paid no attention to her remark. He looked across at Vachell. "We'd better get this job over," he said. "The rest of you will stay here until we've finished. "I'll tell a boy to bring tea."

He led the way through the open flap and across the grass to Lady Baradale's tent. The dead woman's remains had been collected in a sack and carried there, after much protest, by two reluctant natives. The others waited in uneasy silence in the stuffy mess-tent, trying to keep their imaginations from playing with the scene they knew was taking place.

"My God, this is awful," Gordon Catchpole said at last. "I shall *never* forgive myself, *never*. I shouldn't have killed that magnificent beast, leaving his mate to avenge him with poor Lucy's blood. . . . Though I must say, I *don't* think Danny ought to have left Lucy all alone in camp. After all, he's paid to *protect* us."

"He couldn't protect her and get you a lion at the same time, could he?" Chris asked acidly.

"He didn't *get* me a lion," Catchpole said. "I got it for myself. I do really feel that he's rather to blame. Chris, when do you think Cara will be back? There's something so strong and *comforting* about her."

Chris walked to the tent opening and looked out over the white sand and the blue river to the line of the veldt beyond. An immense, formless bank of violet and indigo cloud was massed over the flat horizon, vivid and heavy. The hills to the right looked dark and menacing, and every thorn tree was sharply defined.

"There's a terrific storm going on towards Malabeya," she said. "I'm not sure that Cara *will* get back to-night."

"Oh, dear, this is *too* ghastly," Catchpole wailed. "I wish I'd never come to this awful country."

Chris stepped back to make way for Geydi, tall and impressive in his turban and silk robe, carrying the tea things on a tray. She poured out tea and they sat for a while, awkward and depressed, in a silence broken only by the clinking of cups and saucers.

Five minutes later they heard a step outside and then Vachell's tall, lanky form appeared in the opening. He stooped a little and came in, looking serious and taking nervous puffs at a cigarette. He halted in front of the table and glanced quickly at each face in turn.

"De Mare is talking with Lord Baradale," he said. "He'll be out in a moment. We found out how Lady Baradale died." He paused for a moment, the focus of four unwinking pairs of eyes. "She was shot through the head."

CHAPTER 8: FOR A MOMENT NO ONE SPOKE. Then Catchpole pulled himself half out of his chair and shouted: "That isn't possible! She was found quite close to us—we should have heard the shot!"

"She was shot through the forehead," Vachell went on, "and from the front. It isn't suicide, because there's no weapon near. The bullet must have killed her outright."

Paula gave a gasping cry and started to sob. Chris put one hand on the girl's arm, but her eyes never left Vachell's face.

"Did you find the bullet?" she asked.

Vachell shook his head. "No. It came out at the back of the head—drilled a neat round hole clear through the skull. She wouldn't have suffered any."

"There wasn't a rifle in the car," Rutley exclaimed. "Ask any of the boys, they'll tell you." He was standing near the opening, breathing hard.

"Who said there was a rifle in the car?" Vachell asked.

"No one. But you all think—" he checked himself abruptly and stood there, glowering like an angry bull.

Catchpole stood up suddenly, jerking the table so that the tea slopped over into the saucers. "There's only one explanation!" he exclaimed. "Of course, that's it. Lucy was shot close to where I got the lion, wasn't she? Well, there were two shots. I fired, and hit the lion. Then Danny fired, a second after I did, and missed. The lion was only hit once. Danny's bullet must have ricochetted off something, and hit poor Lucy. Chris, don't you see?"

The tent darkened momentarily and they all looked up, as though their necks had been manipulated by a single cord, to see de Mare in the opening of the tent. He took off his hat and walked with long, jerky strides to the table.

"What's the excitement, Gordon?" he asked.

"Oh, my poor Danny," Catchpole exclaimed, compassion in his voice. "It's *too* awful for you. It's one chance in a million, and it's too *cruel*, but it must have happened. The shot you fired at the lion, the one that missed, was the fatal shot. *You* killed Lucy!"

De Mare's mouth tightened into a hard line and he thrust his hands into the pockets of his shorts. It was a gesture of sudden self-control.

"Save your sympathy," he said. "You might need it for yourself. If either of us shot her, it was you."

"But it couldn't have been, Danny. It was *my* bullet that killed the lion. Your gun-bearer brought it to me himself—he'd cut it out of the carcass. Look, I've got it here!"

Catchpole dug his hand into his pocket and threw a twisted, shapeless scrap of metal on to the table. It was a spent bullet. "My rifle's a .315," he went on, "and that's a .315 bullet. So it couldn't have been *my* bullet that killed Lucy. It was yours."

"You did not shoot that lion," de Mare said. He spoke slowly and distinctly. "I did. My job as a white hunter is to see that my clients shoot the animals they want to shoot, and have paid for on their licence. If they're such damned bad shots they couldn't hit the Albert Hall at twenty yards, I have to shoot the animals for them. But I have to be careful that they don't know I've done it. That lion was killed by a bullet through the vertebræ of the neck at eighty yards while he was moving. Do you seriously think you could make a shot like that?"

"But the bullet," Gordon wailed. "They found my bullet!"

"They found nothing of the sort," de Mare said. "That bullet on the table was dug out of a zebra you shot a week ago. When I gave instructions to my gun-bearer about skinning the lion this morning, I gave him that bullet and told him to bring it to you, saying that he'd found it in the lion's heart. You missed that lion completely. Your shot went high."

Catchpole's face was white and contorted. He gripped the edge of the table and looked as though he was going to cry.

"I don't believe it!" He stamped one foot on the ground.

"I'd suggest that you call your gun-bearer to confirm that," Vachell said.

De Mare walked to an opening and bellowed "Japhet!" in the direction of the boys' quarters. The gun-bearer came running—a tall, beefy African with an intelligent, friendly expression, who carried himself like a soldier. He was dressed in khaki shorts, a bush shirt, and sandals made from an old car tyre. He stood smartly at attention in the opening of the tent and said "Bwana," in a crisp military tone.

De Mare nodded to Vachell. "You ask the question," he said.

"Listen, Japhet," Vachell began. "Who shot the lion that died this morning?"

"Bwana Danny shot it," Japhet answered without hesitation.

"And this other bwana, bwana Catchpole, did he shoot it also?"

Japhet shook his head emphatically. "No. There were two shots, but only one bullet in the lion's body."

"Did you see the bwana fire?"

"No, because I was walking through the bush close to the river, with a man who works as a tracker. Bwana Danny told me to stay close to the river so as to drive back the lion if he tried to escape in that direction, and then to walk up the gulley so as to drive him ahead. I was going slowly up the river when I heard the rifle speak twice, very close together, and I ran up quickly, and I saw the lion lying in the grass—quite dead."

"You only heard the rifle speak twice?"

"Yes, twice only. The first time very close, and the second time very near to it. Then I stayed with the lion to drive away the vultures and the tracker went back to camp to fetch the skinners. The skinners came and did their work, and I found the bullet from bwana Danny's rifle in the neck."

"Was that the bullet you brought to bwana Catchpole, and said was his?"

"No, bwana." Japhet shook his head. "Bwana Danny told me to throw away the bullet that killed the lion, and to bring instead a bullet that he gave me, and that had been fired from bwana Catchpole's gun. So I smeared it with the lion's blood, and then I took it to bwana Catchpole, and I said what I had been told to say."

"Are you positive that the bullet you found in the lion's neck was from bwana Danny's gun?"

"Yes, bwana," Japhet spoke emphatically, and his voice rose several keys. "Have I not been bwana Danny's gun-bearer for ten years? Have I not cleaned his rifle every day, and seen him kill many, many animals—lions, elephants, and buffaloes?"

"Have you got the bullet still?"

Japhet hesitated and looked rather embarrassed. Then he grinned, showing a fine array of white pointed teeth. "Yes, I kept it because a bullet that has killed a lion brings strength and good luck to the owner."

"Show it to me, then."

Japhet groped in the breast pocket of his shirt and extracted a slug of metal, which he handed to his interrogator. Its tip was slightly flattened from impact with the bone but its shape was intact, and Vachell had no difficulty in establishing that it was of the same bore as a cartridge from de Mare's pocket which fitted the hunter's Mannlicher-Schonnauer .375 magazine rifle.

"I guess that proves the story," Vachell said.

De Mare nodded dismissal to Japhet. The gun-bearer turned on his heel like an askari and left the tent.

"I'm sorry, Gordon," de Mare said. "But you needn't worry. That's one of the commonest hunter's tricks on this sort of safari. We all do it on occasion. And it couldn't have been your bullet that killed Lady Baradale. You fired straight ahead across the gulley and her—remains were found a hundred yards to the right, up the slope."

"Were you with Sir Gordon all morning?" Vachell asked the hunter.

"Yes, after we left camp a little before ten. We tracked the lion from the kill and beat the gulleys for about an hour and a half, I should think, before we got a shot. You and Chris flew over the hippo pool, quite close to us, about five minutes after we got him—that ought to help you to fix the time. Lucky it wasn't five minutes before, incidentally; you made an awful racket starting up the engine. After we shot him, we hung about taking measurements and so forth for a bit, and got back to camp between twelve and half-past. We were together all the time."

"And you didn't hear another shot?"

De Mare shook his head. "No, I can swear to that."

"Do you confirm that statement, Sir Gordon? You were with de Mare all morning?"

"Of course I was with Danny every *instant*!" Catchpole exclaimed. "And I *know* I didn't hear another shot. Your mind is full of the most *degrading* innuendoes! I don't see what it's got to do with you, either. I think you're being absolutely *horrid*!"

"Not I," Vachell said. "There's some one else around here who's being horrid!"

"Yes, but that's no reason to pick on me," Catchpole complained. "*I* didn't shoot poor Lucy. Since no one heard another shot, she couldn't have been killed *there*, could she? No one saw her after she left Rutley at the drift.

We've only got Rutley's word for it that she ever went to the drift at all."

Rutley stepped forward from the side of the tent where he had been standing, his jaw thrust out and his fists clenched. "If you're suggesting that I had anything to do with this—" he said, and stopped.

Gordon Catchpole hit the table with the flat palm of his hand. "I'm not suggesting anything!" he said hysterically. "*You're* all suggesting things. First Danny says I never shot the lion at all, and now Vachell tries to make out that I sneaked off and killed Lucy when Danny wasn't looking. I won't stand it, I tell you, I *won't*!"

"Take it easy, Sir Gordon," Vachell said. "No one's picking on you." He turned to Paula, who was sitting, stiff and scared, rigidly in her chair. "Did you hear those two shots here in camp this morning?" he asked.

She shook her head. "No, not those. That is, I don't think so. I wasn't listening."

"The camp's up-wind of where we got the lion," de Mare put in. "I don't think you'd be likely to hear the shots up here."

"What time was it," Vachell asked slowly, "when you heard the other shot?"

Paula ran her tongue over her lips and swallowed hard.

"I never said I heard another shot," she said in a dry voice. "I didn't hear a thing."

"What the hell has it got to do with you?" Rutley demanded. His fists were still clenched and his jaw thrust forward. "You keep out of this."

Vachell turned and looked at him steadily. His face was grave and set.

"You thought I came up from Marula to replace Engle-brecht," he said. "Well, I didn't. I'm a detective from the Chania C.I.D. I was called here by Lady Baradale to investigate the theft of her jewels three days ago. Now it's turned into a murder case, and there's going to be an investigation. From now on, I'm in charge."

CHAPTER 9: SHADOWS FROM THE THORN trees were lying in dark bars across the bleached pale-green grass, and the evening light was clear and golden, when Vachell finished his investigation on the spot. The storm had spent itself in the west, and the sun was setting like a shining dove in a fleecy nest of red and violet shreds of cloud over the hills toward Malabeya.

The examination yielded negative results. Vachell ruled out a ricochet from Catchpole's rifle, for there were no rocks or trees so placed as to deflect the bullet. Nor, apparently, could the possibility that Catchpole had shot Lady Baradale deliberately be entertained. De Mare had picked out, without hesitation, the place where they had stood to fire at the lion across the gulley; and from this spot Lady Baradale, advancing through the bush, would have been invisible. A rocky knoll on the right cut off the view. In any case, Catchpole had been slightly in the lead, and if he had swung his rifle around to aim at a target to his right, de Mare could not have failed to see the movement. The hunter was emphatic on this point. As for de Mare, since his bullet had been recovered from the lion's back-bone it could not, obviously, have killed his employer as well.

"God, what a mess," de Mare commented as they walked back together towards the camp. "If I hadn't seen the bullet-hole in her skull with my own eyes, I wouldn't have believed it. How can a woman be shot without any one hearing the report? It isn't possible."

"There isn't any evidence to show where she was when the killer shot her," Vachell reminded him. "Dead bodies often get shifted around."

"I suppose so. But it's a bit of a coincidence that it should be shifted so close to that lion."

"I don't care for coincidences in a murder case. Maybe this isn't one."

"What do you mean?"

"How do you ever find a dead body in the African bush?" Vachell countered.

"By the vultures, in the daytime," de Mare answered promptly, "if you find it at all."

"Right. Now suppose, for the sake of argument, that Lady Baradale was shot some place else, and the killer just left the body where it lay. Pretty soon the vultures would start to come around. Natives are lynx-eyed on details like that. The chances are they'd spot these vultures right away, and just as soon as Lady Baradale was reported missing, they'd go along there to investigate. Check?"

"I see," de Mare said slowly. "You mean that she may have been shot somewhere else and the body moved close to the dead lion? Every one would expect vultures to collect there in any case, so no one would suspect there was a second kill, and with a bit of luck the body would never be found.

"You got the idea," Vachell agreed.

"It didn't work."

"Not altogether. It did to this extent—by the time we found her, it was too late to decide just how long she'd been dead. That's always to a murderer's advantage."

The camp came into sight, its white tents gleaming like mushroom tops in the slanting sunlight. It looked peaceful, and full of the normal activities of evening. Blue columns of wood smoke rose into the air in graceful spirals, and an inviting smell of burning logs and cooking drifted towards them on the wind.

"Now for Lord Baradale," Vachell said. "I guess he'll be hard to handle. How did he react when you found the body?"

"Characteristically. He's only got one reaction to anything unpleasant or unintelligible—he loses his temper. It's a sort of hang-over from the feudal system, I think, when barons were barons, and lost tempers got results. He upped with his rifle and picked off three vultures from an adjacent tree. It was rather pathetic."

"It was good shooting," Vachell said.

Lord Baradale had emerged from his tent, and was sitting at the table under the acacia tree, watching the shadows fall over the sands and the gurgling river. The shrikes were sending their pure and mournful notes clearly through the still air, and a pair of flycatchers were chirping cheerfully among the myriad pale flowers of the acacia.

He didn't, Vachell thought, look particularly bereaved; but then he was not the sort of man to parade his sorrow, if indeed he felt it. Vachell didn't know much about the English aristocracy, but reserve before strangers and an unshaken front in the face of disaster were, he'd always heard, two of their chief characteristics. Lord Baradale seemed to be displaying both, together with a third, and perhaps more plebeian, trait—recourse to artificial stimulation at a time of crisis. A bottle of champagne was open on the table, and his complexion was a little flushed.

Vachell pulled up a chair and uttered some stock phrases of sympathy as sincerely as he could. Lord Baradale bobbed his head in a formal bow of acknowledgement and poured out some more champagne.

"Most amazing thing I ever heard of in my life," he said. "My wife had no enemies, nothing to fear. It *must* have been an accident."

"I think not, sir," Vachell said. "She may have had no personal enemies, but there's one guy in this outfit who had every reason to be scared to death of her."

"Who the devil do you mean?" Lord Baradale demanded.

"The man—or woman, maybe—who stole her jewels."

Lord Baradale sat up suddenly in his chair, spilling his wine. His surprise at the news of the theft seemed to be genuine. He listened, bug-eyed with astonishment, to Vachell's account of the situation.

"So you see, sir," the superintendent concluded, "I reckon Lady Baradale was murdered because she guessed who stole her jewels, and guessed right. Have you any idea who she suspected?"

Lord Baradale took several gulps of champagne and glared ferociously at the peaceful scene below him. "I've got a damned good idea who took them," he said, "the blasted parasite. But you must find that out for yourself. You say you're a policeman, and that's your job. I've no proof, no proof at all."

"There are a number of routine questions we have to ask," Vachell went on. He lit a cigarette and pushed the charred match into the ground. "About the will, for instance. Who inherits Lady Baradale's money?"

"So far as I know, my wife left half her fortune to her daughter by a previous marriage, and half to me—apart from various bequests, of course."

"How big were the sums involved, sir?"

Lord Baradale frowned and lit a small cigar before replying. It was clear that he resented the questions.

"That's got nothing to do with the matter at issue," he snapped. "My wife was a rich woman."

"Then I take it you'll inherit a pretty sizeable fortune —over the million mark, maybe."

Lord Baradale poured himself out another glass of champagne with a shaky hand. He reminded Vachell of a kettle on the boil, with jets of steam struggling to push up the lid.

"You can take it as you please, young fellow," he said.

"Thanks, sir," Vachell continued easily. "Where is Lady Baradale's daughter's home?"

"She's married to a young man in Hollywood who's got something to do with the films. Not an actor, thank God—writes scripts, whatever they are. My wife goes over to California to see her sometimes. She'll be a rich woman now, I suppose, if that damned fellow Roosevelt doesn't pinch everything before she gets it. American death duties are nearly as bad as ours now."

"About these bequests," Vachell persisted. "Does your daughter Cara get anything in the will?"

"Confound you, sir, how the devil do you dare to ask questions like that!" the angry peer exploded. "What the blazes has it got to do with you how much—" He checked himself in mid-sentence, took a puff at his cigar, and then smiled—a pleasant, friendly smile which banished his ferocity in a flash.

"I beg your pardon," he said. "It's hard to remember that you're a police officer doing your duty, and not a white hunter being inquisitive. Yes, my daughter does receive a bequest. I see no reason to disclose its amount, but the sum is, by most standards, a large one."

"Thanks a lot," Vachell said. "There's one more question. What were your movements during the morning?"

"I was in my tent, developing," Lord Baradale replied. "I've been experimenting with a new colour film on the Leica. It's a patent just got out by a small company I'm interested in, and the developing, though simplified, is still a tricky business. But I've got good results with some excellent studies of a pair of golden orioles and their nest, which ought to be unique."

"You didn't see Lady Baradale at all?"

"No. She never disturbs me when I'm busy with photography."

"Did you hear any rifle shots during the morning?"

"No, not that I can remember." Lord Baradale frowned, sipping his wine. "Wait, though, I think I did. Yes, now you come to mention it, there were two shots, close to-gether—soon after eleven, I think it was. That was when Gordon got the lion, I suppose."

"You heard no shots," Vachell persisted, "from any other direction?"

Lord Baradale shook his head and winced at the movement. He drained his glass and rose, a little unsteadily, to his feet.

"What the devil's become of that girl!" he exclaimed. "Damned little idiot, going off with that half-witted lout of a Dutchman, and coming back from Malabeya alone. I won't *have* her driving about all over Africa by her-self. . . ." His voice tailed off to an indistinct mumble as he walked, with a good deal of concentration, to his tent.

Vachell looked at his watch in the failing light. It was six-thirty. The camp was unusually silent, and though the table was loaded with bottles ready for sun-downers, the chairs were empty. He helped himself to a Scotch-and-soda and tried not to think of his sunburnt knees. They were bright red, and felt like twin furnaces. The pain, he found, made concentration difficult. He walked across to his tent, unearthed a bottle of Pond's Extract, and dabbed some on his sore knees with cotton. A few minutes later Kimotho came in carrying a four-gallon gasolene-tin full of steaming water, and announced firmly that he had brought the bath. Vachell frowned at his knees, thinking how much they would sting in hot water.

"All right, Kimotho," he said. "What is the news?"

The boy arranged an inflated rubber bath-tub in the

end of the tent which had been partitioned off as a bathroom, and shook his head.

"The news is bad," he said. "Very bad. This camp is not good. These Europeans have great wealth, but their cook refuses to give me rice to eat. He gives me maize meal, as if I was a savage."

"Perhaps I will speak to him," Vachell said, dabbing on more Pond's. "But I do not wish to hear about food. What do the boys here say about the memsahib who was killed to-day?"

Kimotho shrugged his shoulders. "They say much, but they do not know. How should we know? We were here in camp all day."

"Who else was in the camp this morning—the white folk, I mean?"

"You went far away and high up in the sky in the bird with a memsahib, and then——"

"Listen, Kimotho," Vachell said patiently, "I know where I went. I do not walk in my sleep. I want to know about the others. Did you see bwana Lordi to-day?"

Kimotho shook his head. "No. Perhaps he was in his tent. No one is allowed to go near him but the Somali, Geydi. He is a very bad man."

"Why?"

"He thinks that he is greater than a white man, and he goes with lying stories to the Europeans. It is true that he knows English and can take photographs and drive a car and make European drinks and shoot with a rifle, but others can do these things too. He——"

"All right, all right. Enough. Now tell me about bwana Rutley. Did you see him to-day?"

"Yes, I saw him go out in a car with the memsahib who is now dead. I did not see him return, but later he went out with a gun."

Vachell sat up suddenly on the bed and spilt some of the Pond's. "He did, huh? Did you see him? Where did he go?"

"Yes, I saw him," Kimotho said. "I had gone down to the river to wash one of your shirts. The work in this camp is very hard. I went up-stream until I found a good place, and then I sat down to wash. Presently, I saw bwana Rutley walking along in the sand beside the river, with a gun in his hand."

"By himself?"

"Yes, by himself. He went up the river towards the hills."

"At what time was this?"

"Perhaps eleven o'clock. Later on I heard the gun speak from above, in the hills, and I thought that perhaps he had shot a buck."

"You heard a gun speak!" Vachell exclaimed. He was sitting bolt upright on the bed, his sunburn forgotten. "What time was this?"

Kimotho shrugged his shoulders again. "It was not yet mid-day. I have no clock."

Vachell thought for a few moments, rubbing the back of his neck. "Did you hear the noise of two guns from down the river?" he asked.

Kimotho shook his head. "No, only the gun that spoke

from the hills. I could hear it because the wind came from that side. If a gun spoke or a man shouted from down the river, I would not have heard, unless it was close, because the wind would blow the sound away to Malabeya."

Kimotho emptied the contents of the gasolene-tin into the tub with a splash. He seemed to imply that this idle chatter had gone far enough. "The bath is ready," he remarked, and made towards the exit. "The cook says that there is no more meat for the boys," he added. "It would be good if you were to shoot some, bwana. Here we are without meat, and there are antelope all round us. If I went to a wedding feast, should I be without beer?"

The question was clearly rhetorical, for Kimotho left without waiting for an answer. Vachell sat on the bed for a few minutes longer, pensively rubbing his knees and staring down at the ground-sheet. Something that de Mare had said in Marula about the art of hunting came into his mind. "Watch the wind—that's the first rule," the hunter had told him. He reflected, as he kicked off his shoes and tested the heat of the water, that Lord Baradale had been foolish to ignore such sound advice.

CHAPTER 10: IT WAS RUTLEY'S MELANcholy task to make the coffin. Vachell found him in his workshop, a grass hut that had been erected near the carpark to house the tools and implements needed to keep the mechanical side of the camp in working order. With fourteen trucks, four cars, an electric light plant, a twelve-tube radio, a plumbing system and a network of electric bells connecting the tents with the natives' quarters, there was a good deal to be kept in order.

Rutley looked up when Vachell entered and nodded curtly. He wore a pair of navy-blue shorts and a white shirt stained in places with engine oil. His hair lay in dark, thick waves over a well shaped head. A cigarette drooped from the corner of his mouth and smoke rose in a lazy spiral towards the naked electric light bulb overhead. Tools and pieces of machinery lay about, and the sharp smell of engine grease was in the air. Rutley was knocking together a long box out of three semi-demolished packing-cases with Gordon's London Gin stencilled on them in tall black letters.

"Evening," he said, and went on with his work. Vachell peeled a piece of gum, folded it into his mouth, and watched the chauffeur for a few moments, chewing steadily.

Rutley stood it for a little and then said irritably:

"Must you do your chewing here? It's like a bloody cow waiting to be milked, or something. I'm busy."

"Why," Vachell asked in conversational tones, "did you say you were here in camp all morning, when you took a walk in the hills with a gun?"

Rutley swung around as quick as a wheeling horse and glared at his questioner. He gripped a hammer in his hand and half-raised it to his shoulder.

"It's a bloody lie!" he shouted. "I didn't go out with a gun—I stayed here. You can ask Paula; she saw me." His voice tailed off towards the end of the sentence and he turned back to his work and hammered in a couple of nails.

"Can't you see I'm busy?" he went on. "I've got nothing to tell you. I don't know anything about all this. I wouldn't want to shoot my employer, would I? She was generous to me, I'll say that. I'll be out of a job now." He gave a quick smile. "The old man isn't likely to keep me, I can tell you that."

Vachell regarded him for a few moments with an expressionless face, his jaws slowly champing the gum, his hands in his pockets.

"It isn't any use," he said finally. "This isn't a gag. My boy saw you with the gun. And he heard a shot."

Rutley's back stiffened and the hand that held the hammer remained for a second in mid-air. Then he straightened slowly and turned his head. His confident, rather bullying expression had faded as quickly as the colour fades out of stones on the beach when the sea recedes.

"Well, if I did take a stroll after a buck," he said,

"what's that got to do with you? I walked a little way up the river and back, that's all. I didn't shoot anything. I was back inside an hour."

"What did you fire at?" Vachell asked.

"A buffalo. I ran into a herd about a mile or so up the river—at least, I saw the backside of one in the bush just across the gulley. I had a shot and then there was the hell of a din, and the whole bank opposite turned black with buffaloes. They seemed to sprout out of the ground, and they crashed through the bush like a lot of steam-engines. In the other direction, luckily. I had a look round when they'd cleared off, but there wasn't any sign of the one I'd fired at, so I must have missed."

"Pretty risky business, chasing after buffaloes," Vachell commented.

"Oh, I wasn't chasing buffaloes, particularly," Rutley answered. His hands were fidgeting with the hammer. "I wanted to get a buck. Englebrecht lent me his rifle, and I wanted to try it. He's a decent chap, Englebrecht is— not so damned snooty as the rest of 'em. This camp is lousy with rifles, but no one else ever offered to lend me one."

"He lent you a .470," Vachell said. "That's used for big game, not for buck."

"He said he wanted his light rifles for himself. This was the only one he could spare. He warned me it would blow a small buck to pieces. What the hell does it matter, any-way?"

Vachell made no reply, and studied the ground at his feet. His jaws champed the gum with the regularity of a sleeper's breathing. Rutley watched him, fiddling nervously with the hammer. He took up a tin of Player's on the bench and helped himself to another cigarette.

"Which car did you use this morning," Vachell said at last, "when you took Lady Baradale out riding?"

"One of the two Fords."

"Do you keep a mileage record for the cars?"

Rutley reached for a note-book lying amid an untidy litter of tools on the bench. He seemed relieved at the turn the questioning had taken.

"Yes, I do," he said. "Lady Baradale was very particular about that. She watched the gas like a hawk. I had to enter up the mileage of every trip and take the speedometer readings every morning to see the natives hadn't done any joy-riding on the quiet." He flipped open the book and handed it over. "I checked all the entries before I went out in the Ford this morning," he added. "I couldn't check either of the Plymouths, though. One went to Malabeya with Miss Baradale, and you and Mrs. Davis had the other all the morning."

"Has the second Ford been out to-day?"

"No—not unless some native took it for a joy-ride."

"Thanks," Vachell said. "Guess I'll keep this for the time being."

He switched on his flashlight and walked out of the hut and over to the car-park, about twenty paces away. He went through the line methodically, shining his torch on to the dashboard of each truck in turn, and comparing the reading on the speedometer with the appropriate figure in the note-book in his hand. In every case the two readings corresponded.

At the end of the line was a gap, and then came the two Ford sedans. The speedometer of the first registered 2,489 miles, and the corresponding entry in the book was 2,476. Rutley was all right so far, Vachell thought. He'd said that he took Lady Baradale six or seven miles along the road that morning; and thirteen miles had been added to the speedometer.

He moved on to the other Ford, and read 2,643 on the dial. He flashed the beam on the book in his hand and read 2,614. He looked at the entry again, frowning, and back at the dial. There wasn't any mistake. The second Ford's speedometer had registered twenty-nine extra miles since the mileages had been noted that morning.

The sudden burr of a motor broke the silence of the night. A wide shaft of light sprang out of the darkness and slid rapidly towards him over the ground until it illuminated the fronts of the trucks, making their head-lamps shine like a row of twinkling stars. A car bumped into sight out of the bush and swung into line in the park. The brakes squealed as it stopped abruptly, and then the motor died. Vachell stepped forward and pulled open the door of the Plymouth box-body. The car was thickly spattered with mud and there were chains on the back wheels.

"Good evening, Miss Baradale," he said. "With all that rain, you must have had a tough trip."

"It was a bit foul," she answered. She slipped out of the car and groped in the pocket of her slacks for a cigarette case. "I struck a lousy storm on the way back, but managed to get through with chains. What I need now is a drink."

Vachell switched on his flashlight again, leant over the wheel, and peered at the speedometer. It registered 3,302. He turned the light on to the note-book and read the appropriate entry: 3,076. It was almost exactly a hundred miles to Malabeya. The car had traveled 226 miles since morning.

He flashed his light into the back of the car and it came to rest on a rifle lying on the wooden floor. He reached over for it, balanced his flashlight on the front seat, slipped out the bolt, and squinted down the barrel at the light. The metal shone brightly into his eyes. The barrel had been cleaned since the last time that the rifle had been fired.

"What on earth are you doing?" Cara Baradale's voice sounded astonished and annoyed.

Vachell slipped the flashlight into his pocket, took out a matchbox, and lit her cigarette. He thought her face looked tired and strained in the sudden glow of the match. "Come along, and I'll tell you," he said.

As he steered her towards the tents over the uneven ground he told her the news, bluntly. She stopped dead in her tracks, and he could feel her staring at him through the darkness. "It must have been an accident," she said.

Vachell gave her the facts, briefly. He felt her arm, thin as a match-stick, shiver under his hand as a shudder passed through her body.

"When did it happen?" she asked. There was apprehension in her husky tone.

When Vachell told her, he thought that she was going

to faint. She caught her breath in a sort of choke and put one hand up to her neck. He put his arm round her waist to steady her, and felt her body shiver convulsively. She started to say something, checked herself, and walked on unsteadily in the dark.

"Do you know who . . .?" Her voice was low and shaky.

"Not yet," he answered.

She went straight to her tent and did not emerge until dinner was on the table. The meal was held in the big mess-tent, for the night was heavy with the coming storm. From time to time a few spatters of rain were ejected from the tightly packed sky as if a growing tension had squeezed them out of taut reluctant clouds.

No one expected the meal to be a cheerful one. Lord Baradale, presiding at the head of the table, ate little, drank quantities of champagne, and scarcely spoke. Gordon Catchpole, looking wan and wearing a heavy purple silk dressing-gown embroidered with golden dragons, sat opposite, nibbling at his food and devoting himself mainly to gin. Cara had clearly made an effort to pull herself together, but her brittle manner was an imperfect mask for the tense feeling of strain that lay beneath. The vivid red gash of her lips was the only colour in her long thin face, framed in its dark background of hair.

De Mare ate glumly, his beaky face expressionless and severe. From time to time Chris Davis glanced at him, as if to find reassurance. She barely attempted to deal with the food on her plate. Her eyes looked large and troubled against the pallor of her skin. The radio in a corner of the tent emitted a flow of swing music punctuated by crackles caused by the thunderstorm, until Lord Baradale, swearing under his breath, got up and switched it off.

Conversation was devoted largely to the prospects of getting the safari back to Malabeya, and thence to Marula. Lord Baradale had first announced that his wife was to be buried at dawn the next morning on the outskirts of the camp; but later in the day it had been discovered that no one possessed a prayer-book or could remember any part of the burial service, so he had decided that he and de Mare were to take the body into Malabeya early the next morning. The District Commissioner's office, even though temporarily devoid of a District Commissioner, should be able to produce a prayer-book, and perhaps even a native minister to preside at the last rites.

Cara tried to discourage her father from his plan. "You'll only get hopelessly stuck in the mud," she told him, "and then what would you do with . . . well, you'd be sunk. If it rains to-night, the road will be impassable. We shan't be able to leave here till God knows when, if it goes on."

"I agree with Cara absolutely," Catchpole said. "Besides, Malabeya's so *sordid*. I'm certain that Lucy would infinitely rather stay here, out in the open unspoilt veldt, than be taken to that horrid, dusty little *outpost*. She'd feel so *jostled*. You know how she hated humanity when it got *unsorted*. I think she'd be happiest on some stark eminence, where she could look *down* on everything. Don't you think that would be more in keeping with her nature?"

There was an awkward pause, broken by the pop of a

champagne cork which showed that Geydi, at any rate, had not forgotten himself.

"I'll ask your advice when I want it, Gordon," Lord Baradale said curtly.

"I was only trying to *interpret* her real wishes," Catchpole said plaintively. "I can't bear to think of the *obliteration*. Africa is so *egotistical*, somehow. It simply doesn't *care* what happens to any one. You know, I believe that's why there's such a lot of it in the Empire. We're so *impervious*, somehow. We're really the only nation that can beat Africa at its own game."

"You should speak with authority," de Mare said acidly.

"Take whisky and golf," Catchpole continued. "Both invented by the Scotch to go with a cold, wet, *draughty* climate. We go on drinking one and playing the other in the most *arid* deserts. And eating Californian tinned peaches in the middle of the most *tropical* fertility, and building sanitary abattoirs in native villages, and making it illegal to buy a drink at five past ten in the recesses of the jungle, and making anecdotal after-dinner speeches in mud huts in the most *unconvivial* places. We simply carry on, regardless of how any one else behaves. We're the only nation really in *harmony* with the spirit of Africa."

Lord Baradale gave a snort of disgust and drank a glassful of champagne at a gulp. Cara pushed her plate away and said: "Oh, do shut up, Gordon. No one wants to hear your theories, and anyhow they've got whiskers."

Catchpole gazed fixedly at Cara's face. His eyes gleamed like those of a cat in the bright light of the unshaded electric bulbs.

"You're prejudiced, my sweet," he said. "The empire-building attitude is terribly *contagious*, and I must say you've been moving in very *infected* circles. I only hope that now all obstacles in the path of true love have been so opportunely removed, you won't find the wide open spaces terribly *flat*."

Cara banged her glass of whisky down on the table and looked at her fiancé with narrowed eyes.

"Just what do you mean by that?" she asked. Her voice was trembling on the edge of self-control.

"I'm only wishing you good luck. After all, it's no good being *too* hypocritical, is it? Every one knows that poor Lucy didn't forget you in her will, so now you'll be free as *air* to choose your own fiancés, regardless of any *sordid* questions of finance. In fact, you can be your own mistress—using the phrase *purely* as a façon de parler, my sweet."

"Damn you, Gordon, don't you dare speak like that to Cara!" Lord Baradale exploded from the other end of the table. "Haven't you an atom of decency left? You sit there, within a few hours of Lucy's death, and . . ." Words failed him, and he sat glaring at Catchpole in impotent anger.

"It's all very well to accuse *me* of having no decency," Catchpole said, his voice rising several keys. "It wasn't very decent to steal Lucy's jewels and then kill her, was it? You all behave as if you thought *I* did it; but when a stray white hunter without a *penny* to his name makes a play for Cara because he's after her money, and then sneaks away a few days after Lucy's jewels are stolen, and then Lucy gets shot a few hours after he disappears, you don't say a *thing*! I think you've got the most *distorted* ideas."

"For God's sake hold your tongue," Lord Baradale snapped. De Mare, for once nonplussed, made a despairing face at Chris, who—unable to think of any better strategy—slipped out of her seat and switched on the radio. The caressing voice of a crooner started "It looks like rain in Cherry Blossom Lane."

Cara lit a Balkan Sobranie cigarette with a shaky hand, keeping her eyes on Catchpole's face. "You would say a thing like that," she said in a tense, uneven voice. "It takes a rotten little mind like yours to think of a thing like that. What about you, anyway? Do you imagine that I've ever for a moment thought that you wanted to marry me for any reason except to get a slice of Lucy's money?"

Catchpole bowed at her slightly across the table. Vachell could see by a white pinched look around his nostrils that he was controlling himself with an effort.

"In that case you are now doubly desirable, my sweet, since this morning's sad event."

Cara pushed her unruly dark hair back from her forehead with one hand and gazed at her fiancé with hatred and contempt. "Thank you." She spoke slowly, with a visible effort. "You think that Luke stole Lucy's jewels and I shot her for her money. Your feelings do you credit." She stood up, swayed slightly, and steadied herself against the table. "I can't stand this any more," she said, almost in a whisper. She turned abruptly and walked unsteadily out of the tent.

There was a moment's silence after her departure. Lord Baradale broke it, speaking calmly and quietly, but with a deadly sting in his tone.

"If I were a younger man, Gordon," he remarked, "I should punch your face into a bloody jelly, and even that would give me inadequate satisfaction."

Catchpole's face was as white as ice, and there were beads of sweat on his forehead. "I'm sorry," he said in a quavering voice. "I'll apologize to Cara. I'm so *utterly* worn out that I simply don't know *what* I'm saying. If only I had nerves of steel, like Danny! You don't know what it's like to feel things as I do! How can any of us here be normal?" His voice rose several keys and a look of something close to panic came into his eyes. "There's a murderer in the camp, isn't there—in it, or outside it; somewhere out there in the dark or here in this tent— some one who's ruthless enough to kill to get what he wants! Some one all of us know——"

"Don't be a bloody fool, Gordon," Lord Baradale broke in. "You're tight." In the background the radio started to play "All God's chillun got rhythm" loudly. Sweat made Catchpole's skin glisten, and his eyes glanced wildly from face to face like those of a rat caught in a trap. His sudden naked terror sent an uncomfortable shiver down the backs of the others seated round the table.

"How do we know he's got all that he wants?" Catchpole went on, his voice almost out of control. "How do we know he won't do it again—to-night, perhaps, out there in the darkness? How do we *know*, I say?"

CHAPTER 11: "Sparks certainly start to
fly around when these old English families let their hair
down," Vachell remarked. "Lord Baradale sure would like
to beat the daylights out of Sir Gordon." He sat with de
Mare and Chris in the mess-tent over a second brew of
coffee. Lord Baradale and Catchpole had departed, and
the others were feeling at once spent and restless after the
strain of the day. The air was stuffy, and the distant rum-
ble of thunder came to their ears.

"Gordon deserves it," de Mare said. "This whole
damned safari is getting me down. They're all alike,
though. If I didn't need the money so badly, I'd chuck
up white hunting to-morrow."

"We're all in the same boat," Chris said. "We're all a
lot of parasites, after all, and parasites can't expect their
hosts not to be tiresome at times. Think what ticks must
go through."

"It's a funny thing about the rich," de Mare mused.
"We all pretend to despise them, and the only way we can
escape from them is to become one of them ourselves.
Englebrecht's the only member of this outfit who's got the
right idea. . . . What is it, Japhet?"

The gun-bearer stood at attention in the tent opening,
his thick-skinned black face immobile and his body rigid.
He had come to make his evening report. It was a habit
he had carried over from a period of his life when, as a

police askari, he had accompanied district officers on their tours. De Mare nodded and he recited in a chant:

"News of the camp, bwana. I have counted here 8 Europeans, 36 black men, 18 motor-cars, 10 tents for Europeans, 9 tents for black men, 24 cases of petrol, two tents full of stores, one aeroplane, 16 guns, 26 bags of maize flour, 17 bags of rice, and 18 hides."

De Mare frowned and glanced up at the askari, standing in the opening as solidly as a chunk of basalt rock.

"How many guns?" he asked.

"Sixteen, including three for birds. That is two fewer than before. Bwana Luke took three away, but this new bwana brought two more."

"One is missing, then?"

"One belonging to bwana Lordi. Douglas, the gun-bearer who looks after bwana Lordi, does not know where it has gone. There are three guns belonging to bwana Lordi. Douglas cleaned them all two days ago, but he did not touch them to-day since the bwana did not use any of them. To-night, when he went to make the tally, one was gone from bwana Lordi's tent."

"Just a moment," Vachell said. "Who keeps the cleaning materials belonging to all of the guns in camp?"

"The gun-bearers do," de Mare replied. "Japhet here looks after mine. Englebrecht has his own boy. The Baradales share a bearer called Douglas, Catchpole has one called Suya, and Cara has a fellow named Harrison. Chris looks after her own weapons."

"Could one of the Europeans clean his own gun without the bearers knowing?"

De Mare shook his head. "He'd have to ask the bearers for the materials," he said, "unless of course he'd kept a pull-through or a ramrod and some oil concealed somewhere on purpose."

Vachell spoke direct to Japhet. "Which guns were used to-day?"

"One of bwana Danny's, one of bwana Luke's that he gave to the European who looks after the cars, and one of the small bwana who walks like a baboon," Japhet replied promptly. "I do not know about that of the memsahib of the bird. Those of the memsahib who has died, of the young memsahib and of her father, bwana Lordi, were all clean."

"Did any European call for cleaning materials from the bearers?"

Japhet shook his head. "No, bwana. Only this memsahib"—he pointed at Chris with his chin—"sent her boy for a tin of gun-oil."

"My Revelation suitcase jammed," Chris explained. "You know, the part that slides. I sent for some 3-in-1 to oil it."

"This missing gun may be important," Vachell said. "I'm going to search the camp right now. If some one used a gun to-day, and then found he couldn't clean it, it wouldn't be a bad idea to conceal the gun."

A thorough search through native quarters, the white folk's tents, the cars, the trucks, and even the bush and trees around the camp yielded nothing. Lord Baradale himself could give no help. He couldn't remember, he said, when he had last seen the rifle, and he seemed indifferent as to whether or not it was found. He was silent and preoccupied, and answered only in grunts and mumbles.

It was nearly eleven o'clock before the fruitless search ended, and Vachell and de Mare joined Chris Davis at the table under the acacia. The rain had cleared off for the time being and the clouds had retreated, leaving the sky to the vast and silent company of stars. The veldt beyond the river seemed to stretch forever until it was swallowed by a dark and invisible horizon.

Vachell poured himself a stiff Scotch, squirted a little soda into it, and listened to the noises of the night. Crickets trilled shrilly from the surrounding grass and a chorus of innumerable frogs croaked hoarsely and persistently from the river. Their throaty clamour seemed to surge like waves through the air.

"Those frogs make too much damned noise," de Mare remarked suddenly. He drew a deep breath, tipped back his head, and shouted, with the full strength of his lungs, two words that neither of his companions understood. The frogs' chorus ceased as abruptly as the music of a radio orchestra when the set is switched off. There was a silence in which it seemed that every frog was listening for a repetition of the sound.

"What on earth . . . ?" Chris, startled, asked.

De Mare's spare, bird-like features relaxed into a smile. "It's a native legend in these parts," he said. "Up here they believe that if you shout 'Silence, frogs,' in their own language, they'll stop croaking. Only it's no good shouting in a foreign tongue. These must be Timburu frogs, so I addressed them in Timburu. You see, it works."

The frogs, indeed, remained temporarily hushed, as if startled into silence.

"I'll have to wait until the frogs learn basic English," Vachell said. "Right now I need another lesson in animal customs. When your trackers hit the trail of a herd of game, how close can they estimate the age of the spoor?"

"That depends on a dozen factors," de Mare answered. "Time of day, time of year, amount of cloud, rain, and so on."

"Well, take an instance. Suppose there was a herd of buffalo feeding to-day in those hills in back of the camp. If you took your trackers out there to-morrow morning and asked them what time the buffaloes had been around, could they give you an answer that would hit the time right on the nose?"

"They couldn't specify the exact hour," de Mare answered, "but they could get pretty close to it. Suppose they said the buff had been feeding at a certain spot at noon, for instance. You could reckon that the herd had been there sometime between ten and two."

"Thanks. Will you loan me your best tracker for an hour to-morrow morning, first thing?"

"Surely. What's the idea?"

"I want to find out if buffaloes can prove an alibi," Vachell said.

He wished his companions good night, and strolled over the starlit grass to his tent. Chris, he thought, looked tired out. There was something, over and above Lady Baradale's death, weighing on her mind. Perhaps she was worried about Danny de Mare. Hunters couldn't afford to have their clients murdered on safari. They were like ships' captains; responsibility for every one's safety was theirs, and if anything went wrong they took the rap, whoever was really to blame. He had an idea that Chris cared a good deal for de Mare—more than she'd ever admit. He's in luck, Vachell said to himself, if that's so; she's the sort of girl who'd stick to a guy to hell and gone, and then all the way back.

Vachell was tired, and his camp-bed looked snug and inviting. But the day wasn't over for him. He took out his note-book, sat on the edge of the bed, and drew up a schedule of times and places covering the movements of every one he had questioned that day. Then, with some care, he sketched a map of the camp and its surroundings which he studied for as long as it took him to smoke a cigarette.

Meditation didn't seem to get him any farther. He closed the note-book with a snap, dug into the pocket of his grey flannel slacks for his pocket-book, and extracted from it a fine chain with a key dangling from one end. It was the key of Lady Baradale's safe, taken from her dead body at the post-mortem examination that afternoon.

He made his way through the darkness, the key in one hand and a flashlight in the other, to Lady Baradale's tent. The bundles of letters that he had seen in the safe the evening before, he decided, would bear investigation.

CHAPTER 12: IT WAS PAST MIDNIGHT, AND the camp was shadowy and asleep. The ashes of a wood fire glowed faintly near the big acacia, and by it two forms lay huddled in blankets, inert as logs—guards who were supposed to protect the slumbering occupants of the tents. The frog chorus had dwindled to an occasional burst of croaks. The piercing howl of a hyena twice penetrated the stillness. The sound came from beyond the hippo pool, probably from the lion's carcase, Vachell thought, where those grey and graceless scavengers would be crunching the bones of their betters, gobbling the remnants of the vultures' feast. He wondered whether the lion's mate would stay on to work their joint hunting grounds alone. As if in answer to his thought, he heard the familiar grunt, hollow and chesty, twice repeated. She was hunting down by the hippo pool, probably; there was a track there where the buck came down to drink.

It wasn't possible to lock a canvas flap, and Vachell had only to untie the strings and lift it up to enter Lady Baradale's tent. His nostrils twitched as an indefinable feminine smell, some compound of perfume and powder, tickled his nose. He pressed the switch on the electric light bulb over the dressing-table, but it didn't work. Rutley must have disconnected it, he thought.

He explored the tent with the flashlight's beam. Nothing had been moved. A piece of cretonne stretched across

one corner still bulged with hanging dresses, and a book
lay by the bedside as if it had just been put down. Beside
the bed stood an oblong box covered with coarse calico
which had been tacked over the wooden sides and lid. The
words "Made in Japan," stencilled on the calico, appeared
upside down on one side of the box. A bunch of wilted
wild-flowers rested in a jam-jar on the top.

Catchpole was right, Vachell thought suddenly; there
was something very frightening about Africa's utter indif-
ference to the hopes and fears and little dignities of mankind. Only in Africa could a couple of gin cases covered
with cheap Japanese calico, resting unattended in a tent,
do duty as the coffin of a titled millionairess.

He turned his attention to the safe. It stood where he
had seen it before, black and squat, underneath the dressing-table. Bottles on the table's surface gleamed dully and
silver-backed brushes flashed like stars as he arranged the
torch carefully on the bed, so that its beam fell fully on
to the safe's door. He squatted down on his heels in front
of the table and inserted the key in the lock. It turned
smoothly and silently in his fingers. Easy enough, he
thought, to open the safe without waking even a light
sleeper. He hoped the papers inside might contain a lead.
Funny how often hard-boiled old dames like Lady Baradale went soft over letters, and kept all sorts of com-
promising billets tied up in pink satin ribbon. That bundle,
now, had looked like a bunch of love-letters of some
sort. . . .

His hand froze in mid-air as the steel door swung
silently towards him. He squatted like a stone statue, every

muscle tense, all animation seemingly suspended. A prickly feeling ran up his spine and tingled over his scalp, as though each hair was rising on end. Behind him, in the dense darkness of the tent, he sensed, rather than heard, the muted movement of another living creature.

He held his breath and strained his ears as desperately as a hunted animal to catch the faintest tremor of a sound-wave. Silence wrapped itself heavily around him like a blanket. Above the drumming of the blood in his ears he heard the croak of a frog, the soft hoot of an owl, and then the far-off yap-yap of a peevish jackal. There was no sound in the tent, but he knew, beyond doubt, that some-where behind him in the darkness was something that was alive.

Then, slowly, the flashlight rolled over on the bed. The safe's door was swallowed by darkness, and the beam slid along the side of the dressing-table. Something, brushing against the bed, had jolted the flashlight from its position.

Vachell's breath was driven from his lungs in a muffled gasp as he braced his muscles and threw his weight sud-denly back on to his heels. He started to spring to his feet in a sort of backward leap; and then the unseen hand struck. Something hit the back of his head like the kick of a horse. He pitched forward helplessly and sprawled, mo-tionless, on the floor of the tent. The flashlight toppled off the bed and lay there, its beam ineffectively directed into his unconscious face.

His first thought, when he came to, was that a blinding sun was shining into his eyes; his second, that a giant sledge-hammer was pounding away inside his head. Gradu-

ally he became aware that the light in his eyes came from
an electric torch. He put up one hand, pushed it away,
and sat up shakily, feeling very sick. There was a lump
on the back of his head the size of an orange, and it hurt
abominably. He found that he could stand, but his knees
felt like putty. He looked at his watch and found that it
was ten past one. Then he directed the flashlight's beam on
to the safe. The door was closed, and the key had vanished
from the lock.

Speculation and anger were obliterated from his mind
by an overpowering desire for a drink of water. He walked
unsteadily towards the opening, the flashlight wavering in
his hand. The beam fell on to the improvised coffin and
lit up the jam-jar full of drooping flowers on top. By the
side of it lay two round objects that had not been there
when he entered the tent. He pointed the beam at them
incredulously and wondered whether a crack on the head
could induce optical illusions. Then he closed his hand
over them and said aloud: "Well, I'll be God-damned—
walnuts!"

Two walnuts were sitting on top of Lady Baradale's
home-made coffin. He pushed them into his pocket, feeling
dazed and resentful. Everything was going hay-wire. The
whole situation was hopelessly unreal. "Oh, nuts!" he
thought, and stopped dead, as though suddenly paralysed.
Nuts! Could that be it? A message from the murderer;
an insolent salute to the police? He swore tersely, and
walked unsteadily out of the tent.

It was quiet and still outside, but not raining. The camp
lay in darkness, its fires extinguished. The beam of the

flashlight carved a path through the blackness, flood-lighting every grass-blade. As he moved forward something white gleamed at him from beneath a guy-rope at his feet. He leant down and picked up a half-smoked Player's cigarette. The action caused his head to throb intolerably. He straightened up slowly, and walked on towards his tent.

The night was still as death, and the leaves of the big acacia hung motionless in the air as though they had been carved in stone. Vachell stood for a few moments by the smooth bole, cooling his throbbing head and straining his eyes towards the invisible river. He could hear the water rippling over the rocks, and the noise of unseen birds moving and calling softly in the darkness. The frogs had almost ceased to croak, and the hyenas were silent. A feeling of expectancy seemed to encase the earth.

Vachell was not conscious of the moment when another and alien sound first came to his ears. All of a sudden it was there—a low, deep note like the faint hum of a distant bee. He jerked his head around to the west. At first he could see nothing, but a little later a far-off twinkle of light gleamed at him through the trees down the river. It moved slowly along the horizon, and then vanished as suddenly as it had come.

It was too bright for a traveller's lamp, too low for a shooting star, too small for a grass fire. There was only one thing it could be: the headlights of a car.

Vachell turned suddenly and made for the car-park, stumbling in his haste. The noses of the trucks shone faintly in the starlight. They looked like squat crouching monsters. He counted them carefully: four cars, fourteen trucks, each one in its place.

Somewhere, close to them on the veldt in this vast uninhabited land, was a fifth car, driving over roadless territory at one-thirty in the morning.

The yowl of a hyena broke the silence so suddenly that Vachell jumped and nearly dropped the flashlight. The beast was prowling about beyond the car-park. Another answered from the bush behind. From a long way off the sharp cough of a startled zebra pricked the veil of silence that shrouded the earth.

Vachell shivered a little, although the night was warm and balmy. He walked quickly over to Rutley's workshop, pushed over the creaking wooden door, and played the flashlight over bench and walls. Tools gleamed back at him like dull black eyes. The questing flashlight came to rest upon a plate of oranges and ginger crackers on the table. A pile of orange peel lay beside it. There was something else there too, hiding behind the oranges. Vachell stepped over to the bench and peered down. Walnuts. There were five walnuts on the plate.

He looked at them for a full minute, speculating, before he remembered what he had come for. Then he circled the hut with the beam and brought it back to rest on a heavy jack that lay in a corner. He picked it up, balanced it in his hand, and decided that it would make as good a weapon as any. His next job was to check up on every member of the safari; and he wasn't going to be caught with his pants down twice. He wondered why his assailant hadn't made a job of it in Lady Baradale's tent. Next time, the killer might hit harder, and hit to kill.

He started with the women's section of the camp. Every one slept with the front flap of their tent tied back, and this made his task easier. He skirted guy-ropes and tent-pegs cautiously, and listened outside each flap for the steady noise of breathing.

Chris Davis and Paula were sleeping soundly. He flashed the light on to their beds for a brief instant to make sure. The third tent he came to was Cara's. He couldn't hear her breathing, so he took a chance with the flashlight. The beam fell on to a blank expanse of white pillow. The sheets were not disturbed and a pair of wine-red silk pyjamas lay over a chair by the bedside. Cara Baradale was not at home.

CHAPTER 13: The flame that precedes

the rising of the sun had started to warm a cold grey sky when Kimotho brought hot tea and rattled the cup to wake his employer. Vachell sat up and groaned. The lump on his head was as tender as a boil and his knees were red and sore. He gulped the tea gratefully, pulled on his clothes, and fastened the ready filled cartridge-belt, which he had worn the previous day, around his waist. He took up the .470 and stepped out into the still clear morning, moving carefully so as not to jar his head.

He found de Mare checking over the chains of one of the Plymouths, ready to go. The camp-made coffin was already in the back of the car, and de Mare had added a sack of maize meal to hold the box-body steady over the bumps.

"I can't get a single native to come," he remarked. Vachell thought that he looked pinched and ill, and the naturally sallow tinge of the hunter's complexion was exaggerated in the unflattering grey light of dawn. "Not one of them will share the back with a corpse. It'll be the hell of a business if we stick. With no one to push us out we'll just have to stay there, I suppose, till the road dries up."

"If you don't get back to-night I'll come out in one of the trucks to-morrow to pick you up," Vachell promised. He handed de Mare a sheet of paper on which he had written a brief report of the murder for the Commissioner

of Police. "I'd be grateful if you'd send this off by wire,"
he added. "That'll fetch the Commissioner up here with
a hop, skip, and a jump, or I miss my guess."

The gun-bearer Japhet and a tall, lanky native tracker
in shorts were standing stiffly about twenty paces away,
watching de Mare's activities with wooden faces. They
were ready, the hunter explained, to conduct Vachell on
his buffalo hunt. "For God's sake be careful," he added.
"We don't want any more disasters. And whatever happens, don't let any of the others leave the camp. You're
responsible for their safety while I'm away. If there's any
trouble, you can always count on Chris."

De Mare folded the chains into the tool-box and turned
to greet Lord Baradale, who arrived, escorted by Geydi,
in a clean and pressed pair of grey flannels, an old dirty
woollen sweater, and a brown tweed deerstalker hat pulled
down over his head. Geydi deposited a box of cigars, a
luncheon basket, and several cameras in the car with his
usual disdainful air. Baradale nodded curtly to the two
Europeans and climbed into the front seat without waste
of words. It was clear that his temper was thoroughly
soured.

The car jolted off into the bush with its gruesome cargo.
Vachell called Japhet over and explained the object of
the next expedition, to ascertain whether a herd of buffaloes had grazed, the previous morning, over the hills
behind the camp. The idea behind the quest was simple
enough. If there weren't any traces of a herd of buffaloes,
Vachell reckoned, then Rutley would be proved a liar and
his alibi a fake. If the buffaloes had been there, on the

other hand, part, at any rate, of Rutley's story could be accepted. It wasn't likely that he could have known of the buffaloes unless he had seen them for himself. That, of course, didn't prove that he had fired at them; the shot that Kimotho had heard might have had a more sinister objective. Still, it would clear the ground to prove even fifty per cent. of Rutley's story either false or true.

This certainly was a queer case, Vachell reflected as his little party started out. The thin, lanky-legged tracker, gripping a stick, led the way, and Japhet, clasping his master's heavy rifle, followed behind. If the case ever reached its climax in a court of law, the tracker Konyek, with his bronze graven-image face, curiously Egyptian in its cast of features, and his tattered khaki shorts patched in the seat with a piece of flowered cretonne, might find himself doing duty as an expert witness for the Crown. "Can you explain to the jury, Mr. Konyek, in language as intelligible as possible to the layman, the precise method that you follow when estimating the age of buffalo droppings . . . ?" Vachell thought of Sir Bernard Spilsbury, and smiled. It took all sorts of expert witnesses to make a trial.

Japhet was in an expansive mood. He understood that the bwana was not one who knew safari work, but only a white askari. Well, that was all right; he, Japhet, would protect him; he needn't be scared. Bwana Danny had said so, and he was the greatest hunter in Africa; the elephants and lions that he had shot were as numerous as the goats of a very rich chief.

"What is the talk of the black men in camp?" Vachell asked. "Who do they think killed bwana Lordi's wife?"

Japhet shrugged a pair of broad shoulders encased in a khaki woollen jersey, and spat.

"They do not know, bwana. How should they? They say: why do the white men make such a fuss? She was only a woman. If her husband killed her, he must pay many cattle to her father, and then it is all right. If some one else killed her, then her husband must find the man and get from him the cattle that are his due. It is his affair. But Europeans, they call always for the police. Are they children, then, and are the police their mothers?"

Vachell was trying to think out a suitable retort when he heard a shout from behind. All three stopped dead and turned their heads to see Gordon Catchpole hurrying along the faint game-track which they were following uphill through the bush. He was hatless, and carried a rifle in one hand. He waved it at them to stop. By the time he reached them he was panting hard.

"This altitude!" he exclaimed between gasps. "It's so breath-taking. I wonder if it *really* sends one mad? Why didn't you tell me you were going out shooting? Danny never mentioned it, either. He said nobody was to leave camp, but I saw you *sneaking* off the moment he'd gone. Is this your form of relaxation, or have you discovered a real, red-hot *clue*?"

"Not yet," Vachell answered. "Say, listen, Sir Gordon, this is a sort of a one-man show. I guess you ought to follow out de Mare's instructions and stick around in camp."

A frown came over Catchpole's fair, finely moulded face. He pushed a lock of golden hair off his forehead and exclaimed petulantly: "I really don't see *why* I should. After all, surely one ought to be safe enough with the *police*, if nowhere else. Between us we've got *batteries* of rifles. And I simply must *do* something—something *physical*. I'm absolutely worn out with worry; I didn't sleep a *wink* all night. Besides, I've got something terribly important to tell you. At least, I think it *may* be important, though I didn't know quite *why*, but at any rate it is definitely *odd*."

Vachell raised his eyebrows. "Sounds interesting, Sir Gordon. I'm all attention—shoot."

"I can't tell you till I've verified something," Catchpole said. "It may be a red herring, and I shouldn't *dream* of saying anything that might—well, *compromise* any one, until I'm absolutely *certain*. Let's proceed, and if there's anything in it I'll let you know on the way home to breakfast."

Vachell cursed under his breath, hesitated, and said "okay" in what he hoped was a noncommittal voice. He wanted to send the baronet back, but he didn't know how to do it. If Catchpole refused he couldn't very well sock him on the jaw and carry him bodily back to camp, or tell the gun-bearer to do so. He realized how much a detective's prestige depended on the unseen army of uniformed policemen with truncheons or revolvers that normally stood behind him—on warrants and cells and magistrates, and the threat of force. Stripped of all that, a policeman felt naked. If people refused to do what he said, it was just too bad. In this outfit he would have to call a different play: to say little, see a lot, and use plenty of cunning. The direct method wouldn't work.

The little procession wound a wavering course up the hill, dodging round bushes and at times having to push its way through an extra bit of vegetation. The sun flamed in the sky above the hilltop and spread a golden glow over the dew-drenched grass. Soon they were wet to the waist, but the sun's fresh rays shone warmly on their faces and chests. The sky was robin's-egg blue and cloudless, and a faint wind moved the grass stems. Once or twice Konyek paused to kick up a little cloud of dust from a loose patch of earth with his naked toes. It floated softly back over their legs. The wind was right.

About a mile from camp they came out on a little bluff where they paused for breath. They had climbed up quite a way and the tents gleamed white beneath them. They could see two black figures drawing water from the blue thread of river, and the empty gasolene cans used as containers flashed back the sunrays like a heliograph. Three columns of smoke rose up as straight as pines and then scattered in wisps and spirals into the clear morning air.

"Now, Sir Gordon," Vachell began, "what's this dope you say you have on ——"

He was interrupted by a sudden hiss from behind. He jerked his hand around, looking for a snake. It was no snake, however, but Konyek, who raised one hand with a gesture that could only mean: "Quiet, you fool, I'm listening." The tracker's body was taut, frozen into an attitude of attention. Then his muscles relaxed. He turned without a word and started to move slowly and cautiously up the

hill. Japhet quietly lowered the .450 from his shoulder
and motioned to Vachell to go next. He himself fell in behind and left Gordon Catchpole, clasping his light rifle, to
bring up the rear.

Vachell concentrated on trying to move as noiselessly as
possible through the thick bush. To his straining ears, the
rasp of thorns against his khaki shorts seemed as loud as
the sound of tearing canvas. Japhet, in reply to Vachell's
unspoken question, whispered "buffalo!" They zig-zagged
slowly up the hill, following the line of one of the shoulders. A shallow gulley lay below them on the right.
Vachell's heart began to step up its beats a little. He
moved as if he were treading on thin ice, every sense
wound up to its tightest pitch. Somewhere ahead was a
mob of alert, wary black beasts, invisible and unheard.
The bush was so thick that they might be twenty yards
away and still unseen.

Konyek stopped suddenly and bent down to examine
something on the ground. Vachell stepped forward and
peered over his shoulder. Buffalo droppings. Konyek
turned them over with his toe and whispered softly "yesterday." Japhet grunted agreement. "What time yesterday?"
Vachell whispered back, his mouth close to Konyek's ear.
The tracker prodded them again and breathed back:
"yesterday morning, but not very early." Japhet pointed
with the muzzle of the rifle to another heap of droppings
farther on. "Look," he whispered, "more. Many buffaloes."

So, Vachell thought, at least Rutley was speaking fifty
per cent. of the truth.

Konyek, like a hound searching for scent, had scouted a little way ahead, and was already out of sight. Just as Vachell was opening his mouth to recall the tracker, a low whistle sounded from the wall of bush a little to the left. Japhet jerked his rifle to his shoulder instantaneously and pushed the safety-catch over. Nothing happened for a full minute, and then the whistle sounded again.

Japhet started towards it, motioning Vachell to follow. He moved with redoubled caution. They found Konyek squatting on his heels, examining a blade of grass which he held between finger and thumb. Vachell bent over it and felt the muscles of his throat tighten at what he saw. Across the grass-blade ran a red streak of blood.

He stretched out his hand and took the leaf from the tracker. Then he saw, with mounting excitement, that the blood was wet. That could only mean one thing: that Rutley's random shot, unknown to him, had found its mark. There was a wounded buffalo somewhere, close at hand, in the bush.

Konyek got to his feet and moved on, slipping through the wall of bush like a fish gliding through water. Vachell scrambled after him, going in sideways, with his rifle held out behind him in one hand. Konyek was moving silently and with great care. A few yards farther on the tracker pointed with his stick to a small speck of blood on the leaf of a bush, about waist high. Japhet moved like a cat, with his eyes fixed on the bush ahead and the rifle at full cock.

A minute later Konyek stopped again and pointed to the ground ahead. The grass was bent and trampled and bore the impress of a heavy body that had recently rested there. Blood was spattered over the grass stalks, and in one place there was a dark brown patch where a pool of it had partially congealed.

They all halted, while Konyek and Japhet made a thorough examination of the spot. Catchpole came up a minute later, panting, with scratches on his face and arms. He looked pale and scared. Vachell cursed him, silently, for being there.

Japhet said in a low whisper: "The buffalo rested here last night. He is wounded in the stomach. He has lost much blood, and will be very savage. It would be best to return that way—" he motioned with his hand towards the river—"to camp."

"Which way did the buffalo go?" Vachell whispered back.

Japhet stretched out his arm and pointed in the other direction. "But he is very close. The blood is fresh. Go very carefully. Let Konyek go first."

Vachell hesitated. All his instincts were to follow the wounded beast and finish it off. He hated to leave it wandering around with an abdominal wound. But then there was Catchpole. His own job, he supposed, was to keep people out of danger, not to carry out mercy slayings in the bush. He nodded, and Konyek started, as cautiously as before, to thread his way back through the bush.

They had settled one thing, anyway, Vachell thought. Rutley had been speaking the truth about the shot. A wounded buffalo had proved his alibi.

It was anxious work, easing through the bush in the sun

and listening with every sense alert for the danger signal of a snapping twig. They heard the crack of a branch once, and all four halted as though a lightning flash had paralysed them in the act of movement. They waited, motionless, for several seconds, and then moved slowly on. A stembuck, probably, or some other buck. As they moved away from the wounded buffalo's restingplace Vachell's muscles began to relax a little, and his heart to feel less bumpy. Every step took them farther from the danger zone.

Then, without warning, it happened. There was a crash in the bush to the left and a noise like the roar of an express. Almost simultaneously a black form hurtled down upon them with the velocity of a torpedo. Konyek dived sideways in the split second before it appeared. Vachell was conscious of two huge spreading horns and a black circle at the other end of his sights. He sighted just below the thick bosses, pressed the trigger, and sprang sideways in a single motion. A violent blow caught him in the ribs and knocked him off his feet as if he had been a skittle, and he hit the bush five paces from where he had been standing. Above the drumming of blood in his ears he heard two quick shots and then a frightful bellow, a compound of pain and futile fury that wrenched the nerves at the pit of his stomach. Then another crash, and a sudden silence.

He kicked himself free of the bush and stood up unsteadily, half winded. Blood trickled down his face from scratches and his left side felt battered and numb. He half ran, half lurched a few paces towards the sounds.

Then he stopped dead in his tracks and stared down at the grass by his feet, feeling sick and dizzy.

A slight, khaki-clad figure lay sprawled limply on the ground, one arm flung out towards the rifle which lay by its side. Vachell knelt down and turned the figure over on to its back. The whole of one side was flattened out, the ribs stove in like a broken egg-shell. Blood crept slowly over the torn khaki shirt while he watched, paralysed with horror. A great gash across the chest had ripped open the body as if it had been made of paper. The head sagged limply against Vachell's arms.

The gored body gave a convulsive twitch and Catchpole's eyelids fluttered. He wasn't quite dead. Vachell watched the white, delicate face speechlessly, and saw the eyes open and the lips move a little. Catchpole was trying to say something. He bent down to listen, but the words were blurred and faint. "Tell Cara," he thought he heard; then a mumble, and the word "Luke." Catchpole's right arm contracted in a sort of gripping gesture and his arm jerked feebly back, as if he were trying to reload a rifle. His lips formed a word which sounded like "seen." The rest of the sentence was inaudible until the end, when, in a sort of croak, he said distinctly "shot Lucy." It was the final effort. His head fell back in the flaccid inertia of death, and his lips were still.

CHAPTER 14: WHEN VACHELL LOOKED UP he saw Japhet and Konyek standing silently by his side, gazing with round and terrified eyes at the body in the grass.

"This is a very bad affair," Japhet said. He shook his head slowly from side to side. "What will bwana Danny say? The bwana-who-walks-like-a-baboon was too slow. Konyek jumped, you jumped, and I jumped; but he did not jump with sufficient speed."

"Is the buffalo dead?" Vachell asked. His voice sounded cracked and uneven.

"He is dead. I shot him twice as he turned after he knocked down the bwana—first in the heart, and a second time in the ear. He ran a few paces; then he bellowed, and fell like a tree, and died. He is here."

Japhet led the way around a thorny bush and Vachell saw the buffalo's black bulk lying on its side in the grass. A little bloody froth still clung to its nostrils, and blood oozed from a hole low down behind the shoulder. He bent over it and found a second hole below the ear. It was a big bull with heavy, spreading horns. He grasped one of the horn tips and turned the head so that he could see its forehead. There was no hole there, but there was a small fresh cut in the flesh, such as might have been inflicted by a branch.

"Where did my bullet hit?" he asked.

Japhet shook his head. "Your bullet did not hit, bwana."

Vachell swore and looked again. "It must have hit," he said. "The buffalo was so close that it was impossible to miss. I aimed just below the boss, where this little cut is."

Japhet shook his head again and said: "No. Look, that's all. Only two bullets hit this buffalo. And another which hit yesterday."

He seized the bull by the hind legs and Konyek took the forelegs. Together they heaved and hauled until the buffalo reposed on its other side. Then they could see the third bullet hole. It was low down on the body, about half way between shoulder and haunch. There was clotted blood on the hair all around the wound.

"Listen," Vachell said. "Cut out the bullets, all three of them, that are in the buffalo, and give them to me."

He recovered his rifle, apparently unharmed, from the grass near the bush into which he had been thrown, opened the breech, and extracted an exploded shell. Certainly it had been fired, and certainly the buffalo hadn't been hit. There was only one conclusion: that he was a lousy shot. And yet he'd won medals for his marksmanship in the past. Scoring bulls on a target, of course, was a different thing from stopping a charging buffalo at ten yards. Vachell felt angry and bitterly ashamed. If that shot had gone home, Gordon Catchpole would still be alive. Between his rage was an undertone of bewilderment. He'd have bet a million bucks to a mousetrap that his aim had been true.

A shadow flickered over the grass, and he looked up. Two vultures were wheeling across the clear blue sky overhead, their necks craned down towards the earth—wheeling and waiting their turn. He cursed them savagely, drew out a knife, and cut the strongest stakes he could find in the surrounding bush. He tore his shirt and handkerchief into strips and bound them together to make a rough stretcher. He'd be damned if the vultures were going to get a turn this time.

Half an hour later the party reached camp. Catchpole's body lay limply on the rough stretcher, carried by a frightened and reluctant Japhet and by Vachell, naked to the waist and dizzy in the head. Konyek stalked silently behind. He had refused, with unshakeable conviction, to touch the dead body, or the stretcher on which it lay.

They were greeted by the sound of native laughter and by the smell of sizzling bacon. With a sudden shock Vachell realized that it was time for breakfast. It seemed as though an age had passed since they had started up the hill towards the sunrise.

Gordon Catchpole's body was deposited on the camp bed in his tent in silence, and covered with a sheet. Vachell walked slowly across to his own tent, feeling sick and shaky at the knees, and leant against the pole. His mind was a jumble of half-formed thoughts, all unpleasant. One predominated: if he hadn't missed, Catchpole's crumpled body wouldn't be lying, lifeless, on the bed.

He hardly noticed Chris Davis's approach. She looked cool and competent in her freshly pressed safari slacks and she wasted no time in useless words.

"I'm sorry," she said. "It's ghastly. You're covered with scratches and you'll be lucky if you haven't any broken ribs. Lie down on the bed and let me clean those cuts at once."

Vachell was too dispirited to argue. Chris shouted for hot water, opened the first-aid case in his tent, and went to work. She bathed the scratches and doused them with iodine, and then dressed the bruises on his side. He'd been caught by the tip of the horn just as he was leaping aside, so that his body hadn't offered any resistance to the blow. There were no ribs broken, she said.

He told her the tragic story jerkily, lying on his side while she sat on the edge of the bed and applied a hot compress to his bruised ribs. He noticed that her arms were graceful and that her long fingers worked with sensitivity and deftness. He observed again how the pallor of her face made her eyes seem large and of a deeper shade than blue. It was soothing to watch a girl fussing over his scratches, even if she couldn't treat the deeper gashes in his pride.

She listened in silence to the story. When he'd finished with the buffalo he told her about the events of the night before, the attack in Lady Baradale's tent, and the head-lamps shining through the darkness from the fifth car. It was a relief to have some one to talk to. Indiscreet, perhaps, but Chris was the sort of girl who knew how to keep things under her hat.

"That accounts for Cara's behaviour," she commented. "I knew there was something behind it."

"Why, what has Cara done?"

"She nearly went off her head when I told her about Gordon just now, while you were—were putting him in the tent. I think she's on the edge of a nervous break-down anyway. She didn't seem to take it in at first, and then she burst into peals of laughter. Hysterics, of course. I gave her some brandy and then she said: 'Well, at least they can't accuse Luke of turning into a buffalo.' I said: 'Don't be silly, no one's accused Luke of anything,' and she said: 'You'll see, they will.' I said: 'How can they, he was with you and on the way to Malabeya when it happened,' and then she burst into tears and refused to say another word. I couldn't understand what she was getting at, but I suppose they didn't go to Malabeya at all."

Vachell searched out a cigarette and lit it, lying on his side. The warmth of the compress was deliciously soothing to the pain.

"They must have gone to Malabeya to pick up Engle-brecht's car," he said. "He left it there on his way through. The way I figure it is, they decided they'd see Lady Bara-dale in hell before they let her drive Englebrecht out and break up their affair, so they drove back from Malabeya in the two cars and fixed up a camp some place down the river. Englebrecht was to stick around and be on hand in the evenings so Cara could meet him and tell him how things were coming along. Maybe she thought she'd be able to work on her father and get him to see things her way. Then some one bumped off Lady Baradale, and that balled everything up."

"Do you think that Luke . . . ?" Chris said.

"I don't know. I have to find him first, and then ask questions."

"Cara gets £100,000 under Lady Baradale's will," Chris remarked.

"How do you know that?"

"She told me. Her father told her, I think."

"Does she mean to marry Englebrecht?"

"I don't believe she *can* be really in love with him, though apparently she thinks she is. But she's so obstinate I'm certain she'd have married him to spite her stepmother. You can hardly blame her, really; Lady Baradale drove her into it. Of course she wouldn't have got the money if she'd married him while Lady Baradale was alive."

"She'd have got the air," Vachell said.

Chris finished dressing his ribs, rubbed an ointment into them, and strapped them up in elastoplast. Vachell swung his legs off the bed and sat up, feeling much better.

"There's one small item to go on the credit side," he remarked. "I guess that buffalo has put Rutley in the clear."

"I suppose it proves his alibi after eleven o'clock yesterday morning," Chris agreed. "But how do you know he didn't shoot Lady Baradale somewhere beyond the drift between ten and eleven, dump the body, come back to camp, and *then* go up the hill and get mixed up with the buffalo?"

"Here's why," Vachell answered. "Rutley drove Lady Baradale thirteen miles between ten and eleven. I got that from the speedometer. So he wasn't hanging around the drift; he must have driven along the track, like he said. Well, suppose he shot her. His natural instinct would be to throw the body out somewhere in the bush, and hope it wouldn't be found before the hyenas had a chance to clean up."

"Yes," Chris agreed, "except that we might be guided to the place where he left it by the vultures, when we started to look."

"Then why bring the body right close into camp, where we could almost see the vultures from our own front porch? Catchpole's lion wasn't killed until around 11.30, and Rutley was up the hill with the buffaloes by then. If he bumped Lady Baradale before eleven, why would he bring the body back and dump it practically on our doorstep? If he did that, he's nuts."

"It does seem odd," Chris admitted.

"It's screwy. And here's another thing. This river has crocodiles in it. Crocs have trunk murderers and guys who push bodies into incinerators, or bury them in quicklime, licked before they begin. They do a swell disposal job. Why didn't this murderer use them, once he'd decided to move the body around?"

"Heaven knows. On the other hand, surely Lady Baradale couldn't have been killed close to the hippo pool without some one hearing the shot. There were plenty of people about, and Japhet and Konyek wouldn't make a mistake like that."

"It doesn't make sense either way," Vachell said. He got to his feet and found that he was steadier on his legs. His side ached persistently, but his head was clear again, and he felt hungry.

"I hope to Heaven you clear it up soon," Chris remarked. She put away the bandages and closed the medicine-chest.

"Now poor Gordon's got killed it will just about finish Danny's career as a white hunter, I'm afraid. It'll be even worse if the thing remains a mystery. In a way, I suppose, we'll all be under suspicion, and he's in charge of the safari. It's awful."

Vachell felt an unreasoning annoyance prick his mind like the bite of a mosquito. Why the hell did she spend so much time worrying about how Danny de Mare would come out? It was obvious he didn't give a damn for her, except as a competent assistant. She was throwing her sympathy away.

"It isn't so hot for any of us," he said. "I shall feel pretty smart when I walk into Armitage's office and say: 'H'ya, Commissioner, the jewels are gone and their owner has been knocked off and another guy got trod to pieces by a buffalo, but it's all right, we got the buffalo.'"

"I'm sorry," Chris said quickly. "I know it's just as important to you as it is to Danny. Let me know if there's anything I can do to help."

"Thanks." Vachell felt a little embarrassed. He looked up and met her eyes, blue and sincere, and thought how attractively her thick blonde hair grew back from her forehead. "Here's another thing that's cockeyed," he said. "The way I missed that buffalo. Is it possible for a bullet to ricochet off the horns, if it hits squarely on the boss?"

"Oh, yes, that's happened. But not with a solid bullet at ten yards, I should think. Are you certain the cartridges aren't old?"

"I bought them this week," Vachell said. He dug the empty shell out of his pocket and handed it over to Chris.

"Don't brood over it," she said. "Even if you'd hit the buff, he might have gone on and killed Gordon just the same."

He looked down at her and smiled. "Swell of you to say that," he said, "but you know it isn't true. I guess I'm just a bum shot, and that's all there is to it."

"You're honest with yourself, anyway," she said, "and that's unusual, you know."

Vachell grinned broadly at her and said: "Sure, but then, you see, I'm different." He went over to his suitcase and extracted a clean shirt. It hurt a lot to bend. He poked his head inside the shirt and struggled as gently as he could into the sleeves, for his arms were tender from scratches. The worst ones were now covered with adhesive tape, so that he had a curious patched appearance. When he finally got his shirt on he looked around and saw that Chris was sitting on the bed, holding the empty shell to the light and examining it with close attention.

"Look at this a moment, will you?" Her voice had a note of urgency in it. He sat beside her and took the shell. At first he could see nothing, but then he noticed a few faint scratches around the rim, where the copper case containing the explosive powder clasped the lead bullet. He extracted a magnifying glass from his box of detective's apparatus on the table by the bed, and examined the case again. He made out a series of small scratches around the rim and two very slight dents, too small to be seen with the naked eye, in the sides of the shell's circular base.

"What the hell!" Vachell's face expressed bewilderment

and doubt. "These cartridges are new. I opened the box yesterday. And cartridges don't come with scratched shells."

Still frowning, he walked over to a corner of the tent and picked up the cartridge-belt which he had thrown aside when he lay down for Chris to dress his scratches. He had worn it that morning. There were two rows of slots to hold cartridges, ten on the left of the belt and ten on the right. The left-hand slots held soft-nosed ammunition, five rounds for the .470 and five for the .275. On the right were the solids, five rounds per rifle. There were three .470 cartridges left in the belt.

He extracted them from their slots and examined them one by one, his lips clamped into a tight line across his bony brown face. Each cartridge had similar little scratches along the upper rim of the copper shell, where the bullet fitted in. He put down the magnifying glass and looked at Chris. His face was grim and a little savage. "Jesus!" he said. "Then that's a second murder."

CHAPTER 15: CHRIS HAD GONE AS WHITE AS the river sand at mid-day, and the pupils of her eyes were distended with fear. She put one hand to her neck in an instinctive gesture. It looked brown as a Rhode Island egg on a white tablecloth. He jumped to his feet and put an arm around her shoulders, afraid she was going to faint. She swallowed once and bit her lip, as if to bring back the feeling.

"I'm all right," she said. Her voice was faint and low. "It's rather a shock, isn't it?"

"I'll say it is," Vachell agreed. "Murder by proxy. I never ran into anything like this before. This guy must be smart as hell. But how could he know there was a wounded buffalo roaming around those hills? I don't see it. No one could have known about that bull except Rutley. I'll need to figure this out."

He found that his arm was still around Chris's shoulders and removed it, feeling a little foolish. "Stay here and rest a while if you want to," he added. "I have to look in to this."

"I'm all right." Her voice sounded more normal now, and she got to her feet. "I must go and see how Cara is. This seems so terribly—well, calculated, I suppose. This must have been meant for you, mustn't it? They may try again. . . . Don't go and get killed too. Please be careful."

He looked back from the tent opening and smiled at

her. "You bet," he said. There were several strips of elasto-plast on his face, and smiling was difficult. "With all this adhesive tape, I'm practically in armour."

Rutley, Vachell supposed, was still at breakfast. Anyway, his shop was empty. The detective pushed open the rough door and went over to the bench. He took one of the scratched cartridges and clamped it, bullet upwards, into a small vice. He selected a strong pair of pliers from a case lying open on the bench, gripped the bullet in their arms, and tugged. It was like extracting a tooth. He worked the bullet around, and after a few grinding motions he felt it give. A minute later it came out with a little plop.

He took the shell out of the vice and emptied the nitro-cellulose powder out of it on to a sheet of paper on the table. Then he repeated the whole operation on a .470 cartridge taken straight out of a new box, and free from scratches. The bullet was harder to extract, but he got it out, and emptied the black powder into a second heap. He examined the two heaps on the table. The first was considerably smaller, perhaps two-thirds as large as the second. A weighing operation, of course, would be needed to establish proof. But Vachell needed no scales to convince him that part of the powder from the five cartridges in his belt had been removed.

The next step was to put the bullets back. This was not so easy. The neck of the copper case had gripped the bullet so tightly that it had contracted when the lead was removed, and now its diameter seemed to be smaller than that of the bullet's base.

This was the same problem, Vachell thought, that the murderer had faced. He rummaged about the bench for inspiration, and came upon a thin steel bar with one end tapered to a point. He inserted the thin end into the cartridge-case, rammed it down as far as it would go, and tapped gently on the other end with a hammer. When he withdrew it the neck of the shell was so wide that he slipped the bullet in easily. He clamped the rim of copper case tightly on to the base of the lead with the pliers, and in half a minute the cartridge was reassembled.

He swivelled the handle of the vice, released the cartridge, and examined it with his lens. That was the trick, all right. Along the rim of the neck was a series of scratches, made by the pliers, exactly similar to those of the doctored cartridges. And on the base of the shell, where the vice had gripped it, with two faint dents—twins of those he had examined a few minutes before in his tent.

Only one more discovery was needed to clinch the proof. There were three pairs of pliers in the tool-case. He examined their gripping surfaces with great care under the magnifier. On one of the pliers he detected a faint, almost invisible trace of glittering metallic powder. He wrapped the pliers carefully in a piece of paper and slipped them into his pocket. There was no doubt in his mind that an expert in the Government laboratories at Marula would be able to identify these few metallic specks as traces of cupronickel, such as that in which the lead of bullets is encased.

It was a neat trick, he reflected. A misfire was crude: it led inevitably to an examination of rifle and ammunition. In this case the powder exploded and the bullet left the

barrel, but it lacked the punch which made it deadly. If
the man who fired such doctored bullets were killed by a
charging animal, no one would be likely to suspect the real
reason. They'd put it down as an ordinary miss. Vachell
himself had done so, until Chris spotted the scratches. If
it hadn't been for her he'd still have been worrying over
his bad shooting. He knew now that he had hit the buffalo
in the spot at which he aimed, but that the bullet had
lacked the strength to do more than inflict a small cut in
the bull's thick hide. That was the one bright spot in the
whole affair.

He added the pliers to a collection of potential exhibits
that was beginning to accumulate in the wooden box containing his detective's outfit. So far the collection comprised
the bullet with which de Mare had shot the lion, the
Player's cigarette-stub picked up outside Lady Baradale's
tent after he had been attacked, and two walnuts. To it he
added the three remaining .470 cartridges with scratches
on their shells, and the empty shell from the bullet he had
fired that morning. He was locking up the box when
Japhet arrived with another contribution—the bullet cut
out of the wounded buffalo's stomach. It was a soft-nosed
bullet, and had flattened out into a twisted mushroom-
shaped slug of lead. This made it hard for Vachell to identify the bore with certainty, but the base had retained its
shape, and he felt reasonably convinced that the bullet belonged to a .470 rifle. Rutley, he remembered, had been
using Englebrecht's rifle—a .470 like his own. He wrapped
it up and packed it with the other potential exhibits. An expert would soon make sure.

It was ten o'clock, and Vachell was reminded of breakfast. He shouted to Kimotho to bring a meal at once, moved his table and chair into the veranda formed by an extension of the tent's fly, and sat down with his note-book open in front of him. Although it was still early, the day was hot. The sun blazed down fiercely from a deep and cloudless sky, and sharp, hard pools of shadow lay on the grey-green grass below the tents and the yellow-trunked acacias. All activity seemed to have been suspended until the shadows started to lengthen again.

Sometimes, on an African noon, Vachell had the feeling that the sun had stunned the vegetation with some form of physical force. But this daze of quiescence had not fallen on the camp itself. It seemed like a whirlpool of activity in a sea of quiet. The voices of natives sounded sharply against an even background of droning cicadas. In the boys' quarters people were walking to and fro continuously, gathering in little knots to talk in low tones, and quickly dispersing again, as logs being carried down a river will catch against some obstruction, form a restless island, and part again before the insistent pressure of flowing water.

The camp was disturbed and upset. Vachell could feel it in the air. Natives were always uneasy when a dead body was in their midst. Perhaps they feared that a curse had descended on the camp, that the gods were angry. They might even suspect that witchcraft was at work. If this was so things would get difficult. Luckily there wasn't anywhere close by where deserters could seek refuge. Malabeya was too far—he hoped. For all that, he had heard of natives doing crazier things than foot-slog for a hundred miles to run away from witchcraft.

Kimotho arrived with a handful of knives, forks, and plates, and started to lay the table. He, too, seemed upset; he was unusually silent as he padded back and forth on his bare feet. He wore a blue shirt and a pair of shorts; usually he was meticulously careful to put on his white kanzu and red taboosh when he served a meal.

Some advice that Armitage, the Police Commissioner, had given Vachell when he took up his new job as Superintendent a year ago came to his mind. "Never neglect native gossip, my boy," Armitage had said. "It's astonishin' how these wogs get hold of information. Things get a bit garbled, of course, but often enough it's bazaar gossip that puts us on the right track." He decided to test this theory on Kimotho.

"Listen," he said. "I want news from the tents of the black men. What are they saying about the death of bwana Catchpole?"

"They say it is a very bad affair."

"They say the truth. What else?"

Kimotho adjusted the angle of a knife and fork and removed the top of a marmalade jar without answering. His face remained impassive, but Vachell sensed, without knowing how he could tell, a faint feeling of embarrassment on the native's part.

"Tell me," he urged.

"Their words are not good. They are only ignorant savages—particularly the cook. Now he is giving me rice, but he refuses onions, and he keeps all the meat for himself. He says that it is finished, but I ——"

"Leave the meat, Kimotho, and speak sense. You know what I wish to hear."

"Yes, bwana. The boys say many things, and they tell many lies. They say that if bwana Danny had been here, this other white man—he who the boys call the bwana-who-walks-like-a-baboon—they say he would not have died. They say bwana Danny knows very well how to shoot."

Vachell continued to stare out into the sunlight, apparently absorbed in the behaviour of two plum-coloured waxbills who were hopping anxiously about near the tent wondering how close they dared approach in search of crumbs. Two muscles in his jaw, below the high cheek-bones, twitched a little at Kimotho's remark. His lean, tight-drawn face was sunburnt, but below the bronze it was pale, and his eyes looked larger than normal in their deep sockets. Strips of plaster ran down one cheek from eye to jaw.

"Go on, Kimotho," he said.

"They also say," Kimotho continued, reassured that he was not venturing too far on to dangerous ground, "that bwana Danny would not have gone so close to a buffalo that had been wounded in the stomach. Buffaloes are very bad, and when they are wounded they are completely bad. The black men think this is a bad camp, and would like to go home."

"We go home to-morrow or the day after, if rain does not spoil the road. Do the black men know who killed the memsahib?"

Kimotho shook his head. "No. What sort of eggs do you want? I will tell the cook."

"Listen, Kimotho. When I ask what is being said by the black men I want to know. It is your job to tell me. Who do they say killed her?"

There was no doubt about Kimotho's embarrassment now. He fiddled with the butter-dish and avoided his employer's eyes. He had a hunted look. "I do not know," he said.

"You tell a lie. What sort of behaviour is this? Speak."

Kimotho, to Vachell's surprise, flashed a row of white teeth in a broad grin, and laughed. "All right. You have asked; it is your affair. The black men say: who is this white man who came here with bwana Danny? Is it true that he is a police bwana, as he says, or does he only pretend? We have seen many police bwanas; they do not behave as he does. They wear very smart clothes and take askaris everywhere to salute them when they speak. This white man's clothes are not at all smart, and he has no askaris. Before he came, everything here was very good. There was much meat, and no trouble. Then he came, and immediately afterwards the white woman was shot; and now the bwana-who-walks-like-a-baboon has been killed by a buffalo. Is it not strange, that these things should happen when the new white man comes? Why did they not occur before? Perhaps it is this white man who killed the memsahib. These are the words that are being spoken, bwana. You asked me, and I have told the truth."

The recital brought a grin to Vachell's face, and at the end he threw back his chin and laughed.

"So I killed the memsahib," he said. "All right, Kimotho. What reason do they say I have?"

"They say that perhaps you wish to buy bwana Lordi's daughter and that her mother refused, so you killed the old woman. And that when the bwana-who-walks-like-a-baboon objected too, because he wished to buy her for himself, you took him close to the wounded buffalo so that it would kill him. They say also that you are a fool to wish to buy bwana Lordi's daughter, because she is very thin and will not bear many children."

"They know everything," Vachell remarked. "They see more than God. What do you think?"

"I do not think that you killed the memsahib," Kimotho said seriously. "I have told these ignorant savages that you are a very big police bwana, and that when you wish to kill a person you do not do it yourself, but you give the person to the Government and they do it for you with a rope. Do you want your eggs boiled, fried, or scrambled?"

"Scrambled. But wait. Have you heard ——"

"It would be best if I fetched your breakfast," Kimotho interrupted. "That cook is so bad that if I do not tell him now he will say that there are no more eggs."

Kimotho strode off to the kitchen, which consisted of the customary three large stones placed in a shallow hole in a roughly built grass hut, while Vachell made jottings in his note-book over another cigarette. When the eggs and bacon arrived he found that he was ravenously hungry. Kimotho watched him eat approvingly, and remarked:

"That buffalo hit you very hard. The skin should belong to you."

"You want it, I suppose," Vachell said.

"Not all of it, bwana. I wish to have a pair of buffalo-hide sandals, like those that Konyek wears. They are very good for safari."

Vachell took a large mouthful of egg and grunted non-committally. Even here, he thought, even on safari, the problem of keeping up with the Joneses overshadows almost everything else.

"There is another matter," Kimotho went on. "It concerns Geydi, bwana Lordi's boy—that Somali. He is not a good man. I have heard strange things about him."

"What things?"

"Some men of the Timburu tribe have been near the camp. The trackers, who know this country, say that the Timburu cattle are far away—perhaps ten days' journey from here—where they always go for grazing at this time of year. But they have seen Timburu warriors close to the camp."

"What has that to do with Geydi?"

"Bwana Danny sent two trackers, two Wabenda, to look for elephant. They searched all day, and it was night before they returned. As they were approaching camp, they heard voices in the dark. They crept up to see what had occurred, and they found Geydi talking to three Timburu men, young men with spears and shields and warriors' head-dress. These Wabenda could not understand what was being said, for the words were in Somali, but presently Geydi gave them some money and they went away. Geydi did not know that the trackers had seen him."

Vachell frowned, and buttered some toast. This sounded

like the Timburu poachers, the gang that was wanted for the murder of a Game Department scout. Probably Geydi was doing some illegal poaching deal with them—buying rhino horn, perhaps, to smuggle with the Baradales' kit down to the coast. If he got the facts, he might be able to use them to put the screws on Geydi. He had an idea that the supercilious Somali knew more than he'd say.

"When did this happen?" he asked.

"The evening that we came here from Marula. The trackers did not speak before, because they were afraid that Geydi would make trouble for them with the white men. But they told me, because we are of the same tribe, and they believe that you are a police bwana. Timburu are very bad men. They are very fierce, and Wabenda are afraid of them."

"Tell these friends of yours to search near the camp," Vachell instructed, "and to come to me if they find where the Timburu are hidden."

"Yes, bwana. There is another thing." Something in Kimotho's voice made Vachell suspect that the native was indulging in one of his favourite tricks, that of keeping his tidbit until the last.

"Tell me then, quickly. I have work to do."

Kimotho gathered up the dirty plates and stacked them on a tray. His manner said, as plainly as if he had spoken, "Yeah? So have I."

"You told me to ask which of the white people left camp yesterday morning. I have told you what I have found. First you and the memsahib who flies above in the bird, then bwana Rutley and the dead memsahib, then bwana

Danny and the white man-who-walks-like-a-baboon. Then bwana Rutley came back alone and climbed the hill with a gun to look ——"

"Yes, I know all that," Vachell interrupted. Africa was teaching him patience, but sometimes he found native repetitions too much. Kimotho paid no attention.

"To look for meat," he went on calmly. "I was washing your shirts in the river, so that I could not see what happened in camp. But yesterday I talked to one of the men who cuts firewood, and he told me this. He was coming back to camp by the road that goes to Malabeya, carrying firewood; and when he had almost reached camp, he met a car, coming fast but quietly, so fast that he had to jump in the bushes to avoid it. He was annoyed because he dropped some of the wood, and then he ——"

"God damn it," Vachell exclaimed, "why didn't you tell me this before? Who was driving?"

"Geydi, bwana. He was by himself, driving very fast and away from camp."

"What time was this?"

Kimotho shrugged his shoulders. "This wood-cutter is a savage; he does not know times. He said that the sun was not yet overhead. Perhaps it was ten o'clock, perhaps eleven. Later, that afternoon, Geydi found this wood-boy and forbade him to tell what he had seen. Geydi threatened to tie the wood-boy up at night with a dead zebra, so that the lions would eat him slowly, if he spoke."

"But he told you?"

"Yes, bwana. I told him that the police have eyes like vultures and see all things; and if he did not tell everything you would tie him to stakes driven into an ant-heap until he was eaten alive by biting ants, beginning with his eyes. He is afraid of Geydi, but now he is still more afraid of the police."

"Kimotho," Vachell exclaimed, "I have told you a thousand times that you are not to tell such lies!"

Kimotho smiled cheerfully, hitched up his shorts, and lifted the tray. "I know," he said, "but I have also promised him a shilling. Give it to me, and I will take it to him."

Vachell sighed, took a shilling out of his pocket and threw it on to the tray. "News is cheap here," he said. "Find out if any boy has heard a rifle speak far away from the camp, and tell them to listen for one to-day. And bring hot water at once."

Kimotho stalked off into the sunlight, rattling the tray. Vachell extinguished his cigarette, and started to assemble his razor, a puzzled frown on his face. It was hard to piece together all the odd, seemingly unconnected bits of information. One thing, at least, seemed clear: the Ford sedan that had made the unrecorded twenty-nine-mile journey on the morning of the murder had had Geydi for its driver.

Suddenly an idea came to him, and he whistled softly, standing stock-still in the tent with the razor in his hand. The idea expanded into a theory while he stood there, as a Japanese paper flower, of the kind that street-sellers used to offer, expands from a speck into a full-blown blossom when you drop it into a glass of water. He sat down abruptly on the bed, pulled out his sketch-map from his pocket, and scribbled a rough calculation of times based on the movements of a herd of elephants.

CHAPTER 16: A VOICE SAID "HODI" AND THE
tent darkened as Rutley's big form loomed in the opening.
Vachell had just finishing shaving. He put down the razor,
and said "Come."

"I came to ask what you want done about this—well,
about Sir Gordon," Rutley said. He lowered himself on
to the bed, took off his cork helmet, and wiped his face
with a large silk handkerchief. His curly black hair was
as well combed and shiny as ever, and his moustache neatly
clipped. "This camp's turned into a ruddy morgue, if you
ask me," he went on. "Now I've had the job of undertaker
shoved on to me. This safari ought to have taken an em-
balmer along. I suppose I'd better rig up another coffin.
It's lucky they keep pace with the gin, or we'd be running
out of cases."

His attempt to be facetious sounded forced and uncon-
vincing. Vachell thought that he could detect a trace of
uneasiness beneath the chauffeur's cocky manner. "You'd
better make another coffin right away," he said. "After
that, it's up to Lord Baradale. I'll help you fix the body
when the coffin's ready."

"Okay," Rutley said. He looked curiously at Vachell's
face and arms. "You had a narrow shave this morning.
Mrs. Davis says it was the buff I fired at yesterday. That
correct?"

Vachell nodded, and began to comb his hair.

"I'd no idea I hit the bastard, honestly. I'd have warned you if I'd thought I had. It was back luck about Sir Gordon —though I can't say I think he'll be missed, to be honest. I can't stick these she-men, especially when they think they're Lord God Almighty, like he did. Still, it's a bit awkward, a thing like that happening, especially with Lord Baradale and Mr. de Mare away."

"You're telling me," Vachell said.

"A bit awkward for you, too. You thought I shot Lady Baradale, didn't you? You wouldn't believe I'd gone up the hill to shoot a buck. Well, I can't blame you altogether. I'll admit it *did* look a bit fishy. That's why I didn't let on about it to start with. Now you know I was speaking the honest-to-God truth. I don't know who shot Lady Baradale. All I know is, it wasn't me. The only thing I get out of it is the sack, and I'll tell you frankly, as billets go, this was a soft one."

Vachell decided that he'd had enough. He swung around suddenly, and looked directly at the chauffeur's face. "Rutley," he said, "what have you done with the letters you took last night?"

Rutley's face was wooden. He stared back for several seconds, and then asked: "What letters?" in an expressionless voice.

"You know what letters," Vachell said. "Your letters to Lady Baradale. The ones you took out of her tent last night. The ones that told her you were through, that the affair was all washed up, that if she tried to stop you marrying Paula, you'd rub her out. The letters that gave you a motive for putting her out of the way."

Rutley jumped up from the bed, and his sun-helmet rolled across the floor of the tent. His face was flushed and his fists clenched.

"Blast your bloody eyes, stop that!" he shouted. "You're a goddamned liar, that's what you are! You know I didn't kill her, and you're trying to frame me because you can't find out who did. By God, I'd like to—" He broke off, half choking with anger, his face dark and menacing. "Oh, hell, it's waste of time talking," he said, in a calmer tone. He stooped to pick up his hat. "You flat-foots are all the same. You make a mess of your job, and then you try to take it out on some one else. Well, carry on. Why don't you start by finding those jewels? That's what you came here for."

"All I have to do is to dig up every inch of sod two feet down within a radius of five miles of the camp, and put it through a sieve, and the stuff's mine," Vachell said. "Sure, that's easy. Now I'll tell one. Lady Baradale kept the key of the safe in her pocket all day and under her pillow all night. You're the only guy in this camp who was liable to be fooling around her pillow and no questions asked. You took the jewels, and you took the letters, and ——"

"And you'll take a sock on the jaw!" Rutley shouted. "You've no right to accuse me like that! You pick on me because I'm just a poor bloody mechanic, not fit to eat a meal with their high and mighty lordships in the west-end part of the camp. Well, I'm not going to be the goat, not this time. You think the members of the English ruling classes couldn't murder or steal, don't you? They're all too much the gentleman, aren't they—wouldn't ever do a

thing like that. Oh, no. Well, you're bloody well wrong.
I can tell you ——"

Rutley's voice tailed off into silence. He stood in the
middle of the tent panting slightly, his face thrust forward,
in an attitude that reminded Vachell of an angry bull
thwarted by a wire fence. He looked uncomfortable, as
though he had said too much. "Anyway, you won't find
the swag in *my* direction," he concluded. "I haven't got it,
and I didn't pinch those letters from out of the safe, either."

Vachell's eyes, narrowed into slits, gleamed with triumph. "Just a minute, Rutley," he said quietly. "I said
you'd taken those letters out of Lady Baradale's tent. I
didn't mention any safe. Just how did you know they were
in the safe?"

"I've had enough of this," Rutley said. His voice was
only just under control and the muscles of his face were
twitching. "I'm not going to stand here and let you trip
me up with your bloody theories. Take back what you
said, you son of a ——"

"Take it easy," Vachell said sharply. "Right now you
haven't any spanner in your hand."

Rutley lunged forward and shot out his right fist at the
same moment as Vachell jumped to one side with the
agility of a klipspringer, bringing the tent pole in between
them. Then Vachell stepped forward and slammed his right
fist into the side of Rutley's head. It smacked against the
chauffeur's temple and caught him off balance, knocking
him sprawling on to the bed. He sat up and shook his head
like a dog coming out of a pool of water.

"All right," he said savagely. "You're a bloody cop,

and if I knock that grinning face of yours to blazes you'll send me to jug. You win this time, but don't think I'll forget it. I'll get you one day, so help me, and when I've finished with your face your own mother won't ever recognize it again."

"Thanks for the warning," Vachell said. "Next time, I'd advise a wrench. A spanner's a bit on the light side, I guess."

Rutley scowled again, grabbed his helmet, and stalked out of the tent. Vachell sighed, and called to Kimotho for a glass of water. All this he-man stuff, he decided, was hot, hard work. His head throbbed, his mouth felt dry and stringy, and his side ached. He sat down in a camp-chair, and noticed that his hand was shaking as he lit a match.

A tide of despondency crept over him as he sipped the water. The case was all around him, all over him, and the farther he went the more confusing everything became. He couldn't even clear up one simple problem: who had knocked him out the previous night in Lady Baradale's tent. He'd tried to bluff Rutley into believing that he'd given himself away over the letters; but it was a thin bluff. The chances were that Rutley had known where the letters were kept ever since he had started to write them. And there might have been other papers in the safe that other people wanted.

And then there were those walnuts. They were like a signature—surely not Rutley's; they didn't fit. There was a touch of macabre humour about them, of boastful contempt for the things that organized society respected: the dead, the panoply of burial, the enforcement of law. Nuts to the bunch of them, the signature said; nuts to it all.

"To hell with the nuts," Vachell said aloud. "I'm going nuts myself, with that crazy gag on my mind." He jumped to his feet, shouted for Kimotho, and gave instructions for Geydi to be summoned to the tent.

It was fifteen minutes before the Somali appeared, walking slowly, and dressed in a newly pressed white suit with a green open-necked shirt and a red tarboosh. He looked, as usual, sulky and supercilious. His lithe body swayed gracefully as he walked, and his whole appearance reminded Vachell of a young poplar in a wind. His face was the colour of milk-chocolate; effeminate in its full lips, big eyes and soft skin, yet with a hint of the underlying ruthlessness and fanaticism latent in Somali men. He stood erect, his hands hanging loosely at his sides, and said: "Yes, bwana," in a tired, low voice, as though the effort required to speak distinctly was more trouble than the occasion warranted. He had a trick of speaking almost without moving his lips.

"First, Geydi," Vachell said, "there is the matter of the gun that disappeared yesterday from bwana Lordi's tent. When did you see it last?"

Geydi paused for so long before answering that Vachell began to think that he was going to ignore the question altogether. Then he mumbled: "I don't know. Perhaps the day before yesterday," and was silent again, as though the effort had exhausted him.

"Did you see it yesterday morning, when you made the bed?"

Geydi shook his head.

"Was it stolen, then, in the night?"

"I do not know."

Vachell turned to Kimotho, and said: "Fetch the two trackers who saw the Timburu, and the wood-boy who saw Geydi in a car." Kimotho disappeared at the double, and Vachell tried again.

"Listen, Geydi," he said. "You are telling lies, and if you lie to the police you will be sent to prison. I have witnesses, and if you lie any more I shall arrest you."

Geydi made no reply, but stared over his inquisitor's head. Silence prevailed for several minutes. The sun, high in the sky, beat down heavily on the canvas, and the tent was hot and stuffy. At last a small column approached in single file, Kimotho in the lead, and halted outside the tent. Vachell called upon each man in turn to tell his story. The two trackers did so without hesitation, but the wood-boy kept glancing nervously at Geydi, and required a good deal of prompting. The facts, however, were as Kimotho had stated.

When they had finished, Vachell fixed his eyes on the Somali's face, and said: "You hear what these men say. What do you answer? Why did you summon these Timburu warriors, and why did you pay them money?"

Geydi turned his head slowly, and gazed with dark, soft eyes at the faces of the trackers. "Perhaps these men saw spirits," he said, still almost inaudible. "They are savages. I talked to no Timburu warriors."

"So they lie, huh? And perhaps this wood-boy lies too? Perhaps he saw a ghost driving bwana Lordi's car? But I have proof here that you cannot deny. Do you not know that when a car travels it leaves the number of miles written on a clock? Are you so ignorant that you do not know this? The car that you took added twenty-nine miles to its clock yesterday. Now tell me where you went."

Geydi turned his head again, and looked Vachell full in the face. It was a look of insolence and contempt.

"I know, of course, that the miles are written. I am bwana Lordi's driver. He has told me that when I want to drive his cars, I can drive them wherever I like. Enough. Yesterday I did so. That is bwana Lordi's affair, not yours."

Vachell felt a strong desire to punch the Somali on the nose. He resisted it, and said: "Why did you say nothing of this before?"

Geydi shrugged his shoulders again. "You did not ask."

"Did you tell bwana Lordi?"

"No."

"Where did you go?"

"Along the road."

"Did you leave the road at all?"

"No."

"What time did you leave camp?"

"Perhaps ten o'clock. Perhaps later."

"How long were you away?"

"Perhaps an hour. Perhaps longer."

Vachell leant forward and pointed his finger at the Somali's chest. "Then how was it," he said, "that you did not meet bwana Rutley driving his car back to camp?"

Geydi shrugged his shoulders again, apparently indifferent to the obvious discrepancy. He mumbled, "I did not see him," and stared dreamily at his feet. He's so damned sure of himself, Vachell thought, that he won't even bother to invent a decent lie.

"All right," he said. "You refuse to speak. But here, in this camp, I am the police, and I shall make you. And understand this: you uttered threats against this wood-boy, telling him that he was not to speak. He has spoken, and now he is under the protection of the police. If anything evil befalls him, you shall be severely punished. Enough. You can go."

Geydi moved his head to look at the wood-boy, his face a mask of contempt. "I do not touch hyenas," he said. He turned without another word and walked towards his quarters, arrogance in his stride. Vachell watched him go in silence. There seemed to be no way to make him open up. The next attempt must be directed towards the Somali's master.

A few minutes later he found Chris Davis standing hatless in the sun beside the kitchen, being talked to by the one-eyed Swahili cook. The fat native looked thoroughly disgruntled. "And another thing," he was saying as Vachell came up, "what sort of food are all of us to eat? Where is the meat? There are animals walking about everywhere, and many guns, and yet meat is lacking. It is a very bad affair."

"All right," Chris said. "I will shoot you meat to-day."

The cook said "Good," without much enthusiasm.

"There'll be a sit-down strike if I don't," Chris added, turning to Vachell. "Paula can look after Cara while I'm away."

"Okay," Vachell said. "I want the answer to another question. About elephants. Are they as scared when they get a native's wind as they are when they smell a white man?"

Chris frowned and looked thoughtful. "That depends," she said. "In districts where natives hunt ivory with poisoned arrows they're every bit as nervous. But up here, where the local natives never hunt them, that isn't so. I've seen elephant feeding peacefully within a hundred yards of native cattle, with the herds wandering about and the elephant paying no attention at all. But as soon as they get a whiff of a white man, they're off like a shot out of a gun."

"That fits in," Vachell said. "You remember those elephants we flew over yesterday? Well, do you recollect just where they were when we first saw them?"

"I think so, more or less. I think I could find the place."

"That's swell. Now, will you do a job for me?"

"I'd love to."

"Swell again. Here it is. Take a car, check time and speedometer, and drive just as fast as you can to the place where we first saw the elephants from the plane. If you can hit it right on the nose, so much the better, but if you can't, use your judgment and pick a place about the same distance from here. Check time and mileage again, and come back to tell me. Do you get it?"

Chris nodded. "That sounds easy, though not very good for the car. May I ask what this is all about?"

"I'll tell you later," Vachell said. "Right now it's just a smart idea, and it may develop into a flop. Watch out for pig-holes, and don't dispute the right-of-way with any rhinos."

Chris smiled, and he observed how laughter put lightness and buoyancy into her face and created a dimple on one side. Her hair shone brightly in the sun, and he was reminded again of granulated honey.

"I'll be all right," she said. "This camp seems to be the danger zone. For God's sake don't let anything else happen. Remember those emasculated cartridges. There might be another attempt. . . . You *will* be careful, won't you?"

Vachell grinned broadly, and felt as though a warm, exhilarating wave was rippling through his body from scalp to toes. "You bet I will," he said. "Good luck." He watched her walk towards her tent, slim and upright in khaki slacks and a white silk shirt, with a green-and-white scarf knotted around her neck. There were darned few girls, he thought, with as much guts. . . .

"There is another matter," the cook's voice said behind him. "It is about the rice. That boy of yours ———"

"Oh, to hell with the rice," Vachell said.

CHAPTER 17: CHRIS DAVIS TOOK TWO

rifles, one light and one heavy, and the tracker Konyek, because he knew the country well. It was 11.30 when she started. The sun was fierce and biting, and she could feel by the heaviness in the air that rain was close at hand. Flies stuck to her arms as if their feet had been dipped in glue.

It was rough going, and she was sorry for Lord Baradale's car. The country to the south-west was flat and fairly open, but there was plenty of bush to dodge, and big rocks, half concealed by grass, that would bust the crank-case to bits or tear the batteries out by the roots if they weren't properly avoided. The car jolted along, much of the time in second, lurching like a tired camel, and sometimes emitting a harsh groan as the chassis slammed down on the back springs.

Progress was noisy, and, Chris felt, likely to disturb the most phlegmatic elephant. She kept one eye on the grass in front of the wheels and one on the surrounding bush, in case of rhinos. They came upon a herd of startled giraffe, who cocked their foolish heads, perched on stiff necks like sparrows on a flagpole, at the interlopers, and on a party of oryx beisa, who cantered along for some distance by the side of the car under the impression that they were running away. Konyek sat in the passenger's seat with the heavy rifle across his knee. He clung to the side with one hand

and stared fixedly ahead, saying nothing. He was an unsophisticated native, and not very used to cars.

All veldt country looked alike from the ground, and the hills to the left were the only landmarks. Dry, bush-flanked watercourses scarred their sides with deep cuts, each one a dark streak running from the forest which clothed the top of the range to merge into the plain below. In places bare rock jutted out of the hill-sides and provided fixed points on which bearings could be taken.

Chris was glad to have something to do. It gave her mind defences against the grim thoughts that had been crowding in on it for the last twenty-four hours—thoughts of vulture-pecked remains nailed down in a gin-case coffin; of Cara Baradale's hysteria and fear; of Gordon Catchpole's self-assured vitality trampled into bloody oblivion; of the havoc being played with Danny's career. And, above and behind all this, the black dread of what was still to be revealed; the paralysing fear that the truth would strike suddenly like a snake from the branches of a tree, and then . . .

She thought of Vachell, and of how much he really knew. More than he'd say, of course. She couldn't make him out at all. He didn't look like a detective, somehow. Detectives were either patient, plodding, polite men in derbies from Scotland Yard, or else tough, lean, abrupt-mannered G-men with two-dimensional guns flat in the pockets of their perfectly tailored clothes, and soft hats tipped over one eye. It was true that Vachell had a felt hat, and tipped it over his eyes sometimes, or else on the back of his head, and that he was lean and wiry, but there the resemblance ended. He had a slow, deliberate manner of speech that she found puzzling; it was hard to know when he was serious and when he was pulling some one's leg. You couldn't tell how much he knew. He never got ruffled, and he didn't jump at conclusions. He might be clever. . . . The front wheels hit a hidden stump, and the car bounced into the air like a high-spirited baby. It came down with a loud protest from the springs, and an echoing squawk from Konyek. Chris fixed her attention again on the driving, and tried to put everything else out of her mind.

Some time later Konyek gripped her arm and pointed to something over on the right. She slipped the clutch, braked the car, and followed his gaze. There was a dry, rocky watercourse just below them, and beyond it the bush-speckled plain rolled on a horizon that wavered in the heat haze. About five hundred yards away a patch of thick bush and scrubby acacias marked the site of an underground pool. Chris saw a flicker of grey against the dark background, and focused her field-glasses on the spot. No doubt about it: elephant. They'd been lucky. She took rough bearings on the hills to the left, the sun, and the line of the Kiboko river. No doubt about that either: she had struck the right spot, and the elephants had returned to the same place to shelter in the heat of the day after drinking at the river. She checked mileage and time, and jotted them down in a note-book: 14.2 miles, 46 minutes, going as fast as a car could safely travel.

She watched the elephants for a little through the glasses. There was a small herd, with at least one big bull and several half-grown calves. They were drowsing lazily in the shade, flapping their big ears and from time to time plucking the branch of a tree with their waving trunks. They were upwind, fortunately, and had not heard the car.

"There is one with big tusks," Konyek remarked. "It would be good to shoot it, because then you could sell the tusks for very many shillings."

"No," Chris said. "I do not wish to shoot; and the tusks would belong to bwana Lordi."

"This bwana Lordi, he is very rich," Konyek said thoughtfully. "The cattle that he owns must be numerous as zebra on the plain. Why, then, does he hunt elephants for their tusks? And these Timburu warriors, they are very poor. They sell the horns of rhinos in order to buy wives. Why does the Government forbid them to kill rhinos, but allow bwana Lordi, who is already rich, to kill elephants?"

"Because bwana Lordi pays many shillings to the Government for a licence," Chris replied. "The Timburu pay nothing and have no licence, and they kill many rhinos so that soon there will be none left alive."

"Rhinos are bad," Konyek persisted. "Sometimes they get angry and kill men. Would it not be a good thing if all rhinos were killed? What use have they?"

Chris felt incapable of launching into an explanation of the principles of game preservation. She started the engine, and drove off towards the hills to the east.

"Do the rhinos then belong to the Government?" the tracker persisted.

"Yes."

"But how can they, when they pay no taxes?"

"We are going to shoot meat," Chris said firmly. "Search with your eyes for buck."

They had gone about two miles when Konyek touched her arm and pointed to the left. This time it wasn't elephant, but one or two vultures wheeling idly in the blue sky. Chris shivered a little. Vultures, since yesterday, had acquired a new unpleasantness. These, most likely, were just persistent birds hovering over the remnants of a lion's kill. She decided to pay no attention. A gulley, however, forced them to make a detour, and they found themselves passing almost underneath the hovering scavengers. Konyek evinced a strong desire to investigate, so she stopped the car and got out. He led the way through the bush almost directly to the focus of the birds' attention. A collection of large bones, too large even for the fabulous jaws of hyenas, lay scattered about beside a clump of bush. The grass was heavily trampled, and fouled with the droppings of hyenas. A big vulture flapped noisily into the air as they approached, and retired to watch them from a nearby tree. The bones were picked dry, and every piece of meat was gone.

"Rhino," Konyek said. "It died yesterday."

Chris experienced a feeling of relief. She had almost expected to find another human corpse. Konyek hunted around for several minutes in the bush, and returned carrying a white object in his hand.

"Timburu," he said, holding it out. "Timburu warriors were here yesterday. They killed this rhino. You see, there is no horn. They took it away."

The white object was a small ostrich feather, such as Timburu warriors used to decorate their hair and ankles

when dressed up for war or for a celebration. Konyek let
the feather flutter to the ground, a look of disdain on his
cleanly moulded Egyptian features, and grace in every
movement that he made.

"Bad men," he said. "They are uncircumcised, and they
kill with poisoned spears. When there are no rhinos, they
kill men."

"They were here yesterday, then," Chris repeated.
"Have they gone far?"

"Who can tell? They move swiftly as the cheetah, and
they travel in the night like bats."

As they turned to go, Chris noticed something shining
in the trampled grass. She picked it up, and gave an excla-
mation of surprise. It was the copper shell of a medium-
bore, magnum rifle. They stared at it for a moment in
astonishment.

"Timburu have no European rifles," Chris said. "A
white man has been here."

Konyek shook his head. He looked all at sea.

"I don't know," he said. "Timburu use poisoned spears,
but here is a rifle cartridge. Yet the Timburu were here,
and dressed in warrior's apparel. They left the feather, and
they took away the horn."

"It is very strange."

"Truly," Konyek said.

They jolted on together in the car through a fierce mid-
day heat which rose in waves from the baked earth, making
the bush quiver and shake before their eyes like objects
in a pre-war motion picture. Chris was moist with sweat,
and her arms and shoulders ached with the effort of con-

trolling the bucking wheel. Her throat felt dry and swollen. They came to a patch of more open country as they drew closer to the hills, and in a stretch of fairly bush-free veldt a herd of eland swam into view, their legs invisible in the heat haze. Chris stopped the car and made a long, hot detour on foot, followed by a careful stalk upwind through scattered bush. She dropped a young bull with an easy shot at eighty yards, and Konyek cut it up and loaded it into the car. The meat problem, at any rate, was temporarily solved.

By the time the operation was over, an afternoon thunderstorm had appeared suddenly overhead. It was real rain, there was no doubt about that: the lurid, violet clouds looked solid and heavy as steel. The heat was intense, and the wind that usually blew from the south-west had dropped, leaving a stagnant stillness in the air.

Chris pushed the Plymouth as hard as she dared, but they struck some rocky broken country, and they had not gone more than half-way home before the storm swooped down like a giant angry hawk, with a scream of wind to herald its approach. It came down on to the windshield in a great grey cloud, beating a savage tattoo on the roof and blotting out everything ahead. Chris stopped the car, and she and Konyek struggled with the canvas side-curtains. A fierce wind snatched them out of their hands several times, but finally they were clamped to the body, and the travellers waited inside their ark-like cabin for the storm to abate.

Thirty minutes later the rain had slackened sufficiently to allow the car to proceed. It went at a walking pace,

slithering wildly over slippery grass and treacherous patches
of mud. Twice it careened sideways into a thicket, and
nearly overturned. They stopped to put on chains, and that
helped a little; but when they came to the next gulley they
saw a racing torrent of dark-brown water tearing wildly
down the eroded channel. Konyek got out to investigate,
and reported water up to his knees. Chris turned the car,
and churned a way slowly and dangerously along the
gulley's bank, looking for a place to cross. Then the back
wheels sank abruptly into a patch of soft earth, churned
two deep pits, and the car subsided gently on to the back
axle. Unquestionably, they were stuck.

Chris and Konyek surveyed the situation in a cold, grey
drizzle, and pronounced it hopeless. There was nothing to
be done but to leave the car and return to rescue it when
the ground had dried and the gulley subsided. The tracker
removed one of the eland's haunches from the back of the
car and hoisted it on to his shoulder. Chris checked the
fastenings of the side-curtains, hoping they were hyena-
proof, stripped the sight-protectors from the heavy rifle,
and led the way, stumbling over slippery grass tussocks,
through a steady downpour and towards their distant goal.

It was six o'clock before, wet and weary, they sighted
the feathery grey columns of smoke rising from the camp-
fires. The sky was clear again and the sun's last rays were
slanting across a clean and golden world. Newly washed
canvas gleamed as white as daisies in a May meadow, and
the acacias' boles glowed like marigolds in the sun. Their
blossoms' perfume seemed twice as strong. The grass was
fresh and sparkling, and the birds sang with renewed en-

thusiasm. It was hard to believe, coming back to such a scene of peace and beauty, that the stain of murder lay over the camp.

Natives were busy setting things to rights after the storm, putting out the chairs and tables that had been hastily collected under cover. There was no sign of Vachell, and Cara was not in her tent. Chris, soaked to the skin, finally located Paula in the veranda of her tent. She was sitting at a table varnishing her nails. Her heart-shaped face was as carefully made up as ever, but Chris thought that underneath it she looked tired and sallow. Cara Baradale, she said, was feeling better, and had gone for a short stroll along the river-bed.

"This storm will ditch our chances of getting back to Malabeya to-morrow," Chris remarked. "We should never get the trucks through, and I wouldn't be surprised if this didn't bring the river up."

"The rain sure did come down," Paula said. "I never saw it so bad before. Mr. Vachell sent two of the trucks out this noon, and they aren't back yet. I guess they must've stuck, because about an hour ago he hollered for George and they both went off in another truck with some rope and a whole gang of boys."

"Couldn't get back over the drift, I expect. I wonder where they went," Chris said.

"I dunno. Listen, Mrs. Davis, may I ask you something? I guess you know what's going on around here better than I do. I've seen you talking with the dick. He's been snooping around asking a lot of screwy questions to-day, and picking on George all the time. They don't really

think George did it, Mrs. Davis, do they? They're crazy
if they do. He's on the level, honest he is."

Chris borrowed a nail file, sat down on a gasolene-case,
and started to trim her nails. "I don't know who Mr.
Vachell suspects," she said. "But so long as Rutley had
nothing to do with it, he'll be all right."

"It isn't only the questions," Paula said. She had forgotten all about her nails, and kept her eyes anxiously on
Chris's face, as if hoping to see signs of reassurance there.
"That cop suspects George, I know he does. He thinks
George shot her, and then cracked the cop on the head
last night and took some letters. Well, he didn't. I saw
him when he came into camp yesterday morning. I asked
him where Lady Baradale was and he said: 'The old sour-
puss wanted to hike back, so I'm going to take an hour's
vacation.' I asked him what for, and he said to shoot a
buck. George is crazy for hunting, see, and they never
give him a chance. Well, Mr. Englebrecht had lent him
a gun, so he took it and went out like he said, and when
he came back he told me about this buffalo. Only he said
for me not to tell, as he was afraid there'd be trouble if
Mr. de Mare got to hear about it. And then, of course,
we heard that Lady Baradale got shot that morning. . . .
But he didn't do it, Mrs. Davis, you know that. He's got
an awful quick temper, but he wouldn't ever kill a person, not like that—not in cold blood."

It sounded to Chris a bit as though Paula were whistling
in the dark. Aloud she said:

"I wouldn't worry, then. He can't get into trouble if

he had nothing to do with it. They'll find the murderer eventually, of course."

Paula looked at Chris for a moment in silence. She seemed to be debating something in her mind.

"Mrs. Davis," she said finally, uncertainty in her tones. "If a fellow was suspected of murder, you'd say he'd be right to tell everything he knew, wouldn't you?"

"He'd be a fool if he didn't."

"That's what I say. But suppose, if he told something, it would get him in trouble over something else, see— some other thing, not the murder, but something that he'd done and he didn't want the police to know? See what I mean?"

Chris puzzled this out in silence for a little. "Yes, I think so," she said. "Well, it all depends, I suppose." She put down the nail file and stared steadily at Paula. Her wet clothes were sticking to her everywhere and her hands were stiff and cold. "Why, does Rutley think he knows who did it?"

Paula bit her lip nervously. "Listen, Mrs. Davis," she said. "Don't you repeat this to any one. George would flay me if he knew I'd talked this way. . . . But I'm scared. You see, he thinks he knows—that is, he doesn't *know*, he hasn't any proof or anything, but he says he knows who did it. I don't know how he found out. Well, suppose this person gets to know George is wise, that puts George on the spot, see? Murderers don't go around in kid gloves, do they? See what I mean?"

"Perfectly," Chris said. "Well, why doesn't he confide in Mr. Vachell?"

"He says Mr. Vachell wouldn't believe him, that he'd think it was a gag George thought up to kind of, well, to drag a red herring across the trail. And then, there's other reasons. . . ."

"Do you know whom he suspects?"

Paula shook her head. "He won't say. He's too darned cagey. I wish he'd talk with the cop. Maybe they'd let him out if he told what he knows. . . . It doesn't do to fool around with murder cases. You can be too smart, and first thing you know you've been framed and take the rap, or the guy who did it lays for you and knocks you off. . . . Gee, you look frozen, Mrs. Davis, You shouldn't be sitting here in those wet clothes. I'm sorry, I oughtn't to have talked this way. You won't repeat what I've said, will you?"

"No, I won't," Chris said. "I'm not going to interfere." She rose stiffly and shivered. She stood for a moment looking down at Paula. The girl seemed frightened and forlorn, and a long way from home. She looked out of place in these crude surroundings, with her loosely cut red linen trousers, high-heeled white sandals, and striped, close-fitting jersey, all so clearly designed for Pacific beaches rather than for the African veldt.

"You're in love with Rutley, aren't you?" Chris asked abruptly.

"Sure. We're going to be married."

"He'll be all right," Chris said slowly. "He'll be safe enough—so long as he keeps his suspicions to himself."

"Then you don't think he ought to tell the dick?" Paula said. "You think he shouldn't talk?"

Chris did not answer at once. She stared down at the girl intently, her face white and curiously set in the fading twilight. Something that Paula saw there seemed to scare her. She shrank back a little in her chair and knocked over a bottle of nail varnish with a nervous movement of the hand.

"I think he should keep silent," Chris said. Her voice was low and quiet, but a cold note of menace underlay the words. "That is, if he wants to stay safe."

CHAPTER 18: DARKNESS WAS CLOSING IN
swiftly on the crimson glow of sunset when Rutley and
Vachell got back to camp. They climbed out of the lorry,
cold and stiff, their legs caked with mud up to the knees,
and walked across to the table of drinks under the acacia.

"Those trucks were stuck good and proper," Rutley re-
marked. "I thought we'd never get the blasted things out.
We wouldn't have, either, if it hadn't been for that patent
jack. Prospects don't look too bright for his lordship and
Mr. de Mare, do they? What'll we do with—well, Sir
Gordon's body, if they get stuck?"

"Bury it," Vachell said. "But I guess they'll make it.
A light car has more chance than a heavy truck."

Rutley drained his glass and put it down. "I need a hot
bath," he said. He seemed to have forgotten his anger
against the detective since they had worked together over
the mud-bound trucks. "See here, Mr. Vachell. You talked
this morning about some letters you said I wrote to Lady
Baradale, that gave me some sort of a motive for—well,
turning nasty, you might say. I don't deny how things
were between us. She made me do it, and that's a fact.
Well, I couldn't refuse. You know how these things are.
If I'd kicked up rough I'd have lost my job, and it was
a good job, I'll say that."

"Nice work, if you can get it," Vachell said.

"You think it was lousy," Rutley went on. "Well, you

can think what you like, but I've got to make a living, haven't I? I only took the job temporary, until I could get back into the movies, or something. This gigolo business isn't all it's cracked up to be, you can take it from me. I was going to get out as soon as I could get something better. Well, what I'm trying to tell you is, you don't want to run away with the idea that I had any reason to—well, to do her in, to call a spade a spade. She was crazy about me, and I always treated her right, I swear I did. It was a bit awkward at times. She wouldn't leave me alone. I don't deny I'd have been glad if she'd cooled off a bit, but that doesn't mean I had anything against her. We was on the best of terms, so help me, and that's the truth, Mr. Vachell."

"Sure," Vachell said. "Just a couple of carefree love-birds, billing and cooing."

Rutley looked at the detective's bland face with suspicion. "If you think I'm mixed up in this business you're barking up the wrong tree," he said. "I haven't got a motive, you can see that for yourself. I'm worse off now than I was before. Well, that was what I wanted to tell you. I don't want you to get a wrong impression."

"Thanks a lot," Vachell said drily. "I'll try to avoid that."

Rutley strode back to his tent through the gathering dusk, leaving Vachell to sip his highball and stare reflectively at the river. It was running strongly, with a deep sound that almost approached a roar. Little fringes of froth had accumulated on the edges of pools where the current was churning with a new activity. The sun's afterglow was reflected in the thick muddy water, so that the stream looked like a channel of dark, venous blood.

As he watched the water, half unseeing, a slender figure rounded the bend, walking slowly up the river-bed. Vachell scrambled down the bank and strolled along to meet Cara Baradale. In the fading light her eyes seemed like holes in a chalk-white mask. Her long thin legs, bare below a pair of shorts, looked as brittle as twigs. She said "Good evening" gravely, and leant against a rock.

"Good evening, Miss Baradale," Vachell said. "Well, we failed to locate him."

"Locate who?" Her voice was husky and tired, and trembled a little as she spoke.

"Why don't you tell me where he's camped?" Vachell said. "It would save time, but nothing else. We'll find him anyway, whether you tell or not. If he isn't guilty, he hasn't anything to fear."

Cara moved restlessly against the stone and said: "I don't know what you're talking about. Have you got a cigarette?"

He gave her one, lit it, and took another for himself. They smoked in silence for a while, watching the night creep down the hills and the day fade out of the sky. A dozen different sounds blended into the evening symphony: preliminary croaks from frogs, the distant bark of baboons, the throaty call of francolins, the squawk of guinea-fowl. A dozen nameless, pungent scents came to them, scents of herbs and trees and of the wet earth.

"Listen, Miss Baradale," Vachell said at last. "Why don't you quit holding out on me this way? It isn't getting you anywhere. Take yesterday. You left camp before six in the morning, and got back after seven at night. I know it doesn't take that long for the round trip to Malabeya, and you know I know it. Why don't you tell me what you did?"

"I have told you," Cara answered. Her tone was flat and lifeless. "We drove to Malabeya. We weren't in a hurry, and we stopped for breakfast on the way."

"Quite a breakfast, I should say. Took three-four hours to eat."

"It wasn't only breakfast. We stopped again, not far from Malabeya. Luke saw a kudu from the road that he thought might have a record head, so he went after it. That took some time, and then he had to skin the kudu after he'd shot it."

"How was the head?"

"Oh, it was quite good, but it wasn't a record after all."

"Too bad. What did he do with the skin?"

"What on earth does it matter?" Cara said, irritation sharpening her voice. "You do ask the most fatuous questions. He took it with him, of course. Can't you stop cross-examining people for a second?"

"Sure," Vachell said equably. "I beg your pardon. Maybe you'd rather I told you something for a change. Sir Gordon tried to leave a message for you when he died, but he couldn't get it over. It had something to do with Englebrecht."

Cara dug her toe into the soft wet sand and threw her cigarette stub into the river. Her face was a white blur in the darkness.

"Is that all?" she asked.

"Not quite. Sir Gordon's death was not an accident. I shouldn't tell you this, but I guess you can take it. It was another murder."

"But the buffalo—" Cara exclaimed. She shrank back against the rock, and tried to grip it with her hands.

"The buffalo killed him, sure. But dead buffaloes don't trample people to death, and that buffalo would have been dead before it ever reached Sir Gordon if the bullet I hit it with had penetrated the skull. It didn't, because the cartridge only had half a charge of powder. The rest had been taken out."

"Then it was meant for you?" Cara asked. Vachell got the impression that she had expected something else. "I mean, you were supposed to be the—the victim?"

Vachell nodded, and flicked his cigarette into the water. It hissed faintly, and disappeared.

"Poor Gordon," she said. "He butted in once too often. . . . How did the murderer do the trick?"

"He emptied half the powder out, replaced the bullet, and then he put the cut cartridges back in my belt last night, sometime after eleven o'clock."

He thought he heard Cara catch her breath, but the evening was so full of noises that he couldn't be sure. "What sort of cartridges were they?" she asked.

"You mean the bore? They were .470's. What makes you ask that?"

This time there was no mistake. She gave a sort of gulp, and her body went rigid against the rock. "Nothing," she said. Her voice was hoarse and hard. "Let's go in; I'm cold."

They walked in silence back to camp. Cara poured herself a stiff drink of gin and drank it straight. She walked off to her tent, calling to her boy to bring a bath.

Hot water was gloriously soothing to Vachell's bruised ribs and aching limbs, even though the rubber tub accommodated only half of him at a time. His scratches, under the plaster, were sore and itching. He dressed slowly, in a pair of grey slacks and a dark sweater. There might yet, he suspected, be work to do.

As he sat on the bed to pull on his shoes, the lid of the wooden box containing his detective outfit, standing on the ground opposite, caught his eye. It wasn't quite closed; and he had left the box safely locked. He jumped up and went over to inspect it. Then he swore tersely and flung back the lid. The lock had been roughly forced, and from the box had been taken the package containing all the potential exhibits relating to the Baradale case. Nothing else, so far as he could see, had been touched.

He squatted on his heels by the box, tabulating in his mind the thief's haul. One used bullet, the bullet fired by de Mare into Catchpole's lion; one Player's cigarette stub; one pair of pliers, with traces of capro-nickel dust on their gripping surfaces; one empty .470 shell, with scratches, from the cartridge that hadn't killed the buffalo; three doctored .470 cartridges, with part of their powder gone; and two walnuts.

That was all. Yet one of these unpromising objects must have been the thief's objective. One of them must be a vital clue, whose destruction was essential for some one's safety. One of them had been worth risking detection to secure.

And, for the life of him, Vachell couldn't think which.

Tents could not be locked, and any one might have walked into his during the last two hours, after he had gone out with Rutley to the drift. That meant that any one in camp could have burgled the box—any one, in fact, except Lord Baradale and de Mare, who were still somewhere on the Malabeya road. There was nothing to be gained by thinking along those lines. Kimotho, summoned for inquiries, could contribute nothing. He had seen no suspicious character hanging around his master's quarters, loitering with intent.

Vachell was still puzzling over the matter when he joined Chris Davis under the acacia and poured himself out another Scotch. She had changed into the usual dinner dress of the camp, and looked fresh and self-possessed in a black and crimson dressing-gown over black silk pyjamas. Her hair was like a golden halo in the lamp-light.

"I see the trucks got back," she said. "You must have had fun and games with them in the drift."

"We sure did," Vachell said. "They went down the river to look for Englebrecht, but the rain came on and they had to turn around before they found anything."

"He must be down the river if he's here at all," Chris said. "There's no other water for fifty miles. If you like, I'll take you out to-morrow morning in the plane. If we fly down-stream we can't miss him, and then you can go after him in the car."

"That's a swell suggestion," Vachell said. "I'd like to call that a date. How did you make out to-day?"

Chris recounted three adventures: locating the elephants; finding the rhino carcase with a Timburu feather and an empty rifle shell beside it; and getting stuck in the mud. She handed him the cartridge shell and a sheet of paper on which the time and distance between camp and the elephants were written.

"How does that fit in with your theory?" she asked.

He grinned and raised his glass to her. "You flatter it. It isn't an adult theory yet; it's just a moppet. But what you found out will stimulate its growth. You've been a big help, and thanks a lot."

"You don't give much away, do you?" Chris said.

"I may be going cheap myself in a couple of days. Something tells me the Commissioner will be headed this way when he gets my telegraphed report, and I don't anticipate that he'll be falling over himself with satisfaction at the way things are shaping."

"Don't worry," Chris said consolingly. "If we can't get out, he can't get in. He'll stick in the mud."

Vachell looked at his watch in the strong light of the gasolene-lamp which hissed softly on the table. "Mind if we turn on the radio?" he asked. "The news is just coming on, and I asked headquarters to slip in a message for me at the beginning if there was anything hot."

He brought the portable radio out of the mess-tent and set it on the table. He tuned in to Marula, and they listened in silence to a symphony orchestra record and a lot of static. A voice announced the second news bulletin, copyright reserved. There was a pause, and it came through again.

"Before the second news," it said, "I have a police message for Superintendent Vachell, Chania Police, believed to be somewhere on the Kiboko river, Western Frontier province. Calling Superintendent Vachell, Chania Police. Message begins. Your report received. The Commissioner is leaving Marula to-morrow and hopes to reach Malabeya the following day. He will proceed to your assistance as soon as road conditions permit. The following information received to-day from Malabeya is transmitted for your information. The District Commissioner, Malabeya, reports that at 4 p.m. yesterday the Honourable Cara Baradale and Luke Englebrecht called at his office with the intention of obtaining immediately a special marriage licence. This was refused. Englebrecht has not yet been reported out of the Western Frontier province. You are further warned that a number of Timburu warriors, one or more of whom is wanted for the murder of a Game Department scout, is believed to be at large in your area. Message ends. I will now repeat. Police message for Superintendent Vachell, Chania Police. . . ."

The stilted voice droned on in the darkness, punctuated by the crackle of static and the croaking of frogs. The two listeners sat in silence, glasses clasped in their hands, staring at the radio. A slight breeze ruffled the leaves above them and an owl hooted in the distance. The repeat ended, and the voice said: "This is the B.B.C. Empire Service, second news bulletin, copyright reserved. Heavy casualties are reported from Canton today, where the Japanese launched a fresh aerial attack. . . ."

Vachell got up and switched it off without comment. His face was set and thoughtful in the hard white light. A white-clad form materialized out of the night and started to clear bottles and glasses off the table in readiness for dinner.

"Poor kid," Chris said. "I wonder why on earth she tried to do an idiotic thing like that?"

"I can think of one reason," Vachell answered.

"What's that?"

"Because a wife can't testify against her husband in a court of law," he said.

CHAPTER 19: IT WAS AFTER EIGHT O'CLOCK
when an angry voice, shouting loudly in Kiswahili for a
hot bath, proclaimed the return of Lord Baradale and de
Mare. As soon as they entered the pool of light under the
acacia Vachell could see why they were late. It was clear
that they had made the last part of the journey on foot.
Lord Baradale was thickly encrusted with black mud, and
it was only too evident that at some stage he had slipped
and fallen headlong into a particularly wet patch.

"What in God's name have you been up to in that drift?"
he demanded furiously. He seized the whisky bottle and
splashed some of the contents into a glass. "Having an
all-in wrestling match with an elephant? The whole
damned place is chewed to bits. You could no more get a
car through there than up Mount Everest. Mine's stuck
over the axles, and I should be obliged if you'd kindly
have it brought in before it's washed away. . . . Where's
my daughter?"

"We had a bit of trouble with the trucks," Vachell said.
"Miss Baradale is in her tent, I guess. She isn't feeling
very well. She's had a shock, sir. I'm afraid it will be a
shock to you, too. I hate to tell you this, but the fact
is ——"

"For God's sake, man, out with it!" Lord Baradale
barked. "Do you think I'm a hysterical old woman who'll
throw a fit if she gets a shock?"

"Sir Gordon Catchpole has been killed," Vachell said shortly. He added, after a momentary pause, "by a buffalo."

De Mare said, "Oh, my God!" and dug the butt of his rifle into the soft ground with a gesture of impotent anger or despair. "This is the last straw. How did it happen?"

Lord Baradale said nothing for a moment. He stood and stared at Vachell, his small black eyes wide with astonishment and consternation. He seemed, for once, at a loss for words. He shut his mouth with a snap and sat down heavily in a chair, pulling his glass of Scotch towards him and gulping the contents before he spoke.

"Gordon dead!" he exclaimed dully. "Lucy—then Gordon. . . . There's something behind this! Are you sure it was a buffalo?"

Vachell told the story briefly, omitting all mention of his mutilated cartridges. The faces of his listeners were set and strained in the harsh light of the hissing gasolene-lamp that stood on the centre of the table. A big brown moth banged itself persistently against the lamp-glass while he spoke, until Chris shot out a hand and knocked it to the ground, where it lay stunned.

"God damn it!" Lord Baradale exploded. "You had no right to let him go with you! You, a detective, who's here to protect us—you're responsible for his death!"

"Vachell couldn't help it," de Mare said. He pulled a chair close to the table and sat down. He was as precise as ever in his actions, but his voice was flat and dispirited. His face seemed to become more lean and hawk-like every day, and his eyes to grow larger in their sockets. "Of all big game, I'd sooner meet anything than a buffalo hit too far back. They've killed better men than Catchpole before—better hunters, I mean—and they will again."

Vachell glanced across the table at de Mare and tried to put gratitude into the look. He thought again how curiously sensitive to other people's feelings the hunter sometimes was, for a man whose life was spent in action.

"That bull must have done the old trick of circling round to cut across his own back trail, and then lying in wait," de Mare went on. He seemed to feel that some one ought to speak to fill the sentence. "They wait until you're on top of them, and then let you have it. They mean to get you when they do that. They've killed a good many people that way. If any one's to blame, it's Rutley. He ought to have been able to tell that he'd hit something from the sound of the shot."

Lord Baradale said nothing and stared at his drink. He was breathing heavily. When he spoke at last his bluster had given way to a helpless acceptance of the situation that surprised and almost shocked the others.

"There seems to be some ghastly curse hanging over this camp," he said. "It's terrible, all this, terrible." The remark was somehow pathetic in its banality. "Mr. Vachell, has my daughter told you that she endeavoured to get herself married yesterday—to that infernal young scoundrel of a white hunter my wife sacked just before she . . . met her death?"

"I just heard about it," Vachell said.

"Peto, the D.C., got back to Malabeya yesterday morning—unexpectedly, I understand, as a result of some

trouble with these Timburu poacher fellows," Lord Baradale went on. "Just before he left his office at four o'clock
my daughter and this—this damned young whippersnap-
per appeared, demanding a special licence to be married
at once. Thank God, Peto had the sense to refuse. They
went off in a furious temper, so he said, with that young
scoundrel's car, and came back in this direction. So it looks,
Mr. Vachell, as though Englebrecht is in hiding a few
miles from this camp, waiting to abduct my daughter. And
what's more, he was somewhere within easy reach of this
camp at the time my wife was shot yesterday morning.
I'd suggest, if it's not going beyond my province, that you
have a talk to that young man."

"I've been trying to pull him in to-day, sir," Vachell
said. "Your daughter knows where he is. If she'd spill it,
we'd pick him up right away."

Lord Baradale grunted, finished his drink, and pushed
back his chair with a vicious jerk.

"Cara's on the edge of a nervous breakdown, Lord Baradale," Chris put in. "If any one tries to force the information out of her I'm afraid she ——"

"I believe that I know how to deal with my own daughter, Mrs. Davis," Lord Baradale snapped. He turned
abruptly and strode off towards her tent."

"Hello, Chris," de Mare said. He looked across at her
and smiled. She had pushed her chair back into the half
shadows, and he seemed not to have noticed her before.
"This isn't our lucky safari, is it? Pull up your chair and
have a drink."

"You must have had a foul trip," she said.

"I did. The old man's feeling it more than he shows. I don't think his wife's death broke his heart, but this business about Cara nearly did. Englebrecht's a damned young idiot. I'd like to wring his bloody neck."

Chris shivered a little and hunched her shoulders over her drink. "I wish to God we could pack up the safari and get out," she said.

"Not a hope—not for the trucks. We stuck about ten times in a patch of black cotton about half-way between here and Malabeya, and the water's coming up so fast in the gulleys you can almost see it. We're here for a week, I should think."

The brown moth had revived and started butting its head against the lamp. Chris stabbed at it unsuccessfully with her hand.

"Danny," she said abruptly, "what's come over Luke?"

De Mare's sharp features relaxed in a sudden smile, and he fumbled in his pockets for a pipe. The chorus from the river-bed had started up again, but it was more subdued to-night, almost as though some emanation of the dark emotions of fear and suspicion that permeated the camp had radiated outwards like wireless waves, and penetrated the consciousness of the surrounding frogs.

"I'm surprised that you ask that, Chris," de Mare said. "It comes over us all at times, you know. Just plain, old-fashioned, elemental love—very elemental, like everything else about Luke. He doesn't go in for subtleties, such as wondering whether Cara would be really happy as a white hunter's wife, for instance. He reminds me of the perfect Nazi: blond, muscular, and moronic; and he "thinks with the blood," as good Nazis ought. He wants Cara, and he doesn't see any reason why he shouldn't take her. It's part of the much over-rated nature of the little child—'mama, buy me that' sort of thing. Very likely he thinks she's lucky to get him. Perhaps she is—I don't know."

"I expect you're right," Chris said. "I suppose Cara tried to marry him to get her own back on Lady Baradale. They'd had a row about Luke the day before, and of course Cara was furious about Luke's getting the sack. It all seems very childish. I should have given Luke credit for more sense. Danny, you don't think that perhaps he. . . ."

"Cleared his path to happiness by removing an insurmountable obstacle, in the form of Lady Baradale?" de Mare inquired. "*I* don't know. That's Vachell's job. But it's hard to believe that some one you've lived and worked with for several years can be guilty of murder. Don't you agree, Chris?"

"I think there are worse crimes than murder," Chris answered. She reached for her glass and sipped its contents, staring into the darkness over the river. Her face, Vachell thought, looked as pallid and fragile as a piece of old china.

"Ah, but you let your charity run away with you," de Mare said. "Women are always ready to justify themselves and good-looking young men."

"A lot depends on the motive."

"Murder for money is always inexcusable, don't you think? It's sordid, anti-social, and unscrupulous. Even you, Chris, can't make a noble motive out of that." De Mare was smiling faintly, and there was a sort of barbed banter in his tone. There was some hidden thrust and parry behind their words that Vachell couldn't understand.

"I suppose not," Chris said. She was staring with a set and tense expression across the river. "But it's too late now to make any difference."

"Murder always makes a difference," de Mare said. "I'll leave you to find that out for yourself." He got up and took his rifle off the chair where he had laid it. "Well, murders or no murders, we must still wash." A minute later they heard his voice shouting for hot water.

Chris shivered, although the air was warm under the glittering stars, and stabbed at the blundering moth with a nervous hand. She knocked it on to the table and quickly imprisoned it in an inverted glass. "Damn that beastly moth," she said. "It's getting on my nerves."

CHAPTER 20: DINNER WAS A DIFFICULT meal. Cara failed to appear, and her father ate sparingly with de Mare, Vachell, and Chris. They tried to ignore the subject which continually pushed its way back into their thoughts—the subject of the trampled body that lay in a tent less than twenty paces from the dinner table, unwillingly guarded by a native who squatted on his heels by a small fire outside, his blanket wrapped closely around him.

De Mare and Chris kept up a desultory conversation and Vachell occasionally contributed a remark. Lord Baradale sat in moody silence until something that one of them said about the possibility of striking oil in the Western frontier caught his attention. He launched into a rambling discourse on the future sources of power, developing a wild and complicated theory of his own for harnessing the osmotic force of plants to industrial use. This led him on to an account of a company he had once nearly formed to grow London's vegetables on trays in chemically treated water in a series of wooden towers at Wembley; and finally the conversation returned, by devious routes, to the subject of big-game hunting.

"It's a lot of tommyrot, this so-called sport," he exclaimed forcefully. He had abandoned any attempt to eat and was puffing at a small cigar and drinking liqueur brandy. "It's rotten to the core, like everything else about this modern civilization. Sport! It's no more a sport than

shooting sitting pheasants, if as much. There's only one
sporting way to hunt big game, and that's the old way, the
way these natives follow—to hunt on foot with spears and
bows and arrows, weapons a man can make himself out of
materials ready to his hand. That's fair, and that's fun.
It's a battle of wits between one man and one beast: a test
of which can command the greatest cunning, the keenest
senses, the highest skill. Man, if he uses his wits, can usually win; but it's a victory worth having, because it doesn't
go to the coward or the dolt."

"I agree," de Mare said. "It's skill versus skill, always;
but it's man's superior skill that has led him to invent
gunpowder, and weapons that can use the force of gunpowder. So man is justified in using the modern rifle just
as much as the primitive bow and arrow. They're both
a product of his skill."

"Of mankind's skill," Baradale replied, "not of the indi-
vidual's. You've substituted the skill of one man versus
one beast for the skill of the whole race of man versus one
beast. If you had all men versus, say, all lions, that might
be fair. But lions can't combine. So you have the brains and
resources of every one from geniuses like Priestley and
Pasteur to modern big business combines like I.C.I. and
du Pont, pitted against the wits of one poor African lion.
It isn't sporting; it isn't even exciting. True sport involves
equality between the rivals, you see. They give handicaps
in everything from horse-racing to ping-pong, in order to
achieve a rough equality; but they never give a handicap
to the beast. It isn't sport; it's murder."

There was an uncomfortable pause as the last word,

now charged with a personal and fearful meaning, rang loudly through the silence of the night. Lord Baradale checked himself, realizing too late that he had ventured by a concealed back entrance on to a forbidden ground.

"The beast wins out sometimes," Vachell said quietly.

Lord Baradale darted a quick glance at the detective and drew deeply on his cigar.

"Only by accident," he said, "and carelessness—once in ten thousand times. Bell and Sutherland both claimed to have shot over a thousand elephants, I believe. That's mass-destruction, not a battle of wits. Besides, you're not consistent. You say it was man's skill that invented the high-velocity rifle. True enough. It was his skill, too, that invented machine-guns, airplanes, bombs, and poison gas. Why don't you tackle elephants and rhinos, then, with those products of human skill? You wouldn't pretend that was sport; but why is it more unsporting to bomb a herd of elephants or turn a machine-gun on to a pride of lions than to drive up to them in a motor-car and shoot them with a high-powered rifle? If it's legitimate to use one, why not the other? I can't see the difference myself."

"The difference is in the element of danger," de Mare answered. "There's always some risk in hunting with a rifle."

"Danger!" Lord Baradale snorted. "Danger be damned! There's no danger at all in going after some wretched animal, whose only idea is to escape, armed with a battery of expensive high-velocity rifles and flanked by a couple of professional sharpshooters. There's ten times the risk in a single drive in a fast car along the Kingston by-pass.

If any one wants to hunt, let him use a bow and arrow and match his wits against those of a lion or an elephant, as some of these natives do. If he uses a rifle, he shouldn't pretend it's sport; that's my opinion. But I don't expect you young fellows to agree with me."

"Well, I do," de Mare said unexpectedly. "But then, big-game hunting isn't a sport to me; it's a profession. I don't have to pretend. On my last safari, I cut twenty-five miles of road through the bush to a waterhole where I knew a herd of elephants came regularly to drink, and the man I was taking out flew down from Marula one morning in a chartered plane. I met him in a car at one end of the road and drove him to within a mile of the herd at the other, and he was back in Marula dining at Dane's that night with a very fine tusker to his credit—if you can call it that. No one could say that was sport. It's efficiently conducted execution."

"You must get fed up with your own profession, if you feel like that," Lord Baradale remarked.

"I often do," de Mare said.

Coffee, sweet and fragrant under the rustling leaves of the acacia, came and went, borne by Geydi's deft, walnut-coloured hands. Conversation faded, again, fitfully into silence. Tobacco smoke drifted in blue twirling spirals towards the dark boughs overhead. From the boys' quarters came the occasional sound of raised voices, and once a burst of laughter that died quickly, as though the sound itself was conscious of its impropriety.

Lord Baradale broke the silence abruptly. "Well, I've got some work to do," he said. "Please excuse me, Mrs.

Davis. De Mare, I shall see you in the morning. I suggest
seven o'clock for this very distressing duty we have in
front of us. Mr. Vachell, I wish you good night."

De Mare lit his pipe and excused himself to attend to
the preparation of a grave. The storm had obliterated, with
the road, the possibility of taking Catchpole's body into
Malabeya, and he was to be buried close to camp.

"I ought to go and see how Cara is," Chris remarked.
"I hope the old man didn't bully her about Luke."

"Not he," Vachell said. "He's nuts about her. Let's take
a walk along the creek. If we watch the water long enough
maybe we'll get cool."

"It is stuffy," Chris answered.

They strolled down the bank in the soft darkness, listening to the throaty call of the frogs, the chirping of tree-
crickets, and the whisper of the running water. The air
left no breath of coolness on their faces. It was not a
clammy heat and not uncomfortable, but the threat of
thunderstorms kept the air motionless and heavy. A sky
crammed with stars gave enough light for them to see
their way among the faint shadows suggested by bush and
trees. Chris caught her toe in a root and Vachell took her
arm to steady her, and for a little they walked in silence.

"I wish it was all over," Chris said. The remark had all
the sincerity of a prayer. "It's this waiting for the next
thing to happen that's so awful."

"You mustn't let it get you down," Vachell said.

"I believe you know already who the murderer is."

"If I knew that, he'd be under arrest right now."

Chris laughed apologetically in the darkness. "I wasn't

trying to pump you. It's only that I wondered—I do wish you'd get it over with, and put an end to this suspense."

"I have a hunch we're close to the pay-off," Vachell said. "If things work out the way I've figured that they should, that is. It's so darned fantastic I can hardly swallow it myself, so maybe my theories won't jell. I'm hoping they won't, too, and that's bad."

"I knew you had a theory," Chris said. "It's got something to do with those elephants we flew over, the ones that got scared."

"They're easy. Trouble is, this theory has loose ends."

"Such as?"

"Several things. The position of the body, those screwy walnuts, and the fact that some guy helped himself to—well, to a lot of junk out of my tent this afternoon."

"This afternoon?" Chris repeated. "What sort of junk?"

"A couple of pork pies, a bag of ripe tomatoes, and a signed picture of Stanley Baldwin."

"Oh," Chris said.

They walked along the river bank without speaking. To their right the white sand gleamed softly in the starlight, and a silver lustre shone on the crests of the gurgling torrent. Trees were dark formless shapes, and the grass a dim expanse of pale petrified sea. From a thicket close at hand a dove cooed persistently in the darkness: "Ku ku, ku—u—ku ku; ku ku, k—u—ku ku." The notes were sweet and warm, but a little sickly.

"Well, I guess we should be getting back," Vachell said. They halted close to the thicket. The dove in the branches gurgled once and then was silent, and a rustle from the undergrowth proclaimed the startled movement of a small animal.

"Dik-dik," Chris said. "It had better be careful. Konyek said there was a leopard down at the hippo pool last night."

"Listen, Chris," Vachell said. "I want to ask a favour. It's a hell of a big one, and there won't be any kick if you turn it down. This time factor is getting on top of me, and I have to find Englebrecht. Will you lend me your plane to-morrow for the search?"

"I offered to take you up," Chris said.

"Thanks," Vachell hesitated. "That isn't exactly what I asked. It's kind of hard to explain. I'm asking for the loan of the machine on the drive-yourself plan. I had a pilot's licence up to a couple of years ago, and I promise I won't bust up the machine."

"Why don't you want me to fly her?" Chris asked. Her voice was hurt and cold.

"I'm like Greta Garbo," Vachell said. "I want to be alone. That's not polite, but it's this way—on police work we're supposed to play a lone hand, especially in a murder case. You understand that. If you don't want to loan the plane on those conditions, okay; but you'll be helping the investigation a whole lot if you let me take her up."

"There's something behind this," Chris said slowly. "If you're only going to look for Luke's camp, it can't matter if there's some one with you in the plane."

"It's a matter of principle, I guess."

"You didn't talk about principles when you asked me to measure the distance to the elephants this morning. Something's happened since then." Chris stared up at him, trying to read the expression on his face in the starlight.

"It's up to you," he said.

Chris straightened her shoulders and turned to look at the river. "You don't trust me," she said. "You don't suspect *me*, do you?" She jerked her head round to look at him again, incredulity in her voice. Then she laughed, but without amusement. "I see. I'm in the running for the prize you're going to give to one of us before we get away from here—a pair of handcuffs and a length of rope. Well, you're a policeman, and this is a murder case, and I suppose we've all got to do what you order us to, whether we like it or not. I don't, but that won't do me any good."

"Say, you've got me all wrong," Vachell protested. "I'm not trying to put over any strong-arm official stuff. If you don't want to loan me the plane, that's okay. I can find Englebrecht on foot. It takes longer, that's all, now the cars get bogged if they go a mile out of camp."

"Oh, take the plane, if you want her." Chris turned and started to walk back towards the camp. "For God's sake don't crack her up, that's all. I shouldn't have got annoyed. I thought that you—well, it doesn't matter. I know you're only doing your job."

"That's swell of you, Chris," Vachell said. "You know, you're a swell person. And look: don't talk to any one about this. Keep it under your hat."

"All right," Chris said. "Let's get back to camp."

When they had retraced their steps along the river for a few paces, Chris halted abruptly and stood like a startled antelope, her head turned to one side. Vachell stopped beside her and held his breath. The dove in the thicket behind them gurgled again and flew off with a flapping of wings. A faint rustle came from the thicket, and the sharp snap of a breaking twig. Then the frogs and the whispering water regained their monopoly of the noises of the night.

"There's the dik-dik again," Vachell said. There was a question in his voice.

"No." Chris spoke in a low tone, just above a whisper. "It was too heavy."

Vachell reached out and gripped her arm. It was cold and trembling slightly. They stood for a full minute as motionless as two cranes fishing by the edge of a stream, but they heard no more.

"Some sort of a buck?" Vachell queried.

"A buck wouldn't have stood there close to us while we talked."

"Well then—what?"

"It might have been a man," Chris said.

CHAPTER 21: THEY FOUND THE CAMP IN darkness, save for the log fires that always smouldered through the night, and glimmers of light shining through the scattered trunks and branches from the natives' quarters. Vachell said good night to Chris and walked quickly over to his own section of the camp, beyond the acacia. Two out of three tents were lit: his own and de Mare's. He slipped quietly around the back and shone his flashlight into the third tent, at the end of the line. It was Rutley's, but the bed was empty.

De Mare was sitting at a table in his tent veranda, smoking a pipe and making entries in several ledgers that were open in front of him. He looked up when Vachell appeared, and nodded.

"The poor devil's to be buried at seven," he said. "You'd better be there."

"Sure," Vachell said. "I'm checking on every one in camp. Where's Rutley?"

"Holding Paula's hand over in her tent, I should think. I haven't seen him. I've been here for the last half hour, checking the stores. The cook's been complaining of thefts, as well as of this meat famine. I'm going out first thing to-morrow to replenish the pot."

Rutley was sitting over a blazing camp fire behind Paula's tent, a whisky bottle by his side and a glass in his hand. Paula sat cross-legged at his feet, staring at the crackling logs. Conversation stopped abruptly when Vachell appeared out of the darkness and stepped into the orbit of the fire's glow.

"Have you been out hunting buffaloes again?" he inquired.

"What are you talking about?" Rutley demanded.

"Where have you been for the last half hour?"

"Sitting here, talking to Paula. Why, has anything happened?"

"He's been here all the time," Paula said defiantly. "Is anything wrong?"

"And how about you?" Vachell added. "Have you been right here, outside this tent, all evening?"

"Sure I have—except when I went over to fix a sleeping draught for Miss Baradale, just a little while back. She's been awful sick, but I guess she's sleeping now."

"What's the idea?" Rutley said truculently. "Have we got to send a rocket up every time we move five yards in this camp?"

"Curiosity is an occupational disease," Vachell said, "in the police."

There was no doubt that Cara Baradale was asleep. Her young face, in its frame of dark rumpled hair, looked white and haggard in the beam of Vachell's flashlight; but the light did not wake her. The cars and trucks were all in place in the line, with the exception of the two temporarily abandoned Plymouths that had stuck in the mud. Kimotho reported that all the gun-bearers and trackers and the cook were gathered around a fire, listening to a fascinating account by Geydi of an experience in London, when he was an honoured guest in the palace of a white chief so staggeringly rich that he owned more wives than there were goats in Chania, wives who were kept busy night and day serving food to a countless company of distinguished guests. After further enquiry Vachell identified the palace as one of Lyons' Corner Houses, and wondered if Sir Isidore Salmon was aware of his African reputation for record wife ownership, and of the great prestige that it had brought him.

Lord Baradale's tent was the last port of call. The flap was closed, but a streak of light falling on to the grass outside indicated that the occupant was not asleep. Vachell called "hodi," and had to proclaim his identity rather in the manner, he felt, of a stranger seeking entry outside the gates of a baronial castle in medieval days. Lord Baradale went through life trailing clouds of feudalism, Vachell decided. He was a queer old buzzard; probably never done a day's work in his life and lived on his wife's money, and yet he not only expected universal respect and deference, but apparently got it—at any rate now that his wife was dead. He must have a lot of nerve, to get away with it.

Vachell ducked under the flap and entered, blinking at the strong electric light. It was remarkable that any tent could look so much like a junk-heap. Two folding tables were littered with papers, magazines, enlargements, chemicals, and photographic apparatus. A movie screen stood propped up against one side of the tent, between a rack of guns and rifles and a tool chest, and two projectors occupied the only chairs. The most surprising part of the equipment was a large log mounted on four wooden posts over which a zebra skin had been flung. Nails, hammers, glue, a roll of calico and several tins of paint were strewn about the floor all around it.

"That's a blind," Lord Baradale explained. "I'm going to mount the zebra skin on the frame and hang two curtains, painted brown and green, on each side. That will form a hiding-place underneath, big enough for me to crouch in with the cameras. I shall plant it at a waterhole and leave it there until the animals get used to it."

"Very ingenious," Vachell commented.

"It worked with bears," Lord Baradale said defensively, "in Glacier Park, I think it was, or it may have been in Canada. Fellow dressed up in a she-bear's skin and got some beautiful studies. I read about it in an American paper. The only trouble was, the disguise was almost too good; it was the mating season, and he had some nasty moments with a grizzly. This zebra is a male. Well, you didn't come here to discuss game photography, I take it."

Lord Baradale sat down abruptly on the bed, lit a cigar, and jerked the match across the tent with a flick of the wrist. "I suggest that you come straight to the point, and look sharp about it," he added.

He made no attempt to offer his visitor a chair. Vachell leant against the tent-pole, his hands in his pockets and his eyes on the light bulb, encased in an orange paper shade, that dangled from the ridge-pole. His eyes were heavy and his skin stiff from fatigue. The bruises on his side were aching steadily and he felt a sudden strong impulse to lie down on the bed, relax his muscles, and sink into sleep.

He rubbed one palm over his forehead and through his ruffled sandy hair and said:

"First, sir, I'd like to know about Geydi. He was seen leaving camp yesterday morning in one of your Fords, a little after ten o'clock. He crowded a boy who was toting firewood off the road. Later, he saw this boy and tried to throw a scare into him so he wouldn't talk. Now, sir, what's Geydi's game?"

"How the devil should I know?" Lord Baradale said. He sat bolt upright on the bed, the cigar smoking in his hand, glaring angrily at his inquisitor. "Why don't you ask him, man? *I'm* not Geydi's keeper."

"That bird has something to hide, and I believe, sir, that you know what it is."

"Oh, you do, do you! Confound your impertinence, young man! I'll be damned if I'll sit here and listen to a young puppy of a policeman telling me that I'm a liar. Your superiors shall hear of this. I'm not accustomed ——"

"Take it easy, sir." Vachell's voice betrayed, a little, the strain of keeping his temper. These volatile lords who kept popping like a vat of half-brewed beer, he thought, and went off with a bang whenever any one asked them a plain question, got into his hair. "I guess you want to clean this case up as much as I do," he went on. "Geydi lied about his movements, and I'm going to find out why. And he's your boy. Any suggestions?"

"None whatever, and I'll ask you to keep a civil tongue in your head."

"And there's another thing. He was seen talking with three Timburu warriors on the edge of camp, two nights ago. He gave them something—money, the boys thought. Does anything there strike a chord in your memory, sir?"

"I don't believe a word of it!" Lord Baradale said vigorously. "If you credit every cock-and-bull story brought to you by disgruntled natives, you won't get very far towards solving this damnable crime—or any other, for the matter of that."

Vachell extracted a cigarette from a tin in his pocket, lit it, and rearranged his long, bony body against the hard tent-pole. He wished he wasn't aching in quite so many places.

"Okay," he said. "I guess you realize that, aside from Geydi, there are just three people in this outfit who have no alibi for the time when Lady Baradale was shot?"

"Alibis, young man, are your business—not mine."

"I'm afraid, sir, I have to disagree. Those three people are yourself, Luke Englebrecht, and—your daughter."

"I suppose you consider this sort of tomfoolery to be your duty," Lord Baradale said acidly, a dangerous edge in his voice, "but I must ask you to come to the point of this ridiculous performance immediately."

"Sure. Yesterday you told me that you stopped right here in camp, in your tent, all morning. Does that statement still stand?"

"Of course it stands, you young ape! Are you accusing me of telling lies?"

"Yes," Vachell said, "I am." He squared his shoulders and stood upright, staring down at the indignant face of the peer and hurrying on before the storm broke. "And I can prove it right now. You told me yesterday that you heard two shots, around 11.30 or noon, from beyond the hippo pool. That was the time you knew the lion got drilled. That pool is down-wind from here, and none of the natives heard those shots. But they did hear a single shot, up-wind of here—Rutley's shot that hit the buffalo. You didn't mention that, because you didn't hear it. And you didn't hear it because you weren't here in camp."

"Stuff and nonsense!" Lord Baradale exploded, half rising from the bed. "I've never heard such damned ridiculous infernal impertinence in my life, you young puppy! How dare you speak to me like that, sir? I tell you I was here in this tent, developing. How the blazes could I tell which direction the shots came from? And do you think I stood here and counted them? I hardly noticed them. If this is the way you ——"

"Just a moment, sir," Vachell interrupted. He felt the ground slipping from under his feet. There was nothing for it but to try a bluff. "That's not all. I have two witnesses who saw you leaving this camp shortly after ten o'clock, on foot, with a rifle in one hand and ——"

"That's a lie!" Lord Baradale shouted. "It's a damned lie, I tell you! I didn't have a rifle! I only ——"

He broke off abruptly, and a look of consternation spread over his face like a cloud over the sun. For a moment there was silence in the tent. Lord Baradale's hand, gripping a cigar, was arrested half-way to his mouth. Then his fleshy face suddenly crinkled, and a gust of laughter filled the tent. He sat on the bed and shook and spluttered with mirth, his hands on his knees, rocking to and fro.

"You got me nicely, young man," he gasped, rubbing

a tear out of one eye. "Yes, that was very neat. I gave myself away properly that time. I congratulate you; that was clever. You've earned the truth with that."

"I shall be glad to have it," Vachell said dryly.

Lord Baradale took a puff at his cigar and examined the glowing end. "You shall, you shall," he said. "I was perhaps foolish to prevaricate. I made a statement yesterday on the spur of the moment, without, I'm afraid, taking sufficient thought, and I realized too late that I could not go back on it without putting myself in a totally false position. It's the old story—you allow yourself to get rattled, say the first thing that pops into your head, and find yourself plunged into a labyrinth of deception. I owe you an apology."

"I'd prefer a statement."

"All right, all right. I went down to the hippo pool yesterday morning, soon after ten, with my 16-millimetre cine-Kodak. I've got a hide down there, you know, and I wanted to do some work on the hippos. As I took no boy, there was no one to confirm my statement, and I therefore thought it wiser to say nothing of this. It was foolish, perhaps, but I acted on the spur of the moment, and I couldn't see that it mattered, for I saw or heard nothing at the pool that could possibly have had any bearing on the death of my wife."

"How long were you down there?"

"I was back here about 11.30, I should think. I didn't pay any particular attention to the time. I went straight to my tent to develop the films I had just taken, which I was particularly anxious to see, and I was here until after

Gordon and de Mare returned. In fact, my original statement deviated very little from the truth. I merely omitted to mention my excursion to the pool—shall we put it like that?"

"Quite an omission," Vachell said.

"Not in the least," Lord Baradale retorted, "since it made no difference to the matter in hand. I repeat, I neither saw nor heard anything unusual at the pool. I was entirely preoccupied with the hippos."

"How were the pictures?" Vachell asked.

"Excellent. The best I have obtained, up to date."

Vachell walked over to the flap and threw his cigarette out on the grass. He turned again to Lord Baradale and asked:

"From which side of the pool did you shoot?"

"The hide is on the left bank. Why?"

"You shot the pictures around eleven o'clock?"

Lord Baradale frowned and showed signs of renewed impatience. "About then, yes. I fail to see the relevance of all this. You must accept my word for my movements, young man; I can't produce any witnesses."

"I guess you can, at that," Vachell said. He walked over to one of the tables and turned a reel of movie film over in his hand. "You have your witnesses right here, in among this photographic junk. The hippos you shot at the pool should confirm your story."

Lord Baradale stared at Vachell for several seconds as if he thought the policeman had gone insane, and then brought his hand down on his knee. "By George, you're

right!" he exclaimed. "You mean the film I took yesterday morning at the pool. Yes, I've got it here."

He jumped to his feet and crossed to a cabinet full of
exposed cine-Kodak reels and film packs, and rummaged
about in it for several minutes. Vachell lit another cigarette
and watched his back, a slight frown on his face. Lord
Baradale stood up, waving a reel triumphantly. "This is
it," he said. "I can run it through the projector if you
like." His mood had changed as abruptly as an English
day in spring, and now he seemed to be in high good
humour.

"Go ahead," Vachell said.

As soon as Lord Baradale removed one of the projectors
Vachell sank thankfully into the vacated chair and stretched
out his weary legs. He felt too tired to make an offer of
help. The tent was wired for the projector, and in a short
time the stage was set. Lord Baradale propped the screen
against the bathroom flap, placed the projector on a table
by the opening, connected it, and inserted the film.

"You're certain about this reel?" Vachell asked. "You're
sure it's the one that you shot yesterday morning?"

"Yes, of course," Lord Baradale replied. "You'll have
to move your chair."

Vachell placed it on one side of the projector and sat
down again. The lamp suspended from the ridge-pole
went black, and a white patch of light flickered on to the
screen at the other side of the darkened tent. In the silence
the whirr of the projector sounded harsh and loud.

Rocks and water sprang into sharp relief on the screen.
A grave, spindle-legged bird was standing near the rocks,

immobile. The projector whirred, the bird shot out its neck, plunged its beak into the water, and emerged with a wriggling fish. A gulp, and the fish was gone.

"I took some cranes on the first part of this film," Lord Baradale explained. "Some vulturine guinea-fowl come next, and then the hippos."

A column of guinea-fowl advanced on to the screen, wagging their tufted heads, and vanished in a cloud of fluttering wings. Then the hippo pool appeared, with a background of dark bush, and long shadows from the trees falling across the water. In the foreground a hippo wallowed in the mud. It thrust its big ungainly head, with pig-like eyes popping out of a protruding forehead, almost directly at the camera. It wore a friendly and self-satisfied expression. Presently it lumbered out into deep water, rolling like a tramp steamer, and sank. There were shots of its nostrils protruding above the surface like periscopes, and a final sequence of three beasts clambering slowly out of the water and up the muddy bank and, after some by-play on the top, disappearing into the bush beyond in search of pasture.

The reel clicked to its conclusion and the whirring died. The white screen vanished and the tent's interior sprang into life again as the switch went on. Lord Baradale said, a little suavely: "Now I hope you're satisfied, Mr. Vachell."

"You have a swell picture there," Vachell said. "The finished product should be a knock-out. I guess I won't need to bother you any more."

Beneath the surface courtesy was a hint of wariness,

a sense of words unsaid. Lord Baradale seemed unexpectedly at a loss. He grunted "good night" and looked uncertainly at Vachell. Both faces were expressionless, with the fixity of masks.

"Good night, sir," Vachell said. He pulled the flap aside and ducked into the night. It was sharp and fresh after the stuffiness of heated air that had been imprisoned all day beneath two layers of canvas. Stars in their millions glinted coldly overhead.

He walked slowly across the wet grass, thinking of shadows. For in the moving picture that Lord Baradale had shown him, the shadows of the trees by the pool were long, and from west to east across the water.

CHAPTER 22: VACHELL DIDN'T GO TO BED

at all that night. In spite of an aching weariness, he was uneasy and apprehensive. Most of the time he sat in the mess-tent, smoking and turning over the pages of magazines and occasionally going out into the moonless night to stroll around and make sure that everything was all right. His senses were as taut as an antelope skin pegged out to dry.

At two o'clock he got into one of the cars and bumped over the veldt, scaring nightjars and small buck and a herd of leaping impala, to the air-field. There was a camp-fire near the plane, and two prone log-like forms rolled up in blankets beside it. They were drivers who had been sent down there to mount guard. They were sleeping so soundly that Vachell had to tug at the corners of their blankets to wake them. The boys grunted, sat up, and listened silently to the white man's instructions. One of the two was to be awake and on guard all night, Vachell said, and to watch the plane all the time. They grunted comprehension and threw some more logs on the fire. Vachell doubted, as he drove back, whether his orders would be obeyed.

An hour later storm clouds rolled over the brilliant stars and the darkness grew dense and heavy. A little later it started to rain—a heavy, soaking downpour. Vachell went the rounds of the tents, seeing that they were properly

secured and weren't leaking, and found everybody in bed
and, apparently, asleep. That was around three o'clock. He
inspected the trucks, all in place. The beam of his flashlight caught for a fleeting moment the sloping hindquarters
of a hyena, retreating from the line of cars. Vachell threw
a stone after it; as likely as not it was trying to eat the
tyres, or the leather upholstery. A little later he heard
it howling mournfully in the bush.

At four o'clock he grew suddenly sleepy. He stretched
himself out in a camp chair in the mess-tent, put his feet
up, and dozed uneasily through a grey and watery dawn.
The sun came up through a low bank of clouds which lay
heavily on top of the hills. There was clear sky above,
blue as turquoise; and a little before seven sunlight rolled
across the plain, with the triumphant suddenness of a burst
of music, and drove the raindrops out of the trees and
grass in a silver mist. Birds everywhere put renewed heart
into their song, and grey spirals of smoke curled upwards
to a blue sky with fresh vigour.

There was gaiety and exhilaration in the early morning
air, but none in the hearts of those in the Baradale camp.
There was a melancholy job to be done. Geydi took tea
to his master a little after six, and at seven Lord Baradale
emerged, looking as though he had hardly slept at all, and
shouted to de Mare that he was ready.

Ten minutes later the little party set out, the four white
men carrying a narrow rectangular box on their shoulders.
Rutley and Vachell had to stoop to keep their shoulders
down to the level of Lord Baradale and de Mare. They
walked slowly along a winding route through the bush

towards the hills to the east, into the sunlight. Their pace was slow, and the grass was cold and wet against the bare flesh of their legs.

It was all over inside ten minutes. They walked back in silence, leaving two Africans to throw the wet earth back into the trench where Sir Gordon Catchpole's remains now rested. Vachell wondered, as he watched his long shadow dance before him over the grass, whether to-morrow would see another silent procession to yet another grave.

An hour later he was climbing into Chris's plane, receiving last-minute instructions from its owner. She had gone over the machine thoroughly, checked the controls, and taxied to the end of the runway and back to make sure that the engine was running smoothly. While she was busy Vachell questioned the native guards. They had watched the plane every minute of the night, they said emphatically; but they looked a little sheepish, and Vachell, remembering the rain, suspected that they might be lying.

The natives filled the tank with gas from a dump of cans kept on the edge of the runway in a grass shelter. Vachell put in his .470, a bottle of water and a box of biscuits, wedged himself into the narrow seat, grasped the stick and opened up the throttle. The plane moved off, jolting jerkily on the rough ground, gathered speed quickly, and lifted itself smoothly into the air.

It was some time since he had handled a plane, and at first he felt uncertain and strange, and not a little nervous. The air was calm, however, and the plane hummed along steadily as a flighting bird, its engine running sweetly. He climbed to about a thousand feet, banked cautiously to the right, and swung around in a big arc until he saw the gleam of water immediately below. Then he swung left again, pushed the stick a little forward until he was flying at about five hundred feet, and followed the thread of the river down, his eyes searching the dark border of bush and trees for some sign or movement that might denote the presence of a human being.

For the first twenty minutes he saw nothing, save for a startled herd of impala leaping in all directions at once like a bunch of jumping beans, and the grey boulder-like back of a rhino standing under a bush, bewildered, his head down. When the shadow of the plane passed over him he bolted violently down-wind for a hundred yards, wheeled, and darted off again in another direction, at a loss to know where to run for safety. The bush-flecked plains to the right were dotted with browsing herds of antelope and zebra. They stopped their meals to raise their heads and listen, and then moved off uneasily, alert but not seriously alarmed.

The Kiboko river took a big loop to the south, turned west again, and tumbled over a series of black basalt rocks into a narrow gorge with steep rocky sides, and so on to the plains below. The basalt shone like the polished pates of negroes in the sun. Vachell, peering down through the glare of the sunlight, decided that he must have missed his man. Englebrecht couldn't have gone below the pools. There was nowhere close to the river's edge to camp, for one thing; and you couldn't get a car down, for another.

He pulled the stick back a little and climbed a couple of hundred feet, preparing to bank. The sky looked blue and depthless as the nose of the plane rose in response to his touch. Air swirled past his helmeted ears and the exhilaration of flying enveloped him. The Hawk seemed as sensitive as a well trained polo-pony in his hands. It felt good to be handling a plane again.

Then, suddenly, the knowledge that something was going wrong with the machine gripped his mind. A second later the engine misfired, spluttered, and roared again. He pushed the throttle wide open and held his breath. Again there was a spluttering choke, and the engine wavered and missed. It sent a chill down his spine, as the gasp of a dying man might do. The motor was like a suffocating person struggling vainly for breath. He could feel the plane quiver as the motor stalled, and then begin to lose speed. He pulled the stick back farther to correct the dipping of the nose. Another roar, a splutter, and then a ghastly stillness as the engine gave a last despairing cough, and died.

The sudden silence cracked against his eardrums like a physical blow. His mouth was dry and his heart was pumping wildly. The plane glided on, wobbling a little from side to side as its nose dropped towards the earth and it lost height. It fluttered with the agonizing inevitability of a falling leaf towards the black pools below, and the craggy cliffs. The pools looked suddenly menacing, like giant mouths yawning open to suck in their prey. Around them was rock and dense bush. No place to attempt a forced landing, even if he had the height.

Now the plane was hurtling downwards, its nose headed straight for the grey-green tangle of bush below. Vachell juggled desperately with the stick trying to bring the plane back into control. He saw the earth rushing wildly towards him, and his eyes photographed the flat tops of acacias, the pale gleam of grass. Frantically he unhitched his safety-belt with one hand, a single thought dominating his mind: fire, and the devouring tongues of flame. Behind that monster, a disorderly host of little ogres raced in and out of his mind as the earth advanced: pools, flat black water; the plane stalled before; it backfired, like rifle shots, above the hippo pool; Chris was in the seat behind me; she had rifles; no time to jump; she fixed the plane this morning; she did something to it; relax all muscles before you ——

The Hawk hit the earth at the angle of a racing driver. A violent blow caught Vachell in the chest and simultaneously there was a tearing, ripping sound as the undercarriage crashed through the crown of a thorn tree. Thunderous breakers seemed to be rolling up and sweeping him against the rocks. He hit the ground with an impact that felt sufficient to break his body into pieces as if it had been a dropped plate. For a few seconds he lay stunned, oblivious. Then an explosion crashed in his ears and jolted him into consciousness. Before his dazed eyes leaped a flash of orange flame, and a scalding wave of heat poured over his face.

He never knew how he got out. Afterwards, he realized that the plane must have crashed through the foliage of an acacia and catapulted him out on to the ground. His fall was broken by the branches of the tree. They tore his clothes and scratched his body, but they saved his life.

He crawled, rolled and staggered out of danger, away

from the blazing mass of wreckage in the trees. He stood up gingerly, and found to his amazement that no bones were broken. He was bruised all over from the fall and covered with cuts which bled profusely, but still intact.

After a short search he found his rifle, thrown clear as he had been, some way from the burning wreckage. Leather guards protected the sights, and so far as he could see it was unhurt. He was less fortunate with his hat. He looked everywhere, but it couldn't be found. Still, he reflected, one can't have everything, and he couldn't really complain to fate about the loss of a hat.

He had only one plan: to follow the river back to camp. It must be thirty miles, he reckoned. No doubt de Mare would send a search party down the river later in the day, when he didn't get back, and if the cars could get along they might find him before nightfall. Or he might have to spend a wet and hungry night in the bush.

He had a drink at the river, slipped two solids into the breach of his .470 in case of rhino, and started out. It was slow going. The river-bed was too soft for walking, the banks stony, and the grass above them waist high. Bush grew in thick belts and clumps. He had to cover twice the distance he travelled to get around patches of vegetation too solid to be penetrated. The thick matted grass twisted its stems around his legs and caused him to stumble and curse every few yards of the way.

All through the morning he toiled on, stopping sometimes for a drink and a short rest in the shade of a tree. Sweat poured off in rivulets, and his skin was burning with cuts and bruises. As he progressed the bush seemed to develop more and more branches and sharper and sharper spines. The sun was hot and biting on his unprotected head. Once he was startled into alertness by a sudden crash of breaking branches ahead. He brought his rifle to his shoulder, but the noise grew fainter as a heavy body plunged through the bush in the opposite direction. A rhino, probably. Vachell heaved a sigh of relief and plodded on, cursing the bush, the plane, the case, the profession of detective as followed in Africa, and the whole Baradale outfit, innocent and guilty alike.

All the time his mind was worrying, puzzling, and going around in circles, searching in every recess of his memory for the key to the puzzle. He knew that it was there, lurking somewhere just out of reach. Somewhere there must be a fact, an indication, a sentence, a hint—some pointer that, if he could only grasp its significance, would lead him straight to the mystery's solution. A cloud of odd, unrelated facts, of half suspicions, of not-quite-natural actions wrapped the case around like an autumn mist, concealing the true solution and yet allowing hints of its shape to show through. Somewhere, if he could find it, must be a password that would dispel the mist and reveal the truth, in its stark inevitability, beneath.

He wondered if the final picture that he knew awaiting discovery would include an explanation of the burnt-out Hawk. That was the immediate problem: accident or design, engine failure or attempted murder? For twenty minutes the plane had gone as sweetly as a bird; then, suddenly, the engine had died as though deprived of fuel. But he himself had seen it filled, half an hour ago; and

the gauge had shown a full tank. He didn't see how a
thing like that could have been fixed; nor, after the in-
cident of the cartridges, how the engine failure could have
been a pure coincidence.

By one o'clock he felt hungry, footsore, and dizzy in
the head. An airplane crash, coming on top of a sleepless
night and a difference of opinion with a buffalo, was hardly
a good preparation for a long and hatless country hike in
the sun. He wasn't, he reflected, either a mad dog or an
Englishman. He lay flat on the sand and took a long drink,
bathed his face and arms, and settled down for a rest under
a tall green tree. Luckily, his cigarettes didn't seem to
have suffered. He lit up, drew out his note-book, and
started to compile a list of unsolved problems in the Baradale case, hoping to find some sort of connecting link between them. Before he had scribbled more than half a
dozen lines a wave of drowsiness paralysed his mind. His
head dropped on his chest and he fell fast asleep.

It was nearly four o'clock when he awoke with a dry
throat, a splitting headache, and a guilty feeling. Going
to sleep under a tree didn't seem to be the regulation way
to go about tracking down a dangerous criminal, he
thought. He struggled to his feet, as stiff as an octogenarian,
so stiff that he could hardly move his limbs. Every part
of him felt sore and tender. His arms and legs were covered with congealed blood and there were blisters on both
heels.

Shadows were beginning to lengthen over the white
sand and the racing, muddy water when Vachell started
off again. Every step, at first, was an effort to break through

his stiffness. But the river-bed had broadened out a little, and he was able to travel part of the way on the sand.

About half an hour later he came to a small pool. The banks were flattened, and on his side was a narrow sandy beach, sloping gently up to the veldt above. Such pools were always favourite drinking places for game. He paused by the water's edge to read the story of the morning's activity that was written in the sand. He saw the round, flat footprints of a rhino; a network of zebra's hoofmarks, and a large selection of long, slender impressions of the hoofs of different buck. A trained hunter, of course, would name them all—gerenuk, oryx, waterbuck, Grantii, Tommy, eland, oribi; not only name them but tell, in the case of larger game, whether they were male or female, even good heads or bad.

He shifted his rifle from one shoulder to the other, wiped his forehead, and started laboriously to climb the bank. On the edge of the sandy beach he came upon a new type of spoor: a human foot. And not only human spoor, but the spoor of a man wearing boots. His heart missed a beat in his excitement. At last, he had hit the trail.

The footprints led to the water's edge, and there were none coming back. He collected some clods of earth and loose stones and hurled them into the river with a series of splashes, and then shifted his cartridges, matches, and note-book to the breast pocket of his shirt. Armed with a long branch cut from the bush he waded in, holding his rifle above his head and praying that there were no crocodiles. The water came over his waist, but he got across, and picked up the footprints on the other side. They led up a steep bank and into the bush. After that it became more difficult. There was nothing to go on but a faint trail of bent stems in the thick grass. The man had walked through, evidently, while the grass was still soaked with rain that morning. Now it was dry as tinder.

The trail grew steadily fainter, and in an open patch between two belts of bush Vachell lost it altogether. He was casting around, in hope rather than in confidence, when the smell of decaying flesh assailed his nostrils. It was strong and foetid. He tested the wind with some grass seeds and explored up-wind. In a small open glade he came upon a skeleton. Shreds of flesh still hung from the bones, and a cloud of vultures, gobbling and tearing at the meat, surrounded the carcass.

The vultures rose in a black cloud as he walked forwards, flapping their big wings in protest. They perched in the tops of trees, or sat a little way off on the ground, and watched the invader with a malevolent glare. Vachell approached and examined the scene. Bits of striped hide and some detached hoofs lying around showed that the dead beast was a zebra. So it was a kill, not the victim of Englebrecht's rifle. It was only partially eaten. The two hind legs were gone, and the neck, but there was meat still on the forelegs and ribs. Last night's kill, obviously; the lions, as was their custom, had kept hyenas away. The ground round about was trampled and bloody. Vachell knelt down to examine it, and on a branch of bush nearby he was rewarded by the find of a long, tawny hair from a lion's mane.

He wondered whether Englebrecht had been tracking

the lions, or whether they had just happened to kill close to his camp. He prayed earnestly to the gods of fortune. He was weary, hungry, footsore and bruised. The idea of a foodless night in the open didn't appeal—especially, he thought, with all these lions about.

Lions, he had heard, always returned a second night to their kill. Often they lay up close at hand during the day, and came back at dusk. It was after five o'clock now. No sense in taking risks. He slung his rifle off his shoulder and slipped back the bolt to see if it was properly loaded. Smiling at his own caution, he took out the cartridges, held them up in the sunlight, and examined them closely to make sure that they hadn't been got at. There were no scratches on their copper cases. He took two soft-nosed cartridges from his pocket, slipped them into the breach, and transferred his ammunition and other possessions from his breast pocket back into his shorts. Perhaps, he thought, it would be best to fire a couple of shots into the air to attract Englebrecht's attention. The hunter's camp couldn't be far off, and the noise might bring him out to investigate. . . .

Then, suddenly, something seemed to click in his brain. One glaring, obvious discrepancy in the evidence leapt into his mind and, once there, filled it to the exclusion of every other thought. Now that he had seen the one flaw in the murderer's plan, he could see nothing else; it stood out as blatantly as a nudist at a Royal garden party. Everything suddenly fitted into place; the method, the motive, and the subsequent events. It was so simple, so obvious, even crude. His own elaborate theory of the case tumbled about him in ruins, like a building hit directly by a bomb. He saw it all—saw everything, except the slightest shadow of proof. He realized, as he trudged on with renewed energy through the bush, that he had encountered the almost perfect crime—a murder that, however much the truth might be suspected, never could be proved.

CHAPTER 23: ENGLEBRECHT'S CAMP CON-
sisted of a small tent, without a fly, pitched directly underneath a large acacia with a spreading top, and nothing else.
No one could have seen it from the air. Had it not been
for a curl of smoke rising above the bush from the kitchen
fire, Vachell might have walked within ten paces of the tent
without knowing of its presence. But the fire had been lit
to cook an evening meal, and he stumbled on the camp just
before sunset.

He stood for a few minutes in the shelter of the bush,
taking in the scene. The sun was hanging low above a long
purple line of hills in the west, and the shadows of the
trees were long and deep. The young hunter was seated
on a folding camp-chair by the side of the fire, cleaning a
rifle. Vachell could see, then, why Cara Baradale had
found him so attracitve. There was no doubt about his
good looks. He sat there with a sort of quiet grace, unconscious of scrutiny, and the slanting sunlight turned his
bronzed face, knees and arms and his blond hair the rich
red-gold colour of a ripening peach. He looked the em-
bodiment of health and fitness—like, as de Mare had suggested, a model of the perfect young Nordic male. Perhaps, Vachell thought, even his Teutonic stolidity and lack
of humour had counted as a virtue with Cara, in contrast
to Gordon Catchpole's sophistication and malicious nimble-
ness of tongue.

"Nice evening," he said conversationally, and stepped forward from the shadow of the bush. "I'm glad I found you home."

Englebrecht jumped like a startled antelope, bringing his rifle half-way to his shoulder in a flash. He might look slow and stolid, but he could act on the instant, and his movements had the quick co-ordination of those of an athlete. His round, youthful face betrayed, in quick succession, astonishment, fear and bewilderment. He lowered the rifle slowly, and seemed at a loss for words. Finally he challenged:

"Who are you? What is it you want?"

Vachell laughed, realizing that his appearance must indeed look wild and strange. His clothes were torn to tatters and his face and arms covered with scratches and adhesive tape.

"An arm of the law," he said. "It's getting longer all the time."

Comprehension showed in Englebrecht's face. "I didn't recognize you," he said. "How did you get here? I heard no car. How did you know . . . ?"

Vachell sat down wearily on a chop-box that was lying near the fire, and explained. Englebrecht appeared delighted. "I knew you would use the aeroplane," he said. "That's why I pitched the tent under this tree, so that it would be hidden from the air. I was successful, then. The car, too, is safely hidden."

He frowned and flushed a little, realizing that he had made an admission. His unlined, fresh-cheeked face reflected faithfully each of his emotions.

"You did a good job," Vachell said. "Now it's your turn to answer questions. Why did you sneak out of Malabeya on the day that Lady Baradale was bumped and hide yourself away in the bush so you couldn't be found? And why did you come snooping around the camp in the night like a hyena, the same night some one busted into the tent where the dead body was lying and crowned me with a blunt instrument and took away the key to Lady Baradale's safe?"

"I don't know anything about it," Englebrecht said quickly. His slightly guttural voice was urgent. "Lady Baradale's death, I mean. I knew you would come here to question me. I told Cara it was foolishness to hide. You found out that we had been to the D.C.'s office, eh? I told Cara it would be better to come to you, and that you would believe that I was innocent, but she wouldn't let me. She said that you ——"

"Suppose we start the story at the beginning," Vachell interrupted. "Right after you left camp at six in the morning." He stretched out his aching legs and sat limply on the chop-box, every muscle relaxed. A delicious smell of cooking meat tantalized his nostrils and made his mouth water. Englebrecht remained standing, staring at him apprehensively. He still held the rifle in one hand, and his arm was trembling.

"Yes, that is best," he agreed. He was clearly flustered and the words came rapidly. "I met Cara just outside the camp. That was her idea, too. Lady Baradale had forbidden her to go, so she left her tent when it was still dark and waited for me a little way along the track. She brought some stores, as much as she could carry; we had arranged for this camp, you see. She didn't want me to go away. She thought that if I stayed somewhere near, perhaps the new man—that was you—would not please the others, and then Cara would tell her father that she loved me, and then I would come back again to join the safari as a hunter. Besides, she didn't want to do what the old woman said. She hated her, you see—at least, that is . . ."

Englebrecht's voice tailed off and he looked acutely embarrassed again. Vachell leant his elbows on his knees, cupped his chin in his hands, and said: "Skip it. Stick to what you did."

Englebrecht hesitated for several seconds, looking acutely uncomfortable. "Well, Cara wanted to get married, you see," he finally blurted out. "At least, I did too, you understand, only not at once. I wanted to wait until I had saved money, had some good jobs all fixed—you know. So that she could have something, a house perhaps, when I was on safari. Lady Baradale thought I couldn't make enough to keep a wife, that I wanted Cara for her money, but I tell you—I'm as good as Danny, and soon I shall make as much as he does. He has the reputation, but as a hunter. . . ." Englebrecht shrugged his broad shoulders. "Once he was good, yes, but now it is all conceit. He thinks he is the greatest hunter who ever lived, but he is over, finished, done with, really. I can do better . . . but Cara didn't want to wait. She was afraid of the old woman, who wanted to make her marry Catchpole. So we went to the D.C.'s office, but the D.C. wouldn't do it. He said we must wait three weeks. Cara was very angry, but I think, perhaps, it was just as well."

"It's a four-hour journey to Malabeya," Vachell said. "You left at six and you got there at four in the afternoon. You have six hours to fill to make an alibi. How about it?"

"I can explain," Englebrecht said eagerly. Now that he had broken through the wall of silence, he spoke fluently and seemed anxious to talk. "First, we stopped for breakfast, you see. Then, we went on towards Malabeya, but when we got near we passed a hill on the left of the road where lesser kudu sometimes come. I don't know why, but ask any of the trackers, they will tell you it is so—they call it Kilima Marua, even. I saw a fine bull through the glasses, feeding in thin bush near the top. He had a good head, you see, and I thought perhaps it was a record. Well, I went after him. I had a long stalk, longer than I had intended; he moved on all the time, you see, just out of range; he was a wily one. It took a long time. When I had shot him it took more time to skin him and bring him back to the car. We were delayed for several hours, you see, and that made us late in reaching Malabeya."

"And was the head a record?" Vachell asked.

Englebrecht shook his head. "No, several inches short. I was disappointed. It was only fit to throw away."

"What did you do with the skin?"

"The skin? Oh, I threw that away too."

"I guess you felt kind of reckless on your wedding day," Vachell remarked. "Kudu skins are worth quite a bit of money in Marula, I believe."

"Oh, it is very little; only a few shillings." Englebrecht

sat down again on his folding chair and laid the rifle on the ground. He seemed to have recovered confidence and to be more at ease.

"And then?" Vachell persisted. "Where did you go from there?"

"I had left my own car with an Indian in his warehouse, so I took it out and drove back here, and then I made camp. Cara went back on her own—her car is much faster than mine, and I had to stop on the way to shoot a Tommy for meat. So, you see, I know nothing about the accident to Lady Baradale. How could I? I was close to Malabeya when it happened."

"How did you know about it at all?" Vachell asked. He looked up from his contemplation of the grass at his feet and fixed his sharp blue eyes on the hunter's earnest face.

"I went to the camp that night, to see Cara. We had arranged it before, of course. She said I wasn't to admit to that, but I don't see. . . . I didn't know anything was wrong. I left the car at the drift and walked up, and then she told me about the—the murder, you see. I wanted to come back at once to help her, but she wouldn't listen to that. She said I was to stay hidden until the safari went back to Marula, or else the police would arrest me. . . . But it wasn't me. I didn't shoot her—you believe that, don't you? I don't know who it was. It must have been an accident, I think."

Vachell paid no attention to the question. He kept his eyes fixed on the hunter's face and massaged one ear-lobe gently between finger and thumb. "You loaned Rutley your heavy gun," he remarked. "A smaller rifle would have been right for buck."

"I wanted the other rifles to keep myself in meat; the .470 was the only one I could spare. I was sorry for Rutley. He wanted to shoot, but they never gave him a chance. The old woman didn't treat him right, considering . . . well, you know. She was a mean old skinflint."

"She was pretty generous to Cara in her will," Vachell said. "No funny business with cat's homes or new class-rooms for her Alma Mater. It all stayed in the family."

Englebrecht flushed slightly and looked morosely at his questioner. "I don't know anything about that," he replied. "I haven't been back to the camp since then. Cara told me to keep away, that it wasn't safe, and that she would come to me when she could sneak off without being seen; but now the rains have broken I don't think she will be able to."

Vachell stood up stiffly and stretched his arms. "You don't need to worry about that," he said. "You'll see Cara all right, because we're going to beat it back to camp right now. The veldt has had all day to dry, and I guess we'll make it."

They made it, though not without a good deal of trouble and some vigorous pushing by Vachell and Englebrecht's boy. The car was an old and battered Model A Ford, tied together with wire, that looked like something left over from the aerial bombardment of a city; but it leapt from hummock to hummock through the roadless bush and churned its way out of mudholes with a determination and agility no longer shown by its younger and more stream-

lined brothers. It was a lion-hearted car, and refused to
be daunted even by the muddy drift, which had partially
dried with surprising speed after a day's hot sun.

They reached camp a little before eight. Vachell went
straight to his tent, called for a hot bath, and lay in it in
sections. Kimotho, voluble with excitement, stood by and
bubbled over with news. Two cars had started off at eleven,
Vachell learnt, to search for him, driven by Chris and de
Mare. They had gone down the river until they had stuck
in a sandy gulley, and then de Mare, Japhet and two trackers had gone ahead on foot, on the chance of running into
the wreckage of the plane. Every one in camp had given
him up for dead. The African staff was convinced that the
place was bewitched with a magic of unprecedented evil
and power. Five natives had run away in a panic. Rutley
and Geydi had gone after them in a car, but returned about
nightfall with no news of the fugitives. Cara Baradale was
still sick, and Chris so distraught that she lost her temper
with the cook when he came to tell her that the meat was
finished and to ask for more. The cook had gone on strike
as a result, and refused to prepare any lunch. And only
half an hour ago the D.C. from Malabeya had arrived, and
had been engaged in restoring order in the camp. He had
with him a Timburu prisoner, a boy caught by a flying
column of police who were searching for the poachers.
Before he was caught there had been a fight, and one of
the police askaris had been wounded with a rifle. The cook,
now under arrest, was preparing dinner with a guard of
two six-foot askaris standing over him, loaded rifles in
hand, in the kitchen.

Half an hour later Vachell emerged from his tent still sore and aching, but considerably revived. He had dabbed iodine on all his scratches, sealed the worst of them with tape, and restored his morale with half a glass of straight whisky, a plate of sardines and some ginger crackers. Now he had a warm feeling inside, a slight swimminess in the head, and a full-blown plan of campaign.

He held no cards in his hand. There was only one chance, he decided: to pull a wild and barefaced bluff, hoping for a break. The bluff would be a dangerous one, and might end in a farce or in disaster. It was foolhardy, no doubt, and not the sort of procedure for which police regulations allowed. But it offered the only slender chance, so far as Vachell could see, of getting what he needed so badly and lacked so completely: proof of the murderer's guilt. The Police Commissioner would arrive the next day or the day after, if he could get through. Unless something desperate was done, Vachell would have to face him with the news of two successfully accomplished murders, and without a shred of proof to point to the guilty person.

It was a time for drastic measures and for taking risks. He had decided to borrow a trick from the native hunter's trade. Leopards, wariest of beasts of prey, were sometimes captured in a trap baited with a living goat. That was to be the model. The murderer was the wary, prowling leopard, and Vachell was to be the living goat.

CHAPTER 24: THE DISTRICT COMMISSIONER
was sitting in the mess-tent drinking Scotch and soda and
talking volubly to a tall tribal policeman with a strange
pattern of tattoos and cuts on his cheeks, who stood at attention and punctuated the discourse with the occasional
"Yes, bwana." Peto was a heavily built man, broad shoul-
dered and muscular, with the physique of an ex-rowing
blue, and a shock of white hair above a pair of keen, steely
blue eyes and a round, red-cheeked face.

He was known in Chania as a martinet with a sense of
humour. The nomadic Somalis and Timburu and other
warlike tribes under his control feared and respected him:
they found him capricious, but just and firm. His superiors
in Marula feared and detested him; they found him out-
spoken, independent and deplorably lacking in respect for
those virtues considered sacred by the Secretariat: seniority,
precedent and discretion. They would have fired him long
ago, but he was too efficient. He kept just out of reach of
trouble like a wily antelope eluding the hunter. The Secretariat's strategy was to give him all the difficult districts,
where natives had got out of hand and murderous, and
where a false step would have led to bloodshed among the
tribesmen and a Colonial Office reprimand for the D.C.
This delighted Peto, for his ruling passion in life was plant
collecting, and the rarest specimens were to be found in the
wildest regions. So far he had steered clear of trouble, and

left for each of his successors a reasonably peaceful district and a perfectly irrigated garden, complete with shaded lawns, water-lily ponds, terraces and pergolas. Natives who had done time in jails in Peto's districts were much in demand by Europeans as head gardeners when their terms of imprisonment were over.

Peto looked up as Vachell approached the tent, and said: "You're the missing superintendent. I suppose. We all thought you were dead. Poor Chris was awfully upset about her plane. Sit down and have a drink." He dismissed the tribal policeman, and pushed the whisky bottle across the table. He wore shorts and a blue shirt and a pair of giraffe-hide native sandals.

Vachell helped himself and settled down to give an outline of the history of events since Lady Baradale's death. He needed the D.C.'s help. Peto listened carefully, his head on one side, drumming his finger-tips on the table.

"Your boss will be here to-morrow," he remarked, at the end of the recital. "A wire came through just before I left, to say he was due at Malabeya late to-night. I had to leave him my cook, curse it, and now this blighter of Baradale's tried to go on strike. I've placed him under arrest and told him he'll get two years' hard if he doesn't turn out a damned good meal. That's cooked his goose and now he's cooking ours, I hope—I shot one on the way in. Old Armitage will turn up bristling with warrants and handcuffs, I expect. Any idea who to use them on?"

"Yes," Vachell said, "but I can't prove it."

"One never can," Peto said cheerfully. "I've caught dozens of murderers in my time, but I've very seldom had any proof. My method is to arrest them, and if they're guilty they generally confess, or else some of their pals who want to curry favour with the Government because they haven't paid their poll tax will come along and do it for them. In any case, the appeal court lets them off on a technicality, so it's all the same in the long run."

"In this case we aren't dealing with the confessing type, sir," Vachell said. "If I throw a scare into this murderer, I may get a reaction I can use to get this thing cleaned up. I reckon it's the only chance I've got, and I need your help."

"I can't allow any of your American third-degree stuff, you know," Peto said. "Our methods may be a bit primitive up here at times, but they're fairly respectable."

"It's nothing like that. All I want is for you to post two of your askaris down by the hippo pool at ten o'clock to-night. They're to take their rifles and be ready to use them. I want one on each side of the pool, and they should hide in the bush and keep under cover and watch. They're not to move unless some one fires a shot. Then they're to move like hell, and grab the guy who fired the shot, and hold him. They may have to shoot in self-defence, but I don't want any one killed."

"A bring-'em-back-alive stunt, in fact," Peto remarked. "I keep on expecting to find a battery of cameras and a director with a cigar and a megaphone behind every bush in this camp. It doesn't sound to me the sort of procedure that would commend itself to our pastors and masters in Marula, but that, thank God, is your affair. You shall have your two sharp-shooters, if you promise not to let them get hurt. I can't have anything happening to my askaris. I warn you, if it does, I shall have your blood."

"My blood seems to be in too darned much demand," Vachell remarked. "I can't promise you the first refusal."

Peto grunted his disapproval, and finished his drink. "When you've got the melodrama off your chest," he said, "you might give your attention to another murder that's very nearly taken place."

"Timburu?" Vachell asked.

"Yes. That's what brought me here to-day, as a matter of fact. I leave these European vendettas to the police. But there's a gang of murdering poachers in this district, as you know, and I'm here to catch them."

"They speared a game scout about a week ago, I understand," Vachell said.

"They did. And they damned nearly killed one of my men yesterday. I sent out a patrol to round them up, and the askaris came up with them yesterday morning. There was a bit of a dust-up, and my corporal got a bullet through the chest that only missed his lung by half an inch. The point is, how did they get hold of the rifle? They weren't armed last time we heard of them, apart from spears. That's why I came out here."

"I think I can help you there," Vachell said slowly.

"I hoped you might. My patrol sent the wounded corporal back to Malabeya and went on after the Timburu, and they've caught one of the party. He's here now; they brought him in this evening. Unfortunately he's only an uncircumcised boy, not a warrior—a sort of bottle-washer that they took along, I think. He's scared stiff and won't talk. I'm going to have another go at him when he's got a square meal in his belly. At the moment he thinks I'm going to eat him or deprive him of his manhood at the very least."

"There are some folk in this camp who'd like to deprive him of his powers of speech, I guess," Vachell said. "I'd suggest, sir, that you keep him closely guarded."

"He is—very closely. He's handcuffed to one of my askaris, a very reliable man, and one who never trusts a Timburu a yard. He once had a Timburu wife who ran away, and he never got the goats refunded from her father. Incidentally, Chris tells me that one of Lord Baradale's rifles was pinched three days ago. Since the Timburu turned up with one to-day, that looks fishy, to say the least. The question is, how did it get into the hands of those poacher fellows?"

"The Somali, Geydi, gave it to them," Vachell answered, "in payment for services rendered, I guess."

"What!" Peto sat up in his chair, his hard blue eyes under bushy eyebrows staring unblinkingly at the speaker. "You know that, do you? By God, then, we'll have this Geydi put under arrest at once."

"There's more behind it," Vachell said. "Geydi was acting under orders." He finished his drink and got up stiffly, preparing to go. "I can give you the complete picture, I think, but I'd prefer to wait until this other job is over. Then we'll get down to cases and tie up all the ends."

Sardines and ginger crackers, Vachell decided, hadn't been sufficient to fill a very empty stomach. His head felt more swimmy than ever, and his legs refused to obey his brain efficiently. It was long past dinner-time, but the kitchen rebellion, although now quelled, had delayed the meal. The table was laid, as usual, under the tree. He walked unsteadily towards it and found Chris there, knitting a jumper. She had bathed and changed into her black silk dressing-gown with its scarlet facings. The steel knitting-needles flashed and clicked steadily in the lamplight. The image of Chris seated under the acacia with a half-full glass on the table beside her, her face white against a dark background, and light glinting on the glasses and bottles, had fixed itself in his mind as a sort of hall-mark of the case. Whenever he came to that tree she seemed to be sitting there, waiting, and often the picture flashed unbidden into his mind at odd moments, a picture of the tall, straight-trunked acacia, and under it, in the white lamplight, the silent figure, her thick yellow hair combed back in deep waves, her grave pale face with a little pucker of concentration in the forehead, her sharp pointed chin.

He stood by the table and looked down at her, and she raised her head and met his eyes.

"I'm sorry as hell about the plane," he said. "The engine stalled, and there wasn't a thing I could do."

"So that was it," she said. "The engine was all right when you started. . . . But so long as you're safe, that's the main thing, of course."

A wave of revulsion for the whole case, of a deep disgust with his inevitable duty, swept over him in a sickening rush. He felt as though a load was pressing on his lungs, and a hand gripping him by the throat. He burned with a sudden rage against the smug demands of society, and its obedience to the Mosaic precept of retribution on which it based its criminal law. "I wish to God I'd never started on this case," he said aloud.

He saw Chris's eyelids flicker, and something changed in her face. He was never able to analyse what. It seemed as if her face shrank and grew older, and a look for which no name existed—not ferocity, not hatred, not entreaty, but with something in it of all three—came up from the depths and passed over as quickly as a scudding cloud.

"It's nearly over," she said. Her voice was so low that it was barely audible. Vachell sat down heavily in a chair and covered his eyes with his hands. The light made them smart, and the swimming in his head was bad. When he looked up, the place seemed to be full of people. Cara Baradale's voice said: "You win, Mr. Vachell. I didn't think you'd find him. But it doesn't help, you know. He didn't murder Lucy." She looked thinner and more emaciated than ever, and her face was unnaturally flushed. She poured herself out a glass of straight gin. Englebrecht stood woodenly by her side. Lord Baradale walked over from his tent, looking tired and worn.

"You gave us a nice fright," he said to Vachell. "The camp's been in an uproar all day, and de Mare has only just got back from hunting for you over half of Africa. I suppose you crashed the plane into a tree, or something. You had no right to take her up—an inexperienced pilot. Now I suppose I shall be expected to replace it, since it wasn't Mrs. Davis's fault. Six or seven hundred quid gone west to pay for the caprices of a foolhardy young police-man. I shan't let it rest there, I can assure you. I shall speak to the Governor, and hold the police responsible for the cost."

"The engine stalled," Vachell answered wearily. "Some one monkeyed around with it last night."

There was an awkward silence, broken by a snort from Lord Baradale. "Stuff and nonsense!" he exclaimed. "The plane took off all right. You're using that as an excuse to cloak your own incompetence. I'm delighted to hear that the Commissioner is arriving to-morrow. Then, perhaps, we shall see an end to this ridiculous situation. You seem to forget, young man, that so long as you fail to do your job and arrest the criminal, we have a maniac amongst us, and our lives are in grave danger. Geydi! Bring dinner immediately." He sat down angrily at the head of the table.

"Let's try to forget this ghastly murder, if it's only for an hour," Cara said. "I shall go bats if things go on like this, with everybody suspecting everybody else. Can't we talk of anything else for once? Shoes, ships, sealing-wax—where's Danny? He always thinks of something." She waved her glass in the air, and sat down abruptly in her chair. It was obvious that she had already had several drinks.

Danny de Mare arrived with Peto at the same time as the soup. He had bathed and changed, but he looked worn out. His temper, however, still seemed unshaken. White hunters, Vachell thought, certainly knew how to take it.

"Glad to see you," he said to Vachell. "This camp is getting like a Drury Lane stage with a trap-door and people

disappearing down it one by one. I thought you were a
goner to-day. I've been pushing cars through the mud ever
since noon, trying to find you. If this is modern detective
work, give me Sherlock Holmes in the quiet of his Baker
Street flat, or that American fellow who drinks iced beer—
Nero Wolfe. Have you got to detect by air?"

"This is the last time I try it," Vachell answered. "But
I found what I wanted."

"Englebrecht, you mean?"

"Maybe," he said.

Peto was a strong man, but not silent. At dinner he
kept them entertained with stories of his last solitary trip
by camel through the desert, accompanied only by half a
dozen askaris and his personal staff, in the course of which
he had encountered a foreign military force, officered by
a colonel, a major, three captains, and a quartermaster-
sergeant, trespassing on British territory across the border.
He had ordered them off without any effect, and then in-
vaded their camp under cover of darkness and cut the
guy ropes of the officers' tents, escaping in the pande-
monium that followed. Afterwards he heard that several
soldiers had been shot in the confusion that followed, for
a mutiny had been suspected; but the next day the force
retreated in good order, led by the colonel in full uniform,
with sword and spurs, mounted on a white donkey. More
important, he had discovered a *Stapelia* which he believed
was new to science.

His audience was not very responsive. Lord Baradale
merely grunted, and complained loudly about the food.
Cara talked spasmodically and at random, and once she

turned on Englebrecht, who maintained a stolid silence, and almost shouted: "For God's sake, can't you *say* something?" Only de Mare made a serious effort to back up the D.C. in his attempts to keep the conversation going. It petered out altogether with the coffee, and a silence broken only by the distant voice of the radio from the mess-tent fell upon the party. A crooner was singing "The love bug will get you if you don't watch out." Englebrecht opened his mouth almost for the first time during the evening to say that he was tired, and proposed to go to bed. He walked off without saying good night to Cara, looking sulky and upset.

Vachell was thinking over the words of the announcement that he intended to make when a commotion from the boys' quarters made them all turn their heads and stare across the darkness towards the kitchen. There were several shouts, and a black form raced through the shadows and halted by Peto's side. It was the tribal policeman, and the expression on his broad shiny face was agitated and afraid.

"Bwana," he gasped, "there is bad news. The prisoner, the Timburu uncircumcised youth—he is gone!"

"Gone!" Peto echoed. "What are you saying? How can he be gone? He was fastened with handcuffs to the askari."

"Yes, bwana, but a man has beaten the head of the askari, and now he lies on the ground as if he were dead. He went with the prisoner to eat food. They were in a tent together with the food in front of them when I saw them. I went away for a little, and when I returned I found the askari lying dead and the Timburu gone like a bird."

Peto leant forward, his arms gripping the sides of the chair. "Is he dead?" he demanded.

"I think not, bwana, not yet, but he cannot speak. He was hit on the side of the head by a very strong man who crept up behind, and then opened the handcuffs with the key so that the Timburu could escape. To-night it is very dark, and no one saw him go."

Peto leapt to his feet. "Show me," he commanded. "Turn out the askaris and all the boys, bring them all from their tents. We're going to find out who hit that askari if we have to flay you all alive to do it." He disappeared into the darkness, bellowing for the other askaris.

"What the devil!" Lord Baradale exploded. "Vachell! What does this new outrage mean?"

"It means, sir," Vachell answered, "that some one in this camp has gone to work in earnest to see that the Timburu boy doesn't tell his story."

CHAPTER 25: THE ASKARI WAS SITTING UP
ruefully rubbing the side of his head when the white men
found him. An empty steel bracelet dangled uselessly on
his left wrist, and he looked sheepish, bewildered and sick.
He was bleeding slightly from a cut over the temple. There
was no weapon in the tent, and a thorough search failed
to reveal one anywhere close at hand.

Peto questioned him sharply, but could get no useful
information. He and the Timburu boy had been sitting by
themselves in the opening of one of the natives' tents, shar-
ing a bowl of boiled maize flour and beans, when a violent
blow on the side of the head had laid him out unconscious;
and he knew no more.

The boys, assembled in a circle with Peto and Vachell
in the centre, were questioned one by one, but they had
seen nothing—or, if they had, they could not speak. They
were awed and nervous, for the D.C. was the Government,
and this particular D.C. was known to be a savage man
when the Government's authority was defied. Their solemn, broad-nosed faces shone like onyx in the firelight.
Each native shook his woolly head gravely, and echoed:
"No, bwana. I did not see a person with a piece of iron
in his hand, nor a person hitting the askari. No, I do not
know who did this thing."

Only Geydi appeared perfectly self-possessed. He stood
before Peto, his hands hanging limply at his sides, and

gazed straight into the D.C.'s eyes with a faintly con-
temptuous smile on his full, effeminate lips. He answered,
as usual, in monosyllables. Peto's voice was edged with
exasperation, but Geydi's smile remained.

"Where did you go," Peto demanded, "after you had
taken coffee to the Europeans' table?"

"To my tent."

"Because?" Geydi shrugged his shoulders. "Answer me,"
Peto barked.

"To remove my kanzu."

"Was any one with you in the tent?"

"No."

"How long did you remain there?"

"I don't know."

Peto swore under his breath, and looked round at the
circle of impassive black faces surrounding him. "Did you
others see Geydi go to his tent?" he asked. "Do any of you
know where he was?"

No one broke the silence.

"Are you all idiots?" Peto demanded. "Are you unable
to speak? Answer me, some one, or it will be very bad."

The encircling line wavered in one place, and Kimotho
stepped forward into the ring. He stood at attention in
front of the D.C., looking nervous but at the same time
rather smug. "I saw Geydi after he returned from taking
coffee to the white folk," he said. "I do not think that he
went to his tent. He went over there"—he waved an arm
—"towards the motor-cars. His tent is in the other direction."

Vachell regretfully detected a distinct note of satisfaction in his servant's voice. Altogether, it was a good day for Kimotho, what with the cook under arrest and his other *bête noire* getting in bad with the D.C.

Peto looked again at Geydi. The Somali's face did not change.

"Well," he demanded. "What do you say?" Geydi made no reply. "Answer me, you, or I shall have you handcuffed like the Timburu and tied to a tree."

Geydi turned his big eyes, soft as velvet, in Kimotho's direction, and looked away again as though the sight offended him. "That savage lies," he remarked.

"Askari!" Peto shouted. A uniformed policeman stepped forward smartly, snapped his bare heels together, and stood stiffly at attention. Vachell observed that two of Peto's force of four askaris were missing from the muster, and knew that the D.C. had kept his word. "Arrest this man!" Peto ordered. "Take him to his tent and keep him in custody until further orders. The charge is assaulting a police constable, conspiracy to commit a felony, and obstruction."

Geydi did not move, but a subtle change came over his face. It looked, suddenly, evil and malevolent, and his eyes, fixed unblinkingly on Peto's face, gleamed in the lamplight like an animal's. The askari saluted, turned smartly, and seized Geydi's arm with such force that the Somali could not restrain a wince. The prisoner offered no resistance. He turned and walked with grace and a studied insolence beside the big policeman. He reminded Vachell of a leopard being led away by a lumbering bear.

Peto heaved a sigh, and wiped his face with a large silk

handkerchief. "There's something about that boy that gets under my skin," he said. "I know he's mixed up in this. I could cheerfully strangle him with my own hands. Well, I'll leave him to stew for the night, and we'll get down to brass tacks to-morrow morning. Boy! Bring more coffee."

They rejoined a silent and anxious group at the table, and reported briefly. Englebrecht, his curiosity aroused by the commotion, had rejoined the party. He had not, evidently, retired to bed, for he was fully dressed. The air of tension that had hung over the party all the evening had grown stronger, now, than ever.

"Damn it, sir, you've no right to arrest my servant!" Lord Baradale exploded. "This is iniquitous! You've no charge against him whatever. I can assure you that he knows nothing of these Timburu fellows. How the devil could he? I demand his instant release!"

Peto's mouth was set in a firm line below his clipped white moustache. "I'm sorry, Lord Baradale, but that's quite impossible. He'll be perfectly all right, so long as he behaves himself. If he doesn't, that'll be just too bad for him. The askari who's looking after him won the police heavyweight boxing championship five years ago, and he hasn't forgotten much. And he's a very intelligent man—one of the few police askaris I've ever had who can tell a *Hibiscus* from a *Pavonia*. Geydi should find him an interesting companion."

Vachell glanced at his watch and saw that it was after ten o'clock. Zero hour, he thought; time now to play the last card. Time for the trap to be baited with the living goat. He lit a fresh cigarette, cleared his throat, and plunged into the silence.

"I have an announcement to make," he said. All heads turned towards him and seven pairs of eyes were fixed upon his face. "I'll make it as briefly as possible. It is this: the case is almost over. To-morrow I hope to arrest the murderer of Lady Baradale."

Several people caught their breath sharply in the silence that followed, but no one spoke. A gust of wind made the table-cloth flutter and the gasolene lamp flare up suddenly. De Mare stretched out a hand and turned it lower, and Vachell went on:

"I know now who murdered Lady Baradale, and why, and I'm prepared to prove it. I know who took her jewels, and who shot her to silence her suspicions; and I know how it was done. I know who tried to murder me later, by cutting the powder in my cartridges, and who murdered Sir Gordon Catchpole instead. I know who bust open the box in my tent and stole the evidence I had collected there, and why it was necessary to do so. One of you who's listening now knows that the game is over, and the price is due. And this collector travels with a rope."

"If you know so damned much," Lord Baradale said sharply, "why don't you arrest the fellow, and stop talking like a parson reciting the Shorter Catechism to a confirmation class?"

"Because I haven't got a warrant," Vachell said evenly. "I'll have one by noon to-morrow, but a lot can happen before then. I've told you what I know, and now I'll tell you what I don't know—yet. And it's important. I don't know where Lady Baradale's jewels are hidden. And I don't know where to look."

He paused, and shifted his eyes from one face to the next around the table. They were curiously wooden, as though all wore masks. No one spoke.

"I'm laying my cards on the table, you see," he went on. "It's mighty important to us, to the police, to get those jewels." He spoke in low tones, but every word was clear. "That robbery made the headlines, and we have to get back into the headlines with the recovery of the jewels, or the Chania Police gets a black eye and some of its personnel gets fired."

Again Vachell's eyes flickered from face to face, seeing concentration, bewilderment and surprise. "Go on," Lord Baradale said, an ominous note in his voice.

"I want those jewels back. And I'm not such a dope as to think that an arrested murderer is going to tell me where to look. They're hidden well, and the murderer intends them to stay hidden. But I reckon it's possible that a murderer who hasn't been arrested, but who knows he will be inside a day, might come across—if sufficient inducement were offered."

Again there was a pause, while the speaker drained his coffee and drew on his cigarette.

"I think you've gone bats," Cara Baradale said. "What inducement *can* you offer a murderer? You can't let him off, can you? And a reward isn't much use if you're dead."

"Not to you," Vachell agreed, "but it is to your family. The murderer's family, I mean. People have been known to talk, or not to talk, for that."

"Murderers aren't usually very considerate people, even to their families," de Mare remarked. "I think, if I were the man, I'd want a better inducement than that."

"You might get it," Vachell replied. "I'm speaking off the record now. I can't make promises in behalf of the Chania Police, but I can say this: I want those jewels, and I'm prepared to bargain for them. Now a guy who wants to bargain has to have something to give. Here's what I've got. To-morrow, the Commissioner of Police arrives. He's my boss, and I shall report to him in full—lay it all on the line, so he can draw his own conclusions. And he'll see the case as I saw it, up to a few hours ago. He won't see the discrepancy in the evidence, the little slip the murderer made—unless I tell him. . . . Well, there you have it. There's my collateral. I'm open to a reasonable offer, if it's made right now, to-night."

There was a moment of utter silence when Vachell finished his speech. Blank astonishment showed on every face. Lord Baradale recovered first.

"Well, I'll be damned!" he exclaimed. "Never, in all my born days, have I heard anything to touch that! Do you mean to sit there, an officer in the police force of a British colony, and seriously make an offer to the murderer of my wife to help him to cheat the gallows and evade the law? Of all the cast-iron, brazen, colossal cheek! Mr. Peto, I appeal to you, as a Government official—are you going to let this insolent young puppy get away with the most outrageous attempt to pervert the law that I have ever encountered? I demand that you take action, sir— place him under arrest!"

"Can't do that, I'm afraid, Lord Baradale," Peto replied. He had assumed an air of aloof detachment towards the whole affair. "The police must run their own show according to their own ideas—if they have any. I've never noticed that they have, I must say; fat heads go with flat feet, if you ask me. I shouldn't take them too seriously."

Vachell grinned, and got to his feet. "Sorry you don't care for my offer, Lord Baradale," he said, "but it still stands. I want those jewels, and I'm willing to play ball with the guy who owns them. I'm going to take a walk down the river for maybe half an hour. It's secluded down there. If any one wants to have a chat, they'll know where to find me."

He pushed back his chair in a dead silence, and left the table. When he had gone a few paces a voice said: "Stop." Vachell turned, and saw that de Mare had risen too.

"I don't think you'd better do that," the hunter said.

"Why not?"

"Damn it, two people have been killed already," de Mare answered sharply. "I've issued orders that no one is to leave camp alone, even for a five-minute stroll. I suppose I can't force you to obey them, but for God's sake be reasonable and don't go."

"Thanks for the advice," Vachell said. "But there won't be any trouble. I can take care of myself, I guess. And I carry a gun."

He patted the pocket of his dark tweed jacket, turned on his heel, and strolled off with long strides into the starlit night. From the circle of light under the acacia, seven pairs of eyes watched him go.

CHAPTER 26: IT WAS A CLEAR AND CLOUD-less night. Myriads of stars swam in the endless deep seas of the sky, and the Milky Way was an arch of glittering light supporting the immensities of space beyond. So bright were the stars that they threw faint, misty shadows on the earth, and Vachell could distinguish tufts of grass, dark gleaming stones, and gnarled tree roots beneath his feet. A thread of new moon hung over the crest of the hills behind him. Vachell nodded his head seven times, turned a shilling in his pocket, and wished more ardently than he had ever wished before. It was a simple wish: to be alive next morning when the sun rose.

The rain had cleared off for the time being and the wind had changed, causing the temperature to drop by fifteen or twenty degrees. The night air was sharp and cold in his throat. The river had subsided, but not completely; it still ran swiftly and with an urgency of purpose between its shadowy banks.

Vachell sauntered downstream until he reached the place where the river widened and the banks grew shallow and a pool was formed. On the right bank of the stream the bush was thick and pressed down almost to the water's edge. There were a few game paths leading through it. On the left bank a belt of bush, where Lord Baradale had made his hide, thinned out until, by the pool's lower reaches, the open veldt reached to the water's edge. The bare ground here was scarred with paths made by buffalo and lesser game as they came down to drink.

It was here that Vachell took his stand, in the open, where he could be plainly seen from the thick bush twenty yards across the pool, and from the thinner bush on the same side of the river. He strolled down to the edge of the water and lit a cigarette. The barrel of his revolver was cold against his hand as he slipped the matchbox back into his pocket. It was a night of expectant stillness. The water at his feet lay motionless, a flat gun-metal sheet gleaming dully in the starlight. Across the stream the bush seemed squat and brooding, lying in dense mysterious shadow. He could see no sign of life, although he knew that under the banks the eyes of crocodiles and hippos must be following each movement that he made.

The silence grew so oppressive that his heart jumped and his throat contracted when a plop from the shadows to his right betrayed the sudden movement of a frog or water-rat. A little later a rustling in the bush across the river made him start again. He wondered whether an animal was coming cautiously down to drink, or whether one of the concealed askaris had shifted his position. He could see no sign of them; they were well hidden. His half-smoked cigarette painted a red arc across the darkness and ended in a faint hiss in the water at his feet.

Time crept silently, slowly forward. Despite his resolutions, Vachell felt nervousness grow. His throat and mouth were dry, and an insistent pulse throbbed somewhere in his head. He began to sweat slightly, and his ears strained so closely for the slightest sound that they felt like bursting. He knew that terror, stark, unreasoning terror, was somewhere at the bottom of his soul, fighting feverishly with his self-control to burst through and possess his body. He knew now what the tethered goat would feel, if a goat had human feelings, when the hungry leopard crouched by the gateway of the trap.

He summoned reinforcements from his reason to hold the terror down. Probably the murderer wouldn't come. He didn't expect any one to be so dumb as to swallow the bait of a bargain; the knowledge that Vachell was alone, in the dark, and a mile from camp, was the lure. Vachell's life was the stake, and the chance to catch the murderer red-handed—the only chance to secure any evidence—the prize. But it was a crude trap, and it might never be sprung. Anyway, if some one came, he'd get sufficient warning from a movement in the bush. The chances were twenty-to-one against a shot finding its mark in a light like this. The askaris would prevent a second shot. It was as safe as an evening stroll in Central Park. Safer, in fact.

But all the time a second voice was saying: the killer's tried to get you twice already. This is the last chance: it's now or never. The third attempt can't fail, too. Third time lucky, third time lucky, third time lucky—but not for you. The phrase drummed in his ears with the rhythm of the beat of his heart.

He slipped his hand into his pocket, gripped the cold butt of the revolver, and walked a few paces towards the bush to his right. He tried to pierce the darkness with his eyes, but the bush was a formless belt of shadow packed with menace.

It took the utmost exercise of self-control to turn his back on the threatening bush and retrace his footsteps along the water's edge. Still he heard no alien sound. Across the river the bush seemed to be crouching like a huge black beast. He turned his head to the left, where the open veldt lay pale beneath the starlight. Then he stopped dead in his tracks, and his heart jumped into his throat. He stood rigid and erect as a tree, his head swivelled round. Ahead he saw a vast black mass, twenty paces away, rearing its bulk between him and the sky. As he watched it, something moved like a pendulum across the stars. He was staring directly into the face of an elephant.

He was so taken aback at this development that he forgot his nervousness in surprise. He had expected almost anything, but not an elephant. But you could count on Africa to bring out the one thing you hadn't thought of.

The elephant stood like a rock, its huge ears outspread, nothing stirring but its trunk. It was on its way to water. Vachell wondered what he ought to do. He couldn't walk backwards, for the pool lay there. If he moved forwards the elephant might decide to investigate. He wished passionately that he had brought a rifle.

As he stood staring at its dark bulk and debating on his next move, his ears caught a rustle from the bush behind him. A prickly sensation ran down his spine like a mouse. There was a sharp crack of a snapping twig, then silence. After a short interval, the rustling started again. Some one was moving, cautiously as a stalker, through the bush on his side of the river, twenty paces from where he stood.

Vachell's hand closed on the butt of his revolver. His

scalp was prickling, and he hardly dared to breathe. No time now to think of elephants. He swung around, his back to the great animal, and fixed his eyes on the dark shapeless mass of bush in front.

He could see nothing. Another twig snapped, faintly, and then silence fell again. That last sound had been nearer, and close to the water's edge. Again there was silence, and then from across the river came the hollow grunt of a lion. It was quite close, and it made Vachell's nerves quiver as though they were a tight-stretched string plucked by a musician's finger. It was answered by two distant grunts, away to the left. Two lions, hunting together towards the camp. Silence closed in behind their signals, like a fog. A sudden feeling of fellowship for the animals that were being hunted flooded Vachell's mind. He knew the primitive stab of terror that must pierce their primitive minds.

He pulled out his revolver and waited, his heart bumping, his shoulders hunched. The silence seemed like a taut membrane wrapped around the night. It became something evil, personal, malignant, that stretched itself across his ears.

Then, without warning, the membrane snapped, shattered by the roar of a rifle that crashed through the air and left it lying in a million fragments. Vachell's muscles contracted with a jerk like a dreaming dog's, and in an instant he was sprinting across the open veldt and plunging into the bush towards the sound. Now the air was full of noises. He heard a shout from the bush just ahead and then the noise of a heavy body crashing through. There was another shout from across the river, and the sound of violent cursing down to the left.

Vachell zigzagged through the bush like a running hare, and when it got too thick he crashed through with his head and shoulders, one arm over his face for protection. He hadn't far to go. He burst through the last thorny barrier and emerged on to a shelf of rock above the pool in time to see two figures, locked in struggle, topple over into the water. It wasn't deep, and when they came up he could see that the big black askari had a smaller, spluttering figure helpless in his grip. They waded to the edge of the pool and the askari, panting loudly and emitting little screeches of protest as the booted white man kicked his feet, lifted his captive and himself simultaneously out of the water.

Before they had clambered out Vachell realized that something had gone wrong with his calculations. He pulled a flashlight from his pocket and shone the beam full onto the face of the askari's prisoner. The ray illuminated the angry, hook-nosed face of Lord Baradale.

CHAPTER 27: It was the dripping peer who spoke first.

"What the flaming blazes is the meaning of this outrage?" he shouted. "Who the hell are you, behind that light? Call off this murderous gorilla, tell him to let me go! It's assault, that's what it is, assault! I shall take this up to the governor, I shall. . . ."

He broke off to wriggle violently in his captor's long arms, and to aim a vicious kick at the askari's shins. The black policeman merely grunted "Stop it," and tightened his grip. Vachell picked up two rifles from the ledge and said, "Don't let him go," in Kiswahili.

"Did you fire that shot, Lord Baradale?" he asked.

"Of course I did," the indignant peer answered. "Make this fellow let me go, I tell you."

"Then it's my duty to place you under arrest, and to warn you that anything you say may be ——"

"Don't be a bloody fool," Lord Baradale broke in. "I was trying to save your damned life, not murder you. God knows why; I wish now I'd let the other fellow shoot. Now you've let him go, of course, and thrown me into the river. Exactly like the police, God damn their eyes."

"What other fellow?" Vachell asked. "And don't try to pull anything now; it won't do you a bit of good."

"I was a fool to mix myself up in this," Lord Baradale said disgustedly. "I ought to have known the police would

251

bungle it. There was some one over on the other side of the river, aiming a rifle at you across the pool. I saw the gleam of his rifle-barrel in the starlight, and I fired. I believe I winged him, too. Tell this damned fellow to let me *go*, can't you?"

"My God," Vachell said, "that must have been the other askari."

Lord Baradale's captor released his prisoner reluctantly, on Vachell's orders. The still indignant peer explained that he had come down to the pool with a rifle because he was afraid that there might be another accident, and he wanted to prevent it. Vachell knew this for a lie, and suspected that Lord Baradale had been moved by curiosity and a determination not to miss any of the fun. The second askari arrived from across the river, breathless and excited, to say that another person had been hiding by the pool. He had heard or seen nothing until just before the shot. Then his ears had detected the movements of Lord Baradale across the water; but he had heard no sound from his own side of the pool.

The shot rang out, and after that he heard a crashing in the undergrowth quite close to him, on his side of the stream, and the noise of something running through the bush and up the hill. At first he thought it was a large buck, perhaps a waterbuck, and he still couldn't swear that it was not; but from the way it moved, he thought that it was a man. No, he admitted, he didn't see it; but it made a lot of noise—too much for a buck, certainly not enough for a rhino; about the same as a man.

So that, Vachell thought, was that. If it hadn't been

for Lord Baradale, the interfering old buzzard, the gamble would have worked out. The leopard came after the bait, but a damned hyena sprung the trap. The last chance of securing proof was gone.

Half-way back to camp they were met by Peto and an armed askari, jogging down the gentle slope towards them.

"You haven't shot one of my nice askaris, have you?" Peto called through the darkness. "Ah, I see you haven't. Well, did you get a bite?"

"The fish was all set for a rise," Vachell answered, "but we hooked an old boot instead."

"You're near the end of the chase," Peto said. He turned around and fell into step beside Vachell and Lord Baradale. He was panting slightly after the exertion of his run. "I saw the quarry just now, breaking back and going like hell towards the camp."

"You did?" Vachell exclaimed. "Then why didn't you stop. . . ."

"No chance. I heard a splash in the river below, and all I saw was a dark figure wading through the stream behind me and streaking like blazes up the bank and back towards camp. It had a rifle in its hand. Short of shooting it down, there was nothing to be done. But it was headed in the right direction."

"Do you know who it was?" Vachell asked.

"Too dark to see," Peto said shortly.

There was a sort of excited splutter from behind and the askari who had been with Peto burst into speech. It was evident that he could contain himself no longer.

"Bwana," he said, "bwana! I saw some one running from where the shot was fired towards the camp, just now. I do not know who it was, but I saw the person's hair, and I saw that it was a woman."

"A woman!" Lord Baradale ejaculated. "My God, then it must be . . ." He started to break into a run.

"You needn't worry," Peto said. "Your daughter wasn't out of my sight until after we heard the shot. She kept her young man there, too—she thinks he did it, you know. Absurd, of course; he hasn't the brains to murder an ostrich. Your chauffeur was with us, and the maid. We all sat under the tree with your cherry brandy and talked about the weather. As there are only three women on this safari, that makes it easier for the police to perform one of their well-known feats of brilliant deduction."

"My God!" Lord Baradale said. "I'd never have believed it."

Vachell walked on in silence with long strides, and made no comment.

They found Chris Davis in her tent, seated on her bed beside a safari lamp, dabbing at a bleeding arm with cotton dipped in disinfectant. Her black dressing-gown was thrown aside and her pyjama-clad arm was soaked in blood. She looked up as they lifted the flap of the tent and crowded through the entrance. Vachell was in the lead, followed by Peto and Lord Baradale.

Her face was white as milk and her blonde hair wild and wind-blown. As they entered she drew her lips back in a sort of snarl, like a cornered animal.

"All right," she said, "arrest me, and get it over. I did it. Arrest me, for God's sake, arrest me now."

Vachell reached her side in two strides, lifted the lamp, and bent down to examine the wound. The bullet had passed through the fleshy part of the arm above the elbow. The wound was bleeding badly, but the bone was intact.

"It needs a tourniquet," Vachell said. "I'll need your help, Mr. Peto."

Chris tried to jerk her arm away from Vachell's grip. "Leave me alone, damn you!" she cried. "Arrest me, can't you, and get it over. I don't want your help."

"There's a bandage on the table, sir," Vachell added.

Chris stopped struggling, her features screwed up with pain. "Leave me alone!" she repeated. "I tell you, it was me. Aren't you going to arrest me?"

Vachell looked down on her distraught face for the first time and smiled.

"No," he said.

Chris stared at him for a moment, misery in her eyes, and buried her face in her hand. Her shoulders shook with sobs. He pulled a handkerchief out of his pocket and pushed it into her right hand.

"Here," he said. "It isn't very clean, but I guess it will do."

The crowd at the tent-flap looked on in astounded silence. Peto, bandage in hand, ordered them back in peremptory tones. Lord Baradale, clearly unaccustomed to being treated like one of the gaping crowd outside the church at a fashionable wedding, glared his anger, but obeyed. They retreated from the small veranda, and the figure of Peto's massive tribal retainer filled the opening.

"Bwana," he said. "Here is a letter."

"What on earth . . . ?" Peto ejaculated, busy working over Chris's arm. Vachell stretched out his hand and took the note. "It's addressed to me," he said. Then to the askari: "Who gave it to you?"

Japhet's broad face appeared in the tent opening, peering over the tribal retainer's shoulder. "I brought it, bwana," he said. "Bwana Danny gave it to me. He told me to give it to you."

The letter was in a sealed envelope. Vachell tore it open, unfolded the sheet of paper, and asked:

"Where is bwana Danny now?"

Japhet shrugged his shoulders. "He did not say where he was going, bwana. Half an hour ago he took his rifle and a waterbag and a small sack of salt which he tied to his belt, and many matches, and he went away alone—I do not know where, for it is dark and he would not let me follow him. I said: 'Why do you go away like this, at night, when there are many lions and fierce animals that prowl about in the darkness?' and he answered: 'Why does the duiker run away when the hunting-dogs are after it?' He said that he would not come back. I do not know what he meant, or where he went. It is white man's madness, perhaps."

"Good God," Peto said, straightening his back and staring round-eyed at Vachell. "How many more rabbits have you got in the hat? Don't tell me that Danny de Mare . . ."

"Didn't fall into the trap," Vachell said.

He smoothed out the note, and read it aloud:

"'The fly regretfully declines the spider's kind invitation; he prefers the wide, open spaces to the more restricted atmosphere of the parlour. You win, but you will forgive me if I do not stay to celebrate your triumph. Tell Chris that beasts of prey break their hearts in cages. Good-bye, and good luck.

D. DE MARE.'"

Peto stood motionless for a moment, thunderstruck. "I never would have believed it," he said at last. "Never. To think of Danny . . ."

Vachell looked down at the back of Chris's neck. She sat quietly, no longer sobbing, her face buried in his handkerchief. He put his hand on her shoulder and asked gently:

"You knew all the time, didn't you?"

She nodded her head.

CHAPTER 28: BREAKFAST WAS LATE NEXT morning; and the atmosphere of the camp had undergone a subtle change. The strain of suspense and fear had vanished, and, for the first time since Lady Baradale's death, the meal was a reasonably cheerful one. Nerves were less edgy, and the feeling that a molten volcano lurked underneath a thin crust of civility was no longer there.

Peto and Lord Baradale found a topic of mutual fascination in the study of East African birds, on which the D.C. was a recognized authority. Cara ate with renewed appetite, and talked of going off later in the day with Englebrecht to track the elephant that had been so abruptly rebuffed when it came down to the pool to drink on the previous evening.

"Thank God it's all over," she said. "Though I'm sorry for Danny, and I hope he gets away. The last few days have been absolute hell. I thought Vachell was going to arrest Luke."

"Why should he?" Peto asked. "Luke wasn't guilty. You're suffering from over-development of the female protective instincts. As a matter of fact I think he ought to be arrested anyway—for agreeing to your absurd plan to get married in order to annoy your step-mother. I've heard of a lot of fatuous reasons for getting married, but that's the silliest of the lot."

Cara flushed a little and drank some more black coffee

before replying. "It wasn't to annoy Lucy," she said. "Or, at least, only partly. She was so lousy to Luke. . . . Anyway, the awful thing was, Luke hadn't the ghost of an alibi. You see, when we went off that morning, we picked a place for Luke to camp and got everything ready before we went to Malabeya. It took some time, and after breakfast Luke left me to fix the camp while he went off to shoot a buck for his dinner. He didn't get back till about twelve o'clock, so at the critical time he was wandering about alone in the car with a rifle, and I couldn't have given him an alibi. You see how bad it looked?"

"It wouldn't have to me," Peto said, helping himself liberally to marmalade. "I've known your friend Luke for many years, and much as I respect him, I wouldn't put him down as the scheming Machiavellian type. Did you really think he'd shot your step-mother?"

"No, of course not," Cara said quickly. "I didn't *think* he'd done it, but of course it did look a bit, well, suspicious. I was terrified when I got back to camp and heard about it. I knew how bad it would look for Luke, especially after the way Lucy had behaved to him, and our—the call we made on you that afternoon. So I thought the best thing was for Luke to stay hidden, and then every one would think he'd gone away, and wouldn't worry any more about him. So when he came to the camp that night we cooked up a story about a kudu, only I think Vachell caught us out about that over what Luke did with the skin. It's awfully difficult to think of everything."

" 'Oh, what a tangled web we weave,' " Peto quoted. "Take my advice, if I may speak as one bachelor to another, and give your young man the air. Charming as he is, I doubt whether suspecting your future husband of murder is a good, solid foundation for married life."

Cara started to look aloof, but thought better of it and gave Peto a kindly smile. She stood up, preparing to go, hitched up her shorts and took a cigarette from a silver case out of her pocket. "There may be something in what you say," she remarked. "Anyway, I know now where *not* to apply for a marriage licence."

It was a glorious morning, bright and sparkling, and the blue of the sky was as pure and vivid as the petals of a delphinium. Rain had brought a cloud of new, pale lemon buds to cover the vivid green of the acacias, and the air was full of their delicate scent and of the joyful song of birds.

Only Peto was left at the breakfast-table when Vachell appeared. He puffed wisps of blue tobacco smoke into the still, clear air while the late-comer, rested and refreshed, ate a large meal in silence. The D.C. refrained from questions until the last piece of toast had disappeared. Then he said:

"I'd like to hear the story. I still can't believe it, but I suppose you're right. Incidentally, we've got our little Timburu boy back amongst us again. He panicked in the night —he's only a youngster, and this country's all new to him —and he was afraid he'd get lost if he tried to follow his pals all the way to Timburu-land. So he sneaked back into camp late last night, and the askari he'd been handcuffed to woke up to find him trying to snuggle in under the blankets. He's satisfied, now, that he isn't going to be eaten or mutilated, it seems. He told us who knocked out the askari to let him escape."

"Geydi, of course."

"Quite right. We'll hear the rest of his story later, and you'd better take friend Geydi back to Marula under arrest. The case doesn't seem to be over yet."

"You're darn right, it isn't," Vachell said. "I should make three arrests to-day—apart from Geydi."

"Three?" the D.C. queried. "You'll have to send the Commissioner back for another load of handcuffs. What for?"

"One for accessory after the fact and burglary; one for conspiracy to evade the Firearms Act and connivance in offences against the Game Preservation Act, and one for common assault."

"Safaris have changed a lot since I was a boy," Peto remarked. "In those days Simba Ltd. didn't have much of a criminal clientele. Where did this party start from—Pentonville?"

"This is a screwy sort of a case altogether," Vachell said. "The crimes weren't premeditated, they just developed naturally. And all because—so far as I can figure out—de Mare borrowed a foot-pump from one of the trucks when he went down to Marula."

"Come to my tent and spill the beans," Peto invited. When Vachell had swallowed the last of his coffee they settled themselves in the shade of the small veranda of the D.C.'s tent, which faced the river and the plains beyond. Peto crossed his muscular legs, leant back in the canvas chair, and closed his eyes. "Where do we begin?" he asked. "I suppose the jewels are at the bottom of it all."

"They were at the bottom of it all," Vachell agreed. "I had to keep my mind fixed on that. After I got up here, in amongst the Baradale crowd, it seemed as though most every one had a good working motive for wanting Lady Baradale out of the way—money, sex, and just plain hatred. She was one of those women who go around inviting murder: she had money, gobs of it; she wanted to have affairs, and she didn't have a very pleasant nature. But that's the way it always is, I guess. When a person gets murdered and you start to dig into their past and the state of their personal relationships, you find plenty of people who benefit in one way or another from their death. But these jewels were different. They were a red-hot motive, the real thing. They'd been stolen, and Lady Baradale hinted to me that she knew, or suspected, who'd pulled the job. The next day she was bumped. You don't get coincidences like that in real life. The jewels were the key to the murder, so the first question I had to ask was, who stole them?"

"Well, who did?" Peto asked.

"Rutley. I know it, but I can't prove anything, and it's not likely he'll turn sissy all of a sudden and dump a signed confession in my lap. Why should he? He knows he's sitting pretty. He hasn't got the stuff, and what's more he doesn't know where it is, so we can only guess he took it. The whole of this goddamned case is surmise at that. If Danny de Mare walked into this tent right now, I couldn't hold him. I've got nothing on him. I'm telling you, this is the damnedest case I ever saw."

"In that event," Peto said, "how do you know that Rutley took the jewels?"

"Because no one else could have," Vachell answered. "Except, maybe, the maid. No one else could have swiped the key without knocking Lady Baradale unconscious first. She slung it around her neck all day, and slept on top of it all night. But, for Rutley, that was no problem. He could slip it out from underneath her pillow any night he reported for duty, and burgle the safe when he knew she was sleeping. He had a swell motive, too. He wanted to break away, but he didn't want to lose the pay. If he could get the jewels he could quit his job and go to town with Paula in a big way. And he thought up a dandy little gag to keep them hidden and get them safely out when the time came to pack up and go home."

Vachell paused to light a cigarette. Peto remarked that talking was almost as thirsty work as listening, and called loudly to his boy for beer. "This is all very confusing," he remarked. "If Rutley has the jewels, why did Danny de Mare kill the hag-faced Lady Baradale? Not pure altruism, surely?"

"I'm coming to that," Vachell said. "The night I got here with de Mare, Rutley came out to meet us just as soon as we got in, and the first thing he asked was, where was the foot-pump that de Mare had taken with him to Marula?[1] De Mare said maybe the garage in Marula had swiped it from the car, and Rutley raised hell. At the

[1] See p. 20.

time I thought nothing of it, except that Rutley was a lousy-tempered guy, but looking back on it, I guess that was the key to the whole situation.

"For Rutley, I believe, hid the jewels in one of the foot-pumps. There's a place you could pack them at the end of the cylinder, between the end of the plunger and the base of the cylinder in which the plunger slides up and down. It was a cagey place to pick, for Rutley was in charge of all the cars and no one else was likely to go snooping around among the tools. Nobody would think of looking inside a foot-pump if a search was made, so he'd be able to get the jewels away all right when the safari ended. While the safari was in camp the trucks were almost never used, so he picked a pump belonging to one of the Chevs and left it in the truck, figuring it was the safest place in camp.

"It sure was a tough break for Rutley when de Mare, starting out for Marula early in the morning, found the foot-pump of the Ford was missing, and borrowed another from one of the trucks[1]—borrowed the one pump that happened to have a king's ransom in jewels hidden in its innards. It was sheer chance, and it touched off a whole flock of fireworks. If de Mare had taken the foot-pump out of a different truck, I guess Lady Baradale and Catchpole would have been alive to-day, and Danny de Mare a famous hunter instead of a murderer that's being hunted."

A boy placed a large bottle of beer on the table between them and Peto poured them each a foaming glass. He pushed one across to his companion and remarked:

[1] See p. 20.

"So then de Mare found the jewels, I take it."

"He had a flat tyre on the way down,"[1] Vachell said. "When he tried to put air into the spare tyre he found the pump wasn't in proper shape. He investigated, I guess, and stumbled on the jewels that Rutley had concealed inside it.

"We'll never know what went on inside of him, then. He's a guy who's always getting into jams about money,[2] and he said himself that lately he's been pretty low.[3] I got the impression he was getting sick of his profession and wanted to quit.[4] I guess the temptation was just too strong. De Mare would never plan a theft; I don't believe he ever plans ahead at all. He's an opportunist, the sort of a guy who takes what the gods send him, good or bad. So when they dumped a surprise packet of jewels in his lap, probably he figured that fate had given him a break and that he'd be a fool not to take up the option.

"You see, he knew who stole the jewels—it didn't need much cogitation to work that out. He figured the way I did, that Rutley was the only one with lots of opportunity; besides, he was the only guy who was a smart enough mechanic to fix the pump. And he figured Rutley's tongue would be tied, since to admit he knew the jewels were in the foot-pump was to admit he put them there. So de Mare couldn't see that there'd be any danger. It looked too good a chance to miss.

[1] *Ibid.*
[2] See p. 8.
[3] See p. 95.
[4] See p. 186.

"Anyway, whatever he thought, I know now what he did. He kept the jewels, and hid them somewhere in Marula.

"And this, I think, is where he slipped—he didn't hide them well enough.

"If he had, no amount of police investigation would have bothered him. But it's pretty hard to conceal a package so well that the police can tear everything apart and find nothing, especially if you're a novice at the game for one thing, and you have only one day to do it in for another. De Mare hasn't a home; he lives at the country club when he's in town. He couldn't hide them there. I don't know where he did hide them, but I have a pretty good notion that we'll turn them up without a lot of trouble when we get to Marula—in his baggage, maybe, or on deposit in the bank.

"That was his first mistake. His second was a miscalculation. He felt safe because he'd figured that Rutley wouldn't squawk, but he hadn't reckoned on that baby's temper. It was temper that made Rutley indiscreet."

The monologue was interrupted while its declaimer drank half a glass of beer. It was straight out of the icebox, and it slid deliciously down his throat. Peto, his head tilted back and his hands interlocked behind it, gave every appearance of being asleep. He opened one eye and said: "This is the best story I've heard since little Audrey's day. Please continue."

"Sure," Vachell said. "Well, as soon as de Mare got back to camp from Marula, Rutley found the foot-pump was missing and he was mad as hell. He didn't know

whether or not de Mare's story of leaving the pump at
the garage was true, but he suspected that de Mare had
found the jewels. He has a temper just about as explosive
as a load of T.N.T., and the more he thought about it,
the more it burnt him up. This is more guesswork, and it
will stay guesswork unless I can turn the heat on Rutley
some way and make him kick through. All I know is, when
I talked with Lady Baradale that night at eleven, she
hinted that she had some inside dope on the burglary, and
that she suspected some guy who'd be a big surprise to
every one concerned.[1] She couldn't have meant Rutley,
because he wouldn't have been a big surprise to anyone.

"My guess is, some time between six and eleven, Rutley
went to Lady Baradale and told her that he suspected
de Mare of stealing the jewels. I reckon he got so mad
he thought: 'This guy isn't going to get away with the
jewels *I* risked a ten-year stretch to steal. If I can't have
them, then by God that bastard isn't going to have them
either.' So he told her, maybe, that he'd seen de Mare
acting suspiciously before leaving for Marula—slipping a
package into the car with a furtive air, or something. Anyway, I figure he sold her the idea that de Mare was the
thief, without, of course, giving away his own part in it.
It wasn't a smart thing to do, but then I don't reckon
Rutley's a smart guy; in fact I think he's dumb as the
devil, and has altogether too quick a temper to make even
an average criminal.

"Now here's another part that's merely guesswork. Some
time between six that evening, when we hit the camp, and

[1] See p. 36.

ten o'clock next morning, when the lion hunt began, de Mare found out that Lady Baradale suspected he had the jewels. I know that's so, because he shot her; but I don't know how he found it out. I think most likely she sent for him and said she'd had some information which implicated him. He denied it, of course. Then she said—this is more guesswork—'I'm glad to know this story is a lot of hooey, but at the same time it's true you are the only guy who's left camp since the theft and had a chance to get the stuff away, so I think it would be fair to all if the police in Marula were to search your kit and check up on your movements while you were in town. I intend to tell the story to this cop we've imported, and suggest he get his men at headquarters to search the kit you left in Marula, so we can prove that the mud some one's trying to throw is mud and nothing more, and clear your name completely.'

"Of course de Mare had to agree. That put him on the spot. He'd counted on Rutley keeping silent, and the fact that Rutley had lost his head upset all his calculations. And when Lady Baradale said she'd spill the story to the police, she meant it. If they searched his stuff in Marula, there was more than a chance they'd find the jewels and *he'd* find himself behind the bars. He must have got a hell of a jolt, and felt in pretty bad shape next morning. It began to look as though swiping jewels wasn't so easy after all. I'll bet he was desperate as hell by the time he came to take Catchpole out on the lion hunt."

"So he planned to do her in," Peto said.

"I don't believe so," Vachell answered. "I don't believe

he ever planned it at all. He couldn't have, because he couldn't have known that Lady Baradale would be walking back to camp along the river at just about the time he was hunting lions with Catchpole, and that their paths would cross. De Mare's a man who always acts on impulse. I think that when he caught sight of her in the bush that morning the impulse came on him to shoot her, and he acted on it without another thought.

"Now, here's the part of the story that puts me on the spot. Within a few hours of the shooting I held the proof that de Mare was guilty in my hand; and I never saw it. I didn't see it until I was standing beside a lion's kill yesterday afternoon close to Englebrecht's camp, and I opened the breach of my rifle to see everything was all set in case I met a lion. I noticed that it was loaded up with solid bullets, and I remembered then what de Mare told me in Marula when I bought the rifle—that you always use a soft-nosed bullet to kill a lion."[1]

"Of course you do," Peto said, opening his eyes as the narrator paused to renew his attack on the beer. "They come under the heading of soft-skinned game. What on earth has that got to do with it?"

"Everything," Vachell answered. "De Mare shot that lion with a solid bullet. Japhet dug it out and gave it to me afterwards, in the mess-tent.[2] I checked it with de Mare's cartridges right away—that was easy, because it hadn't lost its shape—and found it was fired from his gun all right; but it never occurred to me that an experienced

[1] See p. 10.
[2] See p. 69.

hunter who was following a lion's trail wouldn't have loaded his rifle up with solid bullets."

"You mean he reloaded his rifle with solids in order to shoot Lady Baradale?" Peto asked. "Why?"

"Because of the superior powers of penetration of the solid bullet. Suppose he'd used a soft-nosed for the job. The bullet would have killed her, all right, but most likely it would have lodged in her body. And de Mare knew that if we found the bullet, we'd be able to trace it back to his rifle. Nothing could have explained that away.

"So what occurred, I think, was this. De Mare and Catchpole were trailing the lion through the bush, without a thought of Lady Baradale. I guess they were just thinking lion. They'd spotted the quarry, and they knew he'd taken refuge in a patch of bush down at the bottom of this gulley. De Mare sent the two natives down the river end of it, to the left, to cut him off if he tried to break back, and to beat up the gulley. The two Europeans walked slowly and cautiously forwards, and climbed to the top of a little knoll on the bank of the gulley, where they halted to search the bush ahead with their eyes for a sign of the lion. They expected to see him break cover any moment, and streak away up the opposite side of the gulley. They were all set to shoot at the drop of the hat, and without waiting to see the whites of his eyes.

"Things are pretty keyed up at a moment like that. Every bit of attention is focused on the bush ahead where the lion is crouching; every sense is straining to catch the first glimpse of him when he moves. After all, there's al-

ways the chance that he may come in the wrong direction
—towards you, instead of away. Your eyesight is like the
beam of a flashlight—it concentrates on one spot, and
everything else is in darkness so far as you are concerned.
You wouldn't see a two-headed monster or even King
Kong at fifty paces in circumstances like that, if they were
out of your line of vision.

"So when, just at that tense moment when de Mare and
Catchpole had their eyes glued on the bush ahead and expected to see a lion pop out of it, Lady Baradale sailed
into sight away over to the right and at least a hundred
yards distant. Catchpole didn't see her. De Mare did,
though. I guess these old-time hunters have a sort of sixth
sense that detects anything that moves, the way an animal
does. He felt there was something moving, and when he
turned his head he saw her walking through the bush towards him, on the way back to camp from her morning
stroll. Either she didn't spot them—and it takes an experienced eye to pick out a stationary object in the African bush
—or she saw from the way they were standing on the knoll
that there was something just ready to break, and stood
still to see what it was all about.

"I believe, when de Mare saw her, the impulse to kill
must have come over him like—well, like a sudden fever,
or a wave of nausea. He was a hunter, and his blood was
up. His whole mind and body were attuned to kill. All
that had to change inside of him was the object at which
his lust to kill was directed. It must have come to him in
a flash—the impulse to shoot the woman instead of the

beast. She had threatened his safety, and so she had to go. It was almost an act of self-defence.

"Here's where de Mare did some fast thinking. He knew no one else had seen Lady Baradale. Catchpole had both eyes and all his mind pinned on the bush where the lion still was. The two boys were out of sight down the gulley. He knew that as soon as the lion broke cover, Catchpole would take the first shot, and he, the hunter, would fire a moment later to drop it. That was the routine. It added up to two shots. He decided—and all this happened inside of a few seconds—to try a trick: to fire his first shot at the same instant as Catchpole's, so that the two shots would combine to make one joint bang. That would give him a second shot to use on Lady Baradale, and there'd still only be two bangs.

"It was difficult, but it had this advantage: the trick shot was to be aimed at the lion, so that if it failed to synchronize with Catchpole's, he could call the murder off and no one would be any the worse or any the wiser.

"Well the breaks were with him and the gag worked. He slipped the soft-nosed cartridges out of his magazine and pushed in a clip of solids. He always carried his ammunition in a clip.[1] A few seconds, maybe, after that, the expected happened: the lion broke cover ahead and streaked off up the opposite bank. He'd been driven out, of course, by the boys who were beating up the gulley below.

"Catchpole was standing just a little way ahead.[2] De Mare gave the word to fire, and drew a bead on the lion's

[1] See p. 10.
[2] See p. 73.

neck. Remember, de Mare was a first-rate shot with reactions like a flash of lightning. His shot and Catchpole's went off almost at the same instant. Not quite, of course; I guess de Mare's was a split second behind. De Mare couldn't have gotten away with it if Catchpole had been an experienced hunter, or a less excitable sort of a guy. But he knew nothing about shooting, and he was so steamed up over the lion he'd hardly have noticed an earthquake.

"De Mare's shot was a honey. His bullet hit the vertebrae of the neck and the lion dropped like a stone in a pond. Catchpole's shot, of course, missed. A second later de Mare swung around to the right, sighted full on Lady Baradale's forehead, and fired the second shot. It was another bull. The solid bullet went clean through her skull, drilling a neat round hole in the bone,[1] and she dropped without a sound. Catchpole most likely went racing ahead towards the lion, convinced that he'd dropped it with a beautiful shot. He heard the second bang, of course, and thought it was de Mare making sure the dead lion would stay dead, the way hunters normally do. This takes a long time to tell about, but I guess it all happened in the inside of a minute.

"Well, the double-shot gag fooled me—that, and another thing. When I went over the territory that afternoon, I marked three points—where the lion was shot; where Lady Baradale was found; and where de Mare told me he and Catchpole had stood to shoot the lion. Now, the place where Lady Baradale's body was lying couldn't be seen

[1] See p. 65.

from the spot where de Mare said he stood to shoot the lion. This rocky knoll I mentioned was in the way. But, you see, it was only de Mare who told me where he'd stood.[1] There was no evidence to confirm that. Japhet and Konyek were out of sight, and Catchpole died before I had a chance to take him out there to check positions. So de Mare took me for a ride. He and Catchpole stood on top of the knoll, not to the left of it—and Lady Baradale was in full view.

"I should have seen it, though, from the first. Chris saw the truth that afternoon, when Japhet handed over the solid bullet he'd taken from the lion. A soft-nosed bullet that had hit the bone would have been flattened out into a shapeless lump of metal,[2] and I'd have had a hard job to decide the calibre of the rifle that fired it.

"And, looking back, there was another pointer that I missed. Japhet and Konyek both agreed that only two shots had been fired, and that helped to convince me that Catchpole and de Mare were on the level. But Japhet said something that should have given me a lead. He said there were two shots, 'the first one very close.'[3] It sounded louder than he expected, and that made it seem close. But I missed the lead he gave me. I'm a dope, and I know it."

"You need consolation," Peto said. "Regrets were made for drowning. Try some more beer."

White foam rose in a frothy column as Peto emptied the bottle into Vachell's glass. The sun was already high

[1] See p. 73.
[2] See pp. 11 and 132.
[3] See p. 68.

overhead, and the air was pleasantly warm and drowsy. "You're assembling a convincing case for your theory," Peto added, "considering that you're making it all up. It fits in with Danny's nature, I'll say that. He always acted on impulse, as you say. A trick like that needs speed, luck, and skill, and Danny had plenty of all three."

"Especially luck," Vachell agreed. "I reckon any one who had a girl like Chris Davis so crazy about him she'd cover up for him when she knew he'd committed a murder is a hell of a lucky guy."

CHAPTER 29: "LADY BARADALE'S MURDER," Vachell went on when the glass of beer in front of him was empty and Peto had resumed his posture of apparent sleep, "was a better piece of strategy, I reckon, than de Mare himself realized when he drilled her with a bullet at around eleven-thirty on a fine African morning, with her prospective son-in-law standing a few feet away. Because it silenced Rutley as well as her."

"I don't see that," Peto said, shifting himself in the chair and rubbing a hand through his thatch of tousled grey hair. "Rutley must have known that de Mare had done her in. Why didn't he tell you about it?"

"Because he didn't know what had happened to the jewels," Vachell said. "Of course, he felt pretty sure that de Mare had dug them out of the foot-pump and had them somewhere salted away. But he didn't *know*. De Mare's story about the foot-pump being swiped by a garage might have been true.

"Suppose he'd accused de Mare of theft and murder. First he'd have had to ante up a reason for his suspicions that would satisfy the police. I'd have been a lot harder to satisfy than Lady Baradale, because on the face of it everything pointed to Rutley himself as the guy who did the stealing. And then suppose, after all, de Mare *hadn't* got the jewels, Rutley would have pushed his own neck right into the noose. For, if the police had found that he'd

276

accused de Mare without reason, they'd naturally assume
that Rutley had stolen the jewels and then knocked off
Lady Baradale when she got suspicious, and was trying
to frame de Mare. It was too much of a risk to take. If
he lost out, he'd most likely take the rap for murder. Rutley's temper had cooled down by then, and he was too
scared to talk.

"There was another reason, too, I guess. Rutley wouldn't
get any percentage on a dead and hanged de Mare, but he
would on a live one who could be squeezed. If he could
secure some sort of proof that de Mare was the killer, he'd
have as sweet a blackmail set-up as you ever saw. He'd be
able to twist the screws so tight he'd wring the marrow out
of de Mare's bones. So he was another member of the
outfit who didn't want the murderer caught.

"He has his troubles, though. He came under suspicion
himself, and that scared him plenty. Motive was his weak
point, and he knew it. More women have been knocked
off because their men friends couldn't think of any other
way to get rid of them than for any other reason, I guess.
Rutley almost admitted there was a bunch of letters in
Lady Baradale's safe that gave him a dandy motive[1]—love
letters at the bottom of the pile and letters that showed he
was through and wanted to quit on top. So he sneaked into
Lady Baradale's tent the night after the murder to see if
there was any way he could dig them out—at least, this is
the way I've figured it—and after a little while I came
along. He hid in the clothes closet, and when he saw me

[1] See p. 166.

just about to turn the key he crowned me with a spanner
and swiped the letters, and the key.

"It was de Mare, of course, who left those walnuts on
the coffin. They didn't mean much, but they bothered me
a lot. They were a gesture, that was all, but it didn't seem
to me that any of the suspects I'd booked in my mind for
the crime would have made a gesture like that. It showed
a sort of flippant, perverted sense of humour, a touch of
bravado, that didn't fit Rutley, or Englebrecht, or Lord
Baradale. It did fit de Mare, but I'd eliminated him. I
couldn't figure it out at all.

"De Mare put them there when he found me lying
unconscious in Lady Baradale's tent, I reckon; he was
checking up on my whereabouts in order to plant five dud
cartridges in the belt I'd left lying in my tent. For he'd
decided that I had to go. I had his bullet—the one found
in the lion, that he told Japhet to throw away[1]—and he
knew that bullet could hang him, once I saw its significance
and started to ask questions. Chris had seen it right away,
and he figured it was only a question of time before I saw
it too. Chris was safe; the tortures of hell wouldn't have
dragged the information out of her. But I was hunting too
close up to his trail. The scent was fresh, and he reckoned
that it was him or me.

"I haven't a shred of proof, but I've no doubt at all
that it was de Mare who cut the powder in my cartridges,
hoping it would get me into trouble. He knew there were
buffalo in the hills, and that I meant to go after them—I

[1] See p. 68.

told him that.[1] I think that goes to prove that he wasn't, by nature, a killer. He might have found a much more certain way of knocking me off, but I think he somehow shrank from the actual commission of a planned, cold-blooded murder. He wanted the buffalo to do the job for him. It was a long shot, but it involved no risk, and if nothing came of it, why, no harm was done.

"The trick worked all right, but it worked on the wrong guy. I got the breaks; and the buffalo trod on Catchpole instead of on me. That was luckier for de Mare than he realized. I believe that Catchpole, who was smart enough underneath his pansy poses, had got suspicious of de Mare. When he died, he was trying to tell me something, and I think he was going to name de Mare. The last words I could catch were ". . . shot Lucy." He may have remembered there was something phony about the shot—the double shot—or he may have thought of another thing: that de Mare *unloaded* his rifle just before they saw the lion. He may have got to wondering why a hunter should change the cartridges in his magazine with a lion all ready to jump a few bushes away. Anyway, he died before he could tell me what was on his mind, and that was a break for de Mare. Then we found Rutley's bullet inside the wounded buffalo. That put Rutley out of the running as a serious suspect; the buffalo gave him an alibi, in fact. I told you this was an unusual case.

"With Rutley out and Catchpole dead, that left Lord Baradale or Englebrecht, with Cara Baradale as an accomplice. Things didn't look so good for Englebrecht, at

[1] See p. 99.

one point. He had a swell motive. Lady Baradale had fired him, and he wanted to marry a girl who inherited a big slice of her dough. The most damning thing of all was Cara's attitude. She thought he'd done it. She was scared to beat hell. That meant that either he'd admitted he'd knocked off her step-mother, or that he'd been away on his own when the shooting was done, and she suspected the worst.

"Then we come to the noble Lord. If ever there was a cagey old buzzard, it's he. He lied like a politician, and up till yesterday evening he was my number one suspect. I'd intended to book him for murder, and by God it's no more than he deserves."

"Ah," Peto interrupted, coming to life again. "There, I think, is where I can contribute a chapter to this saga. I intend shortly to expel Lord Baradale from my district, only unfortunately God and Nature seem to be united in a conspiracy to prevent him from obeying my orders. Let's hear your version first."

Vachell refreshed himself with another drink and lit a fresh cigarette. "Lord Baradale was a very careless liar," he continued. "He lied the first time when he said he'd been in camp all morning, and when I caught him out in that he lied again, and said he'd been taking pictures at the pool. I asked him to show me a movie he claimed to have shot while the murder was going on, more or less, and he ran through a reel which he'd taken on some previous occasion. There were hippos in it, all right, but from the way the shadows fell you could see it was shot around five in the afternoon instead of between ten and eleven in

the morning. Lord Baradale would make a lousy criminal.
He's too darned sure of himself to take any trouble.

"Well, the question was, where had Lord Baradale been?
One of the cars had an extra twenty-nine miles to its credit
that no one knew anything about,[1] so it was a pretty safe
guess he was out in that. I could fix the direction, too, by
a bunch of elephants I flew over with Chris the morning
of the murder. Some one threw such a scare into them
around 10.45 that they made tracks for the hills as fast
as they could travel.[2] So it looked as though Lord Baradale had made a trip to a spot about fourteen miles south-
west of the camp. Chris checked time and distances, and
they fitted. Then a boy came forward to say he'd seen
Geydi driving a car out of camp that morning; so Geydi
was in it too. And Geydi had been seen holding a secret
conference with some Timburu braves who fitted the description of the gang of poachers you're interested in. So it
was pretty clear that Lord Baradale was mixed up with
some shady business with a bunch of Timburu gangsters
who were wanted for murder.

"It was right here that I jumped the tracks. I thought
out a pretty fancy theory. I figured that Lord Baradale,
working through his servant Geydi, had hired these Timburu thugs to bump off his wife. One of his rifles was missing after the murder, so I reckoned that was part of the
price. I had it all figured out—how Lord Baradale had
fetched the Timburu in his car and taken them to the drift,
and then returned to camp while they shot his wife with

[1] See p. 87.
[2] See p. 50.

the rifle, according to instructions, and dragged her body closer in to camp so that the boss would find her and know they'd filled their part of the bargain. It was a swell theory, and nothing was wrong with it except the detail that it was cockeyed from start to finish. I still don't know what monkey business old man Baradale was up to with these poachers, but I guess it was something to do with his movies he's so crazy about."

"I congratulate you," Peto remarked. "Never again shall I accuse the police of lack of imagination. You ought to sell that story to Hollywood. Compared to that, I'm afraid the truth will be milk-and-water to your Château Neuf du Pâpe."

Peto shouted loudly for his boy, who in turn summoned two natives to the D.C.'s presence. One was the stalwart tribal policeman, dressed in a dark blue blanket and a knitted cap, and carrying a rifle. The other was the young Timburu prisoner, a thin and reedy lad with a scared expression like that of a wild animal newly taken into captivity. His woolly hair was cropped short and his body was smeared with earth and sheep's fat so that it gleamed like polished copper. He wore a single white feather stuck into his thick hair, and carried a light spear.

The tribal retainer brought his heels together and saluted with the maximum amount of flourish. Peto settled himself back in his chair, one brawny leg thrown over his knee, tilted his head back, and fixed his bright blue eyes on the prisoner's face.

"Tell this Timburu youth again," he said to the tribal retainer, "that he will not be beaten, but given food and

treated well—provided that he speaks the truth. If he lies
he will be punished by the Government. He will be sent
a long way away from his people and kept there for many
years, so that he will not be circumcised and will therefore
be unable to buy a wife. Ask him what has become of his
poacher friends."

A rapid cross-fire of talk in the liquid, flowing tongue
of the Timburu followed. Then the tribal retainer stood
at attention and translated into Kiswahili in crisp and military style.

"He says that he is not a poacher," the policeman began.
"He has been with some warriors, who are members of
his clan, hunting rhinos with the spear. When the rhinos
are killed, the horns are taken and sold to Somalis who
travel here on camels. . . ."

"Tell him I want to hear about the white man who
gave them a rifle," Peto said.

After more talk in Timburu, the retainer resumed the
tale. "There is a man who is employed here called Geydi,
who took as wife a Timburu woman who is a sister of one
of the warriors who came here to hunt. These warriors
saw the fires of the white men's camp, and came secretly
to see whether the Government had sent askaris to catch
them. They found that there were no askaris, but when
they came at night and called to each other in the darkness like birds, Geydi heard them and answered, for he
knows the secret calls; and they saw and spoke with Geydi.

"Several days later Geydi saw them again and told them
that the camp belonged to a very rich white chief who was
greater than the Government, and that this chief wished

to see how the Timburu hunted rhinos with spears. Geydi promised them a very powerful rifle if they would show this chief; and they agreed. Three days ago they found a rhino with a big horn, and one of their number went to the camp to tell Geydi to fetch the white chief. Geydi gave them money, and said that the chief would come the next morning.

"Next day they waited for the white chief, and when he came in a car he had a strange box in his hand which he held up to his head, and it made strange noises like a lizard. The Timburu thought it was a kind of magic and were afraid, but Geydi told them that it was all right, and they hunted the rhino and killed it while the white chief watched with the box held up to his head. Then Geydi gave them the rifle, and the white chief went away."

"There's your mystery," Peto said to Vachell. He dismissed the retainer and the Timburu boy, and added: "Thanks to Lord Baradale's unbridled passion for photography, those murdering poachers have wounded my favourite corporal. He's not going to be allowed to get away with that, peer or no peer. I'm going to get his blood for violation of the Firearms Act. You can get five years for smuggling arms to natives in a closed area. I suppose he'll appeal and get the sentence commuted to a fine, but I hope it's such a big one that they take fifty cents off the income tax in the next budget—or, more likely, appoint five new assistant deputy colonial secretaries in the Secretariat."

"No wonder he wouldn't tell me where he'd been that morning," Vachell reflected. "He knew darned well he'd committed a very serious offence, one he could go to jail for. And all to get a picture of a Timburu rhino hunt. He sure is hipped on this movie business. Seems to me he's a little crazy."

"Just conceited, I think," Peto said. "It's a mild form of megalomania. He thinks those sort of laws are a lot of red tape, and if they interfere with his wishes he just disregards them. He wanted pictures that no one else in the world had got, and broke the law to get them. Worse things than that have been committed in the interests of a hobby, I suppose. I'm going to have a little chat with his Lordship. And if it's any consolation to you, I'm going to make him squirm."

He stood up and picked his hat off the table.

"Are we going to catch Danny de Mare?" Vachell asked.

"We're going to try," Peto answered. "A week ago, either we'd have caught him or he'd have died of thirst. We can always watch the wells. But that rain has given him a chance. A pretty thin one, but he knows the country backwards, and if he can find rainwater pools and avoid the wells, there's just a chance he may slip over the border into Abyssinia somewhere. That's where he's aiming for, of course. It's one chance in twenty, I should think. I can't help hoping, in a way, that he pulls it off."

"I feel that way too," Vachell said, "although I shall get a hell of a black eye from the Commissioner for letting him escape. But I don't know what we'd have done if he hadn't. We haven't any proof."

Vachell sat on for a little after Peto had left, sipping his beer and gazing out at the sun-flooded landscape across the sparkling river. Trees swam in the misty midday heat, and he felt pleasantly drowsy. A couple of clear fine days like this, he thought, and the safari would be able to strike camp and go home.

Then he thought of de Mare and of the strange phenomenon of a woman's loyalty to a man who neither sought nor wanted such assistance. A queer, self-contained, amoral cuss, he thought; unsatisfactory to love, dangerous to hate.

Presently he strolled over to Chris's tent and found her writing letters in the shade of a tree outside. Her left arm was in a sling, and she looked forlorn and pale. She was, as usual, hatless, and patches of sunlight trickled through green leaves on to her corn-coloured hair. She looked up when she heard his footsteps.

"Have you come to arrest me?" she said. "I suppose I'm an accessory, or something. Sounds so like a handbag. Well, I'll go quietly. I don't much mind."

"You're wrong," he answered, and sat down on the grass beside her. "You're wrong about a lot of things. I can't book you on a charge of accessory until we've brought de Mare to trial."

"You'll never do that," she said quietly.

"Maybe," Vachell said.

"I owe you an apology, I think. When you asked if you could fly my plane alone, I imagined it was because you didn't trust me—you believed I was the murderer, or something. I think I know the real reason now. You were frightened, weren't you, that the plane might be damaged somehow? You knew the flight would be dangerous?"

"I guess so, in a way. I didn't see how the plane could

be got at, but I knew that some one was gunning for me, and—well, you never know. I still don't know. The motor just stalled, and died."

"I think I know. There's one thing he could have done that would have that effect—sugar in the petrol."

Vachel whistled and nodded his head. "I hadn't thought of that. Easy to slip in a handful of sugar in the dark, maybe when the guards were taking shelter from the rain. I guess that must be the answer."

"It crystallizes on the jets," Chris went on, "and blocks them; the effect's much the same as running out of petrol."

"It isn't an effect I go for," Vachell remarked. "From de Mare's viewpoint, it was darned nearly effective. I hope the Government doesn't soak Lord Baradale so heavily he can't afford to buy you a new plane."

They sat in silence for a while, watching a pair of kites wheeling lazily over the river, black against the dazzling blue of the sky. Their shadows slipped easily to and fro over the white sand.

"You know I took those things out of your tent?" Chris asked, a little later. "I suppose that's a crime too. I was so terrified you'd see the significance of that bullet of Danny's, and I got it into my head that if I took it, you wouldn't have any proof. I know it was silly, but it was so awful waiting and wondering what was going to happen, and I think I simply lost my head. I kept on seeing that bullet lying in your hand. It became a sort of obsession."

"You sure had that guy on your mind," Vachell said gently.

Chris ran her hand wearily through her thick wavy hair,

and stared out into the white sunlight that enveloped their cool oasis of shade. "I'm afraid I made my feelings very obvious," she said. "It was silly, because Danny was always —well, out of reach. He never let any one get too close. I'm sorry I was hysterical and stupid, last night. I was afraid Danny would attempt to—to shoot you, so I went down to the pool to try to stop it, I didn't quite know how. I was half crazy with the suspense and the—well, it isn't much fun when some one you're very fond of turns out to be a murderer and a thief. It was rather a nightmare, you know."

Vachell reached over and put a long, bony hand over hers. "It's all over," he said. "There's only one thing you can do now—forget it. And there's only one way you can manage that."

"Is there a way, do you think?"

"Sure there is, Chris. I'll tell you: take an interest in some other guy. De Mare isn't the only man in Africa who's got personality. Next time, play for safety—pick on some one who won't turn out to be a murderer or a share-pusher or even a confidence man, some one right outside of the criminal classes. I'd suggest, for instance, you try the police. Kimotho says that when a policeman wants to commit a murder he gets the Government to do the job for him with a rope. That shows how much influence we have in the highest quarters."

Chris achieved a rather pallid smile. "I've always heard the police were a fine body of men," she said.

"Taken one by one," Vachell agreed. "For instance, take me. We should have a lot in common—we're in the same racket, you know. We both hunt for our living. You chase innocent animals and I chase guilty men; you identify them by their footprints, and I use finger-prints to track them down. Otherwise the game is much the same. We could have a lot of fun comparing notes. I think you'd make a swell detective. In fact, I think you'd be swell at almost anything you did."

"Perhaps, with practice, you might give up your rather alarming habits of walking down-wind into rhinos and tracking elephants backwards," Chris suggested.

"I bet you'd study finger-prints upside down," Vachell retorted, "and walk down-wind into the Police Commissioner before breakfast. The art of estimating the state of the Commissioner's liver calls for a far more delicate judgment than that required for merely testing the direction of the wind. I have a theory that everything depends on the phases of the moon. I'd like your opinion on that. In fact, I think we should get together and work out such important problems of technique."

Chris smiled, and he saw that a faint flush of colour had returned to her cheeks.

"It might be quite a lot of fun," she said.

THE END

THE PERENNIAL LIBRARY MYSTERY SERIES

Delano Ames

FOR OLD CRIME'S SAKE (*available 12/82*)   P 629, $2.84

MURDER, MAESTRO, PLEASE (*available 12/82*)   P 630, $2.84
"If there is a more engaging couple in modern fiction than Jane and
Dagobert Brown, we have not met them."   —*Scotsman*

E. C. Bentley

TRENT'S LAST CASE   P 440, $2.50
"One of the three best detective stories ever written."
          —Agatha Christie

TRENT'S OWN CASE   'P 516, $2.25
"I won't waste time saying that the plot is sound and the detection
satisfying. Trent has not altered a scrap and reappears with all his old
humor and charm."   —Dorothy L. Sayers

Gavin Black

A DRAGON FOR CHRISTMAS   P 473, $1.95
"Potent excitement!"   —*New York Herald Tribune*

THE EYES AROUND ME   P 485, $1.95
"I stayed up until all hours last night reading *The Eyes Around Me,*
which is something I do not do very often, but I was so intrigued by the
ingeniousness of Mr. Black's plotting and the witty way in which he spins
his mystery. I can only say that I enjoyed the book enormously."
          —F. van Wyck Mason

YOU WANT TO DIE, JOHNNY?   P 472, $1.95
"Gavin Black doesn't just develop a pressure plot in suspense, he adds
uninfected wit, character, charm, and sharp knowledge of the Far East
to make rereading as keen as the first race-through."   —*Book Week*

Nicholas Blake

THE CORPSE IN THE SNOWMAN   P 427, $1.95
"If there is a distinction between the novel and the detective story (which
we do not admit), then this book deserves a high place in both catego-
ries."   —*The New York Times*

THE DREADFUL HOLLOW P 493, $1.95
"Pace unhurried, characters excellent, reasoning solid."
—San Francisco Chronicle

END OF CHAPTER P 397, $1.95
". . . admirably solid . . . an adroit formal detective puzzle backed up
by firm characterization and a knowing picture of London publishing."
—The New York Times

HEAD OF A TRAVELER P 398, $2.25
"Another grade A detective story of the right old jigsaw persuasion."
—New York Herald Tribune Book Review

MINUTE FOR MURDER P 419, $1.95
"An outstanding mystery novel. Mr. Blake's writing is a delight in
itself." *—The New York Times*

THE MORNING AFTER DEATH P 520, $1.95
"One of Blake's best." *—Rex Warner*

A PENKNIFE IN MY HEART P 521, $2.25
"Style brilliant . . . and suspenseful." *—San Francisco Chronicle*

THE PRIVATE WOUND P 531, $2.25
"[Blake's] best novel in a dozen years . . . . An intensely penetrating study
of sexual passion . . . . A powerful story of murder and its aftermath."
—Anthony Boucher, The New York Times

A QUESTION OF PROOF P 494, $1.95
"The characters in this story are unusually well drawn, and the suspense
is well sustained." *—The New York Times*

THE SAD VARIETY P 495, $2.25
"It is a stunner. I read it instead of eating, instead of sleeping."
—Dorothy Salisbury Davis

THERE'S TROUBLE BREWING P 569, $3.37
"Nigel Strangeways is a puzzling mixture of simplicity and penetration,
but all the more real for that." *—The Times Literary Supplement*

THOU SHELL OF DEATH P 428, $1.95
"It has all the virtues of culture, intelligence and sensibility that the most
exacting connoisseur could ask of detective fiction."
—The Times Literary Supplement

Marjorie Carleton

VANISHED   P 559, $2.40
"Exceptional . . . a minor triumph."
—Jacques Barzun and Wendell Hertig Taylor, *A Catalogue of Crime*

George Harmon Coxe

MURDER WITH PICTURES   P 527, $2.25
"[Coxe] has hit the bull's-eye with his first shot."
—*The New York Times*

Edmund Crispin

BURIED FOR PLEASURE   P 506, $2.50
"Absolute and unalloyed delight."
—Anthony Boucher, *The New York Times*

Lionel Davidson

THE MENORAH MEN (*available 10/82*)   P 592, $2.84
"Of his fellow thriller writers, only John Le Carré shows the same
instinct for the viscera."   —*Chicago Tribune*

THE NIGHT OF WENCESLAS (*available 10/82*)   P 595, $2.84
"A most ingenious thriller, so enriched with style, wit, and a sense of
serious comedy that it all but transcends its kind."
—*The New Yorker*

THE ROSE OF TIBET (*available 10/82*)   P 593, $2.84
"I hadn't realized how much I missed the genuine Adventure story
. . . until I read *The Rose of Tibet*."   —Graham Greene

D. M. Devine

MY BROTHER'S KILLER   P 558, $2.40
"A most enjoyable crime story which I enjoyed reading down to the last
moment."   —Agatha Christie

Kenneth Fearing

THE BIG CLOCK   P 500, $1.95
"It will be some time before chill-hungry clients meet again so rare a
compound of irony, satire, and icy-fingered narrative. *The Big Clock* is
. . . a psychothriller you won't put down."   —*Weekly Book Review*

Andrew Garve

THE ASHES OF LODA   P 430, $1.50

"Garve . . . embellishes a fine fast adventure story with a more credible picture of the U.S.S.R. than is offered in most thrillers."

—The New York Times Book Review

THE CUCKOO LINE AFFAIR   P 451, $1.95

". . . an agreeable and ingenious piece of work."   *—The New Yorker*

A HERO FOR LEANDA   P 429, $1.50

"One can trust Mr. Garve to put a fresh twist to any situation, and the ending is really a lovely surprise."   *—The Manchester Guardian*

MURDER THROUGH THE LOOKING GLASS   P 449, $1.95

". . . refreshingly out-of-the-way and enjoyable . . . highly recommended to all comers."   *—Saturday Review*

NO TEARS FOR HILDA   P 441, $1.95

"It starts fine and finishes finer. I got behind on breathing watching Max get not only his man but his woman, too."   *—Rex Stout*

THE RIDDLE OF SAMSON   P 450, $1.95

"The story is an excellent one, the people are quite likable, and the writing is superior."   *—Springfield Republican*

Michael Gilbert

BLOOD AND JUDGMENT   P 446, $1.95

"Gilbert readers need scarcely be told that the characters all come alive at first sight, and that his surpassing talent for narration enhances any plot. . . . Don't miss."   *—San Francisco Chronicle*

THE BODY OF A GIRL   P 459, $1.95

"Does what a good mystery should do: open up into all kinds of ramifications, with untold menace behind the action. At the end, there is a bang-up climax, and it is a pleasure to see how skilfully Gilbert wraps everything up."   *—The New York Times Book Review*

THE DANGER WITHIN   P 448, $1.95

"Michael Gilbert has nicely combined some elements of the straight detective story with plenty of action, suspense, and adventure, to produce a superior thriller."   *—Saturday Review*

FEAR TO TREAD   P 458, $1.95

"Merits serious consideration as a work of art."

—The New York Times

C. W. Grafton

BEYOND A REASONABLE DOUBT P 519, $1.95
"A very ingenious tale of murder . . . a brilliant and gripping narrative."
—Jacques Barzun and Wendell Hertig Taylor

Edward Grierson

THE SECOND MAN P 528, $2.25
"One of the best trial-testimony books to have come along in quite a while." —The New Yorker

Cyril Hare

DEATH IS NO SPORTSMAN P 555, $2.40
"You will be thrilled because it succeeds in placing an ingenious story in a new and refreshing setting. . . . The identity of the murderer is really a surprise." —Daily Mirror

DEATH WALKS THE WOODS P 556, $2.40
"Here is a fine formal detective story, with a technically brilliant solution demanding the attention of all connoisseurs of construction."
—Anthony Boucher, The New York Times Book Review

AN ENGLISH MURDER P 455, $2.50
"By a long shot, the best crime story I have read for a long time. Everything is traditional, but originality does not suffer. The setting is perfect. Full marks to Mr. Hare." —Irish Press

TENANT FOR DEATH P 570, $2.84
"The way in which an air of probability is combined both with clear, terse narrative and with a good deal of subtle suburban atmosphere, proves the extreme skill of the writer." —The Spectator

TRAGEDY AT LAW P 522, $2.25
"An extremely urbane and well-written detective story."
—The New York Times

UNTIMELY DEATH P 514, $2.25
"The English detective story at its quiet best, meticulously underplayed, rich in perceivings of the droll human animal and ready at the last with a neat surprise which has been there all the while had we but wits to see it." —New York Herald Tribune Book Review

THE WIND BLOWS DEATH P 589, $2.84
"A plot compounded of musical knowledge, a Dickens allusion, and a subtle point in law is related with delightfully unobtrusive wit, warmth, and style." —The New York Times

Cyril Hare (cont'd)

WITH A BARE BODKIN　　　　　　　　　P 523, $2.25

"One of the best detective stories published for a long time."
　　　　　　　　　　　　　　　　　　　—*The Spectator*

Robert Harling

THE ENORMOUS SHADOW　　　　　　　　P 545, $2.50

"In some ways the best spy story of the modern period. . . . The writing is terse and vivid . . . the ending full of action . . . altogether first-rate."
—Jacques Barzun and Wendell Hertig Taylor, *A Catalogue of Crime*

Matthew Head

THE CABINDA AFFAIR　　　　　　　　　P 541, $2.25

"An absorbing whodunit and a distinguished novel of atmosphere."
　　　　　　　　　—Anthony Boucher, *The New York Times*

THE CONGO VENUS (*available 11/82*)　　　P 597, $2.84

"Terrific. The dialogue is just plain wonderful."
　　　　　　　　　　　　　　　　　—*The Boston Globe*

MURDER AT THE FLEA CLUB　　　　　　P 542, $2.50

"The true delight is in Head's style, its limpid ease combined with humor and an awesome precision of phrase."　　　—*San Francisco Chronicle*

M. V. Heberden

ENGAGED TO MURDER　　　　　　　　　P 533, $2.25

"Smooth plotting."　　　　　　　　　—*The New York Times*

James Hilton

WAS IT MURDER?　　　　　　　　　　　P 501, $1.95

"The story is well planned and well written."
　　　　　　　　　　　　　　　　　—*The New York Times*

P. M. Hubbard

HIGH TIDE　　　　　　　　　　　　　　P 571, $2.40

"A smooth elaboration of mounting horror and danger."
　　　　　　　　　　　　　　　　　　—*Library Journal*

Elspeth Huxley

THE AFRICAN POISON MURDERS   P 540, $2.25

"Obscure venom, maniacal mutilations, deadly bush fire, thrilling climax compose major opus.... Top-flight."

—*Saturday Review of Literature*

MURDER ON SAFARI   P 587, $2.84

"Right now we'd call Mrs. Huxley a dangerous rival to Agatha Christie."   —*Books*

Francis Iles

BEFORE THE FACT   P 517, $1.95

"Not many 'serious' novelists have produced character studies to compare with Iles's internally terrifying portrait of the murderer in *Before the Fact,* his masterpiece and a work truly deserving the appellation of unique and beyond price."   —Howard Haycraft

MALICE AFORETHOUGHT   P 532, $1.95

"It is a long time since I have read anything so good as *Malice Aforethought,* with its cynical humour, acute criminology, plausible detail and rapid movement. It makes you hug yourself with pleasure."

—H. C. Harwood, *Saturday Review*

Michael Innes

DEATH BY WATER   P 574, $2.40

"The amount of ironic social criticism and deft characterization of scenes and people would serve another author for six books."

—Jacques Barzun and Wendell Hertig Taylor

HARE SITTING UP (*available 9/82*)   P 590, $2.84

"There is hardly anyone (in mysteries or mainstream) more exquisitely literate, allusive and Jamesian—and hardly anyone with a firmer sense of melodramatic plot or a more vigorous gift of storytelling."

—Anthony Boucher, *The New York Times*

THE LONG FAREWELL   P 575, $2.40

"A model of the deft, classic detective story, told in the most wittily diverting prose."   —*The New York Times*

THE MAN FROM THE SEA (*available 9/82*)   P 591, $2.84

"The pace is brisk, the adventures exciting and excitingly told, and above all he keeps to the very end the interesting ambiguity of the man from the sea."   —*New Statesman*

THE SECRET VANGUARD   P 584, $2.84
"Innes . . . has mastered the art of swift, exciting and well-organized narrative."   —*The New York Times*

Mary Kelly

THE SPOILT KILL   P 565, $2.40
"Mary Kelly is a new Dorothy Sayers. . . . [An] exciting new novel."
                                           —*Evening News*

Lange Lewis

THE BIRTHDAY MURDER   P 518, $1.95
"Almost perfect in its playlike purity and delightful prose."
                        —Jacques Barzun and Wendell Hertig Taylor

Allan MacKinnon

HOUSE OF DARKNESS   P 582, $2.84
"His best . . . a perfect compendium."
   —Jacques Barzun & Wendell Hertig Taylor, *A Catalogue of Crime*

Arthur Maling

LUCKY DEVIL   P 482, $1.95
"The plot unravels at a fast clip, the writing is breezy and Maling's approach is as fresh as today's stockmarket quotes."
                                —*Louisville Courier Journal*

RIPOFF   P 483, $1.95
"A swiftly paced story of today's big business is larded with intrigue as a Ralph Nader-type investigates an insurance scandal and is soon on the run from a hired gun and his brother. . . . Engrossing and credible."
                                           —*Booklist*

SCHROEDER'S GAME   P 484, $1.95
"As the title indicates, this Schroeder is up to something, and the unravelling of his game is a diverting and sufficiently blood-soaked entertainment."   —*The New Yorker*

Austin Ripley

MINUTE MYSTERIES   P 387, $2.50
More than one hundred of the world's shortest detective stories. Only one possible solution to each case!

Thomas Sterling

THE EVIL OF THE DAY   P 529, $2.50
"Prose as witty and subtle as it is sharp and clear. . .characters unconventionally conceived and richly bodied forth. . . . In short, a novel to be treasured."   —Anthony Boucher, *The New York Times*

Julian Symons

THE BELTING INHERITANCE   P 468, $1.95
"A superb whodunit in the best tradition of the detective story."
                              —August Derleth, *Madison Capital Times*

BLAND BEGINNING   P 469, $1.95
"Mr. Symons displays a deft storytelling skill, a quiet and literate wit, a nice feeling for character, and detectival ingenuity of a high order."
                              —Anthony Boucher, *The New York Times*

BOGUE'S FORTUNE   P 481, $1.95
"There's a touch of the old sardonic humour, and more than a touch of style."   —*The Spectator*

THE BROKEN PENNY   P 480, $1.95
"The most exciting, astonishing and believable spy story to appear in years."   —Anthony Boucher, *The New York Times Book Review*

THE COLOR OF MURDER   P 461, $1.95
"A singularly unostentatious and memorably brilliant detective story."
                              —*New York Herald Tribune Book Review*

THE 31ST OF FEBRUARY   P 460, $1.95
"Nobody has painted a more gruesome picture of the advertising business since Dorothy Sayers wrote 'Murder Must Advertise', and very few people have written a more entertaining or dramatic mystery story."
                                        —*The New Yorker*

Dorothy Stockbridge Tillet
(John Stephen Strange)

THE MAN WHO KILLED FORTESCUE   P 536, $2.25
"Better than average."   —*Saturday Review of Literature*

Simon Troy

THE ROAD TO RHUINE   P 583, $2.84
"Unusual and agreeably told."   —*San Francisco Chronicle*

If you enjoyed this book you'll want to know about
THE PERENNIAL LIBRARY MYSTERY SERIES

Buy them at your local bookstore or use this coupon for ordering:

Qty	P number	Price
————	————	————
————	————	————
————	————	————
————	————	————
————	————	————
————	————	————
————	————	————
————	————	————
————	————	————
————	————	————
————	————	————
————	————	————

	postage and handling charge	$1.00
	———— book(s) @ $0.25	————
	TOTAL	

Prices contained in this coupon are Harper & Row invoice prices only.
They are subject to change without notice, and in no way reflect the prices at
which these books may be sold by other suppliers.

**HARPER & ROW, Mail Order Dept. #PMS, 10 East 53rd St., New
York, N.Y. 10022.**
Please send me the books I have checked above. I am enclosing $————
which includes a postage and handling charge of $1.00 for the first book and
25¢ for each additional book. Send check or money order. No cash or
C.O.D.s please

Name————————————————————————

Address————————————————————————

City———————— State———————— Zip————————
Please allow 4 weeks for delivery. USA only. This offer expires 8/31/83
Please add applicable sales tax.